Britannia Rises

Hope you enjoy!
Thanks for the support

Russell Rumper

Britannia Rises
Published by The Conrad Press Ltd. in the United
Kingdom 2023

Tel: +44(0)1227 472 874

www.theconradpress.com
info@theconradpress.com

ISBN 978-1-915494-79-5

Typesetting and cover design by Michelle Emerson
michelleemerson.co.uk

The Conrad Press logo was designed by Maria Priestley.

Printed and bound in Great Britain by Clays Ltd,
Elcograf S.p.A.

Britannia Rises

RULING THE WAVES WAS
JUST THE BEGINNING

Russell Dumper

For all my friends and family, who have supported me over the years, but especially Dad, who always had faith.

Prologue

It may not have been the coldest November on record, but it might have been the bleakest. Most days the frigid mists lingered past noon. There were odd days where the sun managed to break through for a couple of hours, but the darkness soon took over and the mists swept back in with it. No mist today, though. Today the rain cleared it before breakfast was over.

It was as if the weather was able to sense the mood.

The heavy, grey clouds hung low in the sky and the scent of damp filled the air. There was no traffic around central London today, but the air didn't feel clean. It felt heavy and thick.

The black quickly absorbed the little light that did come from the occasional cloud break. There was black everywhere. Every building had black curtains or blinds closed, most of which had been custom-made for the event. Some of them had writing on, others just had her symbol. There was an especially large banner hanging from Big Ben, the letters 'ER' woven in by thousands of school children, most of whom were standing on the side of the road in their black uniforms, heads bowed and waiting.

The procession left Buckingham Palace and crept along The Mall in the rain, which had eased up a little as the morning progressed. They would end at Westminster Abbey for the service and eulogy. This would be the first public appearance by the new king, so it needed to strike the right note with the public.

After that, they would all move on to Windsor for a private service during her interment, next to her beloved husband and 'Papa'. The public lined the streets all the way from central London to Windsor. Honorary columns were marching through cities, towns and villages all over the country.

Similarly, there were marches and cavalcades shown on the screens in Leicester Square and Piccadilly Circus. Sydney, Delhi, New York, Washington, Accra, Toronto, Beirut, Cairo, Auckland, Cape Town. Every major city, and most smaller ones, had arranged some show of respect for her. It wasn't just that it was their duty as her citizens. The majority of people genuinely loved her.

The long, black Rover idled along at the front of the procession. The single driver was the Prime Minister, who she had personally chosen for this honour. Nobody else rode in the car. In the back was a lead-lined, oak coffin, crafted from a tree grown in Windsor for exactly this purpose over three decades before.

Next were three black figures. The new king and his two sons. They walked slowly, heads bowed, hands clasped at the front, ignoring the rain and refusing to carry an umbrella that would both show a lack of respect and weakness.

Behind them were a vast assortment of royal family members, politicians and dignitaries from all over the world. A few had joined the parade on horseback and were directly behind the new British triumvirate, with the cars and limousines at the rear and a few walkers scattered amongst them all. There were three black Rolls Royces at the front of the convoy, holding the closest members of the Royal Family. The new king's two brothers in one, the wives and children in another and his sister on her own in the third. He had allowed her to come out of exile for the funeral, but she would not be publicly recognised as a member of the Royal family ever again.

Behind this were the heads of state of each country in The British Empire. The assortment of black Bentleys, Rovers, Aston Martins, Jaguars and Minis each carried two flags, held aloft from a pole jammed in the rear windows. One flag was the Union Jack, the other was their national flag.

Next were an assortment of military personnel, handpicked to represent their division or regiment. This was the highest honour any of them could ever have hoped for. Some were on horseback, some pulled gun carriages, others marched. In the middle was a band, but they would be silent until the procession to Windsor, aside from the solemn and lonely beating of a single drum.

At the very rear was one black coach, carrying the extended family of the Sultan of Brunei, who had offered to pay for the funeral as thanks for her assistance when the Japanese had tried to invade his kingdom in the early days of her rule.

They reached Trafalgar Square, with Nelson's Column draped in black, and Prime Minister Beckham eased the Rover all the way around the roundabout. The crowds sobbed, blew kisses and threw lilies of the valley on to the street as the Rover went past. Parents consoled their children and husbands embraced their wives. The only people with their eyes up were the police.

Security was tight. It was, perhaps, the single largest police and army presence for any event in history. Because, although the majority loved her, there were some who did not. She had made enemies over the years. And those people would stop at nothing to ruin the day for everyone else.

As the procession neared the Houses of

Parliament, the king finally lifted his head. His wrinkles had become crevasses of late. His thinning grey hair was almost gone from the top, in a windswept, ailing combover. Anguish filled his blue eyes and he pulled the black scarf a bit tighter around his sagging neck. His protruding ears were especially exposed to the bitter wind sweeping past them, but he ignored it as best he could and cast glances either side of him.

Leopold, his eldest son, walked to his left, as the heir to the throne should. Leo was a lot like his father. They were both getting a little portly, but Leo was broader and taller, so it was less obvious on him. Leo was already losing his fair hair, but his blue eyes looked like they were made of ice. He also did not have the ears of his father and he had a bright smile that still lit up any room he entered.

Christian walked to his right. Chris was rugged and brawny, by far the most physically powerful of the three. His ginger hair was only just starting to thin, but his short beard was getting so dark that it was starting to highlight the baldness creeping in. His eyes were also blue, but they were somehow warmer and brighter than those of his father and brother. King Alfred had never understood why.

'Are you both okay?' he whispered, turning back to face the front and looking down.

'Yes, Father,' they replied together, quietly.

They were arriving at Westminster Abbey and ten, especially selected, members of the Royal

Guard were waiting to carry the coffin inside. The King had demanded he be given time alone with his mother before anyone else be allowed to enter.

He waited until the guards had left and smiled meekly at his sons, who both stood dutifully in the rain. 'I only need a few minutes to say goodbye. I will come and get you when I'm finished, okay?'

They both nodded, so he turned and vanished into the abbey through the enormous stone archway.

Leopold looked across at Christian. 'Did you wear Armani?'

'Yea. So what?'

'An Italian designer? Callous, don't you think?'

'They apologised, Leo. It's done with. Get over it, will you?'

He shrugged his shoulders. 'They should have been more respectful.'

Christian sighed. 'Everyone loved Nan. Look at the turnout. In this weather, no less.'

'She was definitely a force to be reckoned with,' Leopold replied, a half-smile creasing his lips. 'I worry about the future, though.'

'Why?'

'Father isn't even planning to tour. Did you know that?'

'We can tour for him. We should start to take on more, anyway. He's not a young man.'

'No, I disagree,' Leo returned swiftly. 'We should stay and plan for expansion. Father should tour and take his wife with him.'

'Well, he will do as he chooses. He's the king.'

'Let's hope he does something to help prepare for the future.'

'He'll do what's best for The Empire, I'm sure. Nan taught him well.'

Leo scoffed. 'He might do what's best in the short-term, but I'm thinking about the future.'

'Whose future?'

'Ours. Mine. The Empire's. I have big plans for it, brother.'

Chapter 1

The frigid February wind swirled around the courtyard and whipped dust up the old, cold brick walls. The sun was out first thing, but the mornings were colder without clouds insulating the little heat it managed to generate. Now the clouds were starting to form and the drizzle started to fall.

Despite the gloom, Jamie Bayston had a spring in his step as he crossed the grass towards the imposing, old schoolhouse. He had two good reasons; it was both his twenty-fourth birthday and his first placement.

He bounded through the door and into the classroom, eyeing the semi-circles of chairs with their fold-away desks on the arms. There were several students already in place, who looked up at him as he entered, but he turned straight towards Professor Ulinov.

She was a slender woman, tall and pale, with matchsticks for legs and arms. She had inextricably long hair, mostly held in a bun on top of her head, which somehow made her skin seem whiter. Her blue eyes were pale grey in certain lights and her tiny mouth made her voice very soft, almost soothing.

There was a large mirror on the wall, with the Russian flag transferred over it, and he caught a glimpse of himself as he walked past.

Bayston was not tall, not short, a fraction over five feet eight inches, and he was quite broad and muscular, inherited from his father and honed playing rugby at school. His blonde hair rested in a centre parting and was a little longer than the top of his ears. His blue eyes were bright and shiny. He did not consider himself especially handsome, but he also did not struggle to attract the women he liked, something his mother always blamed on his strong jaw.

Ulinov smiled as he approached. She proffered a hand and he shook it gently. 'Hello again, Jamie,' she greeted, her thick accent almost sounding like a cat purring.

'Hi,' he replied, removing his scarf and jacket. 'Where can I leave this?'

She indicated a chair on the far right of the front semi-circle. 'Please, that is your seat for this lesson. I would like for you to observe and take notes on how well you think I am teaching.'

Bayston was a little surprised. 'You want me to do what?'

She chuckled. 'I want your feedback after the lesson.'

He pointed to himself. '*You?* Want *my* feedback?'

She placed her hand on his shoulder. 'Jamie, you will have the freshest eyes in the room and, if I am to improve and become better at my role, I need the advice of many people.'

He smiled gently. 'Okay, great.'

She turned away to continue with her preparations, whilst Bayston moved to his seat. He got comfortable, before removing a pen and a notepad. He watched the students arriving, all of them fourteen or fifteen; young men and women; then looked at the professor.

She was teaching at a mid-level secondary school, yet she was known for being one of the foremost minds in the field of Modern History. His father, the local MP, had insisted that his son have the placement with her, even though she was considered controversial in Westminster and some of the local activists had started a campaign to send her back to Russia.

Others thought she might be a spy and, if he was honest, Bayston had thought it was possible, until he met her. Why else would a noted professor be teaching at this school? When he asked her, the answer was simple.

'I was placed in Hull and this school has the most students per class, so I can reach the maximum amount of ears possible.'

Bayston had then asked her why she needed to reach more ears, to which she smiled knowingly and told him to wait until class.

Now he was here he was finding he could barely wait.

The class began and he watched, an expression of curious wonder across his face, as she thundered away. The tiny frame concealed a booming voice.

'Okay, we finished the last lesson on the Asian Merge. Who wants to recap?' She pointed to a tiny girl. 'Jessica?'

Jessica seemed unprepared for it. 'North Korea, China, Japan, South Korea and Mongolia agreed to form a partnership and that became the Asian Coalition, ratified by the UN in 1995.'

Ulinov smiled. 'Does anyone remember what was their primary reason for doing this?'

A proud voice chirped up from the back. 'To complete with us.'

'Not just that,' she replied softly. 'The EU and Russia were getting more closely aligned in terms of politics and economics. The Middle Eastern countries were looking for allies and Saudi Arabia was coming under increasing pressure to choose a side.' She indicated a map on the wall, The Empire highlighted in royal blue. 'It was a strategic move to remain competitive.'

'Is that why the EU and Russia are so close?' Another question from the back.

She sat on her desk. 'The EU and Russia have a marriage of convenience, in a way. They don't always like each other, but they need each other. It was the same in Asia. Japan and South Korea, in particular, didn't like cooperating with North Korea, but they needed the military strength they brought with them. China and North Korea, between them, have a huge army.'

A slender, freckled boy thrust his arm in the air and didn't wait for permission to speak. 'But why do they need an army? To steal British territory?'

'To protect themselves, or so they say. Who can tell me how many countries the British Empire invaded during the reign of Elizabeth II?' There was pensive silence. 'No, it's not a trick question. The answer is zero. Military force is not a tactic The Empire uses. Does anyone know what weapon they have employed, time and again, with huge success?'

There was another silence and a quiet voice offered an answer eventually from somewhere in the middle. 'Economics.'

'Correct,' she declared, giving the voice a quick applause.

Hands went up. She picked one. 'How does that work?'

Ulinov grinned. 'A very good question and, luckily, we have an economics graduate to explain it to us.' She indicated Bayston. 'Jamie, can you answer that one?'

He blushed as every face turned, expectant eyes fixed on him. 'Erm, I can try.' He stood up. 'So, the main exports from China, before the Asian Coalition, were electronic goods, machinery and clothing. Their main food is rice, as you all know. So, the theory goes, in order to attack their economy, you buy up rice and steel to drive the prices up. You can also introduce tariffs on anything they need to import. So, in this case, soybeans, plastics, oil and metals, especially copper.

They needed all these things to produce the items they wanted to export and, with prices going up, they couldn't stay competitive against the countries that didn't have these tariffs imposed. With rising prices of food, people need higher wages at the exact time the cost of materials is going up.'

'Why didn't the government help, like they do here? When they make more money?'

He nodded fervently. 'Yes, it's called Quantitative Easing. Well, in this case, it's believed that China's debt was being recalled by anyone owning it. That was private, public and business debt. So the government had no money and nor did anyone else. Plus, they were in chaos. There were lots of squabbles in the government, people vying for power, scandals and who knows what else?'

'Who was calling the debt in?' asked a huge boy in the front.

Bayston shrugged his shoulders. 'Nobody really knows. With their closed state finances, there's no way to know who they owed money to. It's likely there were a number of corporations and world banks involved.'

'I read a book recently,' proclaimed a blonde girl in the back, 'that said it was a Korean conspiracy to call in all the debt at the same time.'

'It's one theory,' chuckled Bayston. 'Although the only people who could probably arrange something like that would be us. In truth, though, it's quite common. Once people sense their investment is in danger, they want to get out of it. So, once one debt is recalled, the others get nervous and recall theirs. The domino effect.'

Ulinov took control again in a commanding tone. 'Thank you, Jamie.' She motioned for him to sit back down and turned back to the class. 'So, you see, the various political and economic unions that people have undertaken are a direct response to the British Empire.'

'Are you saying it's our fault?' asked Freckles.

The professor laughed. 'No, not at all. It's cause and effect. The Asian and European countries have reacted to the strength of the British Empire. It doesn't matter if it's a threat, or not. It matters that it's perceived that way by others.'

'But we never attacked them. We helped them.'
Freckles again.

She smiled. 'Hitler, Stalin and Mussolini were a potent force and it's thought that they planned to take over the British Empire. I know it's the perception of the British that they saved Europe from tyrants in both wars, but what if I told you that many Europeans blame the British for those wars?'

The room gasped. 'Why?' asked a tiny boy from front and centre.

'There's evidence to suggest the British Empire actually helped get them into power. It's undeniable that the British sold them weapons as they marched across Europe. There are those who believe that it was a British ploy to take over Europe, but that Hitler, Stalin and Mussolini actually turned on their king.'

The students sat, open-mouthed, for several seconds, before a large, black-haired girl finally squeaked out some words. 'That's ridiculous.'

Ulinov held her arms out and frowned. 'Maybe, maybe not. What I will teach you to do is look at the evidence objectively and decide for yourselves. It's all very grey and muddy. Nobody will ever know for sure what happened to get those three on their rampage. What we do know is how it ended. The Japanese paid the price for joining the war and the nuclear age began.'

'Do you really think this is appropriate content

for this class?' All eyes turned to Francine, a tall, slender brunette with a St George's cross badge on her lapel.

The professor's expression darkened. 'Why wouldn't it be?'

'It's not in the curriculum,' the student sneered. 'If you're going to come here and teach, you should at least stick to the approved curriculum.'

Ulinov folded her arms and indicated the badge. 'I see you're a part of The King's Future.'

'Your purview is to teach us the facts. Not interpret them for us.'

'My purview, Francine,' she hissed, 'is to ensure you *can* interpret the facts. That requires open discussion of every possibility, even the ones you might not like.'

'My parents already think you're a spy. Wait until I tell them what you're teaching us. They will report you, for sure.'

'Report what, Francine? That I have told you there are varied opinions on the subject of Modern History? I don't think that will come as a surprise to most people.'

'No,' she snorted. 'That you're abusing your position to try and brainwash impressionable young minds with your anti-British propaganda.'

Ulinov's eyes flashed with anger. 'Well, these are all widely reported opinions, all of which are available to read in the school library. That's not propaganda, Francine.'

'All I see is you trying to steal young, British minds.'

The professor scoffed. 'My dear Francine, I can assure you that, if I wanted to steal young minds, I wouldn't target one with your grades.' The class chuckled. 'But I do think you should spend the remainder of the lesson outside the head teacher's office. You can discuss it with her.'

Francine stood up sharply and packed her books away into her bag, striding out of the room with her head held high.

'Sorry, miss,' one of the young men said softly after she had gone. 'She don't speak for the rest of us. We like your lesson.'

The professor smiled, her expression failing to hide the fact it had bothered her. 'Thanks, Brian. I appreciate that.' She paused and stared at the door for a few moments, then shook her arms in the air. 'Okay, shake it off. So, where were we? Next we will discuss how the British protected the Pacific from the Asian Merge.'

Chapter 2

Davíd Hughes loved his office. His wife had started remodelling it the moment the election results were announced and she had immaculate taste. It was a perfect, cubic shape and she used symmetry to make it feel organised. The bay window was enormous, so she had ensured it was tinted for her photosensitive husband, although the limited time he spent there made him wonder if it had been worth it.

She had chosen a dark, royal blue carpet and azure paint for the walls. Whilst he had wanted a wooden theme, she had insisted that metallic furnishing made him seem more modern. This included his desk in front of the window, the table in the corner and four chairs around that, the bookcase that was full of Shakespeare and Dickens, even though he hated both, the filing cabinet, even the photo frames. She had even insisted he had a silver laptop and Device to match the ambience. He had originally thought it looked cold, but she was right. It seemed less stuffy and old-fashioned than the offices of his peers.

The only thing that wasn't metal, or looked like it, was his seat, which was black leather. He was sitting back in it, nervously fiddling with a solid silver pen.

The cause of his consternation was sitting opposite him, in one of the uncomfortable metal chairs. He employed this tactic deliberately. That chair would numb the buttocks of any visitor within ten minutes. If Hughes wanted the meeting to last longer than that, he would move it to the corner table and the more comfortable seats around it.

He was hoping this would not even last ten minutes.

Hughes was a large man, with green, searching eyes and brown hair. He had a clean-shaven face, which housed a square jaw and an aquiline nose. Although becoming more portly with age, he exercised regularly, so considered his physique to be something he was proud of.

However, he was dwarfed by the sheer, rugged brawn of his guest.

Edward MacLoughlin had been a beautiful man in his youth. He had enjoyed soft, well-groomed, auburn hair, which was now thinning and was unscrupulously neglected. His large brown eyes, once so full of lustre, were now dulled from forty-eight years of life and recessed in the cavities of their dark sockets. Huge bags had appeared on the weathered face, which had lost the firm, smooth skin long ago, replaced by a scarred, sandpaper cover.

There were so many indentations, and so much crookedness, that pockets of stubble remained after any attempt to shave, which was why he rarely bothered, even before a meeting of great importance. Which was exactly what this was.

MacLoughlin had delivered his diatribe and was eagerly awaiting the MPs response. He had known of Hughes for a long time, and knew they shared anti-Imperial feelings, but it took a brave man to speak out in favour of America. And brave men were in short supply in politics.

'Okay, Mr MacLoughlin-'

'Ed, please,' he urged in his thick, American accent.

'I see you elected a new President, Ed. You must be pleased with that.'

He sighed loudly. That was not a good sign. 'She's not been very vocal about a referendum, so I doubt she'll be putting America first. But, we shall see, I guess.'

'Yes, Ed. Well, I'm not sure what I can do for you.'

'I need support. I need someone close to Prime Minister Beckham, who can convince him to approve a referendum. Hell, even raising it in Parliament would be a start. Then we can get it into Congress and go from there. The feeling over there is that there will be a rebellion soon, unless we do something to stop it. Nobody wants more civil unrest.'

Hughes sat back and rubbed the pen on his lips. The American certainly spoke passionately and convincingly, which was virtuous.

However, these days, virtue could get you killed.

'Your credentials speak for themselves, Ed,' he said finally, eyeing the file on his computer screen. 'But you know very well there's no support for that. These people need America and Canada. Outpost has no future without them.'

'We don't need a vote straight away, just a gesture to lead the way. The conversation needs to start. Others want this, too.'

'What others?' he sneered. 'And how would this even work?'

MacLoughlin indicated one of the frames on the wall. Inside it was a collection of defunct bank notes: Franc, Deutschemark and Peseta he recognised, the others he did not. 'Well, everyone.'

Hughes laughed. 'To what end?'

'To let people be free.'

The MP laughed. He did not want to, he tried to stop himself. He knew it was rude, but the bellowing laugh burst from his lips before he could stifle it.

MacLoughlin levelled a calm, cold stare at his host. 'It's not a laughing matter, Mr Hughes.'

'I'm sorry, I'm sorry.' He chuckled for a few moments more and then returned to fiddling with his pen. 'That was rude. I do apologise.'

'It's fine,' the American replied in a perfunctory tone. 'You can mock me, if you want, as long as you help me.'

'Mr MacLoughlin,' he began.

'Ed.'

' Yes, Ed.' He took a deep breath. 'I'm not even sure what it is you want me to do. You want me to talk the PM into opening up a conversation that nobody in this country wants, at a time when nobody wants it. Is that right?'

'I know it's asking a lot.'

'That's a slight understatement, Ed.' He looked over the screen on his desk. 'Reading your file here, it shows large gaps after your service in the American branch of the SAS. I can only assume that means you were involved in some clandestine activities, so surely you understand the need for caution. Why would you bring this to me? Why would you think I have any interest in it?'

He sighed. 'Friends I trust told me that you support it.'

'I wouldn't say I support it. I don't hate the idea, but they're not the same thing. Do you know why?'

'I'm sure you're about to tell me.'

'You're right, I am,' he spat superciliously. 'The instability you have over there is more trouble than it's worth, in my opinion. You don't understand or appreciate British ideals the way you should. You are given the freedom to, pretty much, manage your own affairs and you do nothing but create criminals and idiots. Good for armies, but not much else. We would need another Anglesey to fit them all in. We should either cut you loose or tighten our grip.'

MacLoughlin leaned back and studied the man opposite him. He was still fiddling with his pen and his eyes were trying to hide his fear. His sneering was too abrasive, almost overcompensating for something. 'Can I ask why you took the meeting if you were just going to laugh in my face?'

'It's a fine question. I'll be asking how you got on my schedule.'

'Peter put me on your schedule, which should tell you something.'

He paused. 'Peter Smythe?'

He nodded. 'Uh-huh.'

'Head of MI6, Peter Smythe?'

'You know more than one?'

The MP fell silent for a few moments and began chewing his pen. 'I'll be having a frank conversation with him, then.'

He waved it away. 'He didn't know what it was about, don't worry.'

'But he knows what you're doing?'

MacLoughlin smiled uncomfortably. 'No.'

Hughes' eyes flashed with ire, but it dissipated quickly. 'You know, in my intelligence briefing a few weeks ago, we were notified that you were here. Do you know what the report said?'

He shrugged his shoulders. 'Nothing too complimentary, at a guess.'

'It said you were a rogue operative, of questionable stability, who loves a conspiracy theory. It said you were old, rusty and not a threat to our security.'

His eyes narrowed querulously. 'That's only true if you ignore me.'

'You have no credibility, Ed.'

'I don't give a fuck about credibility, *Dave*. I care about the future and the freedom of my people.'

'Okay, Ed, I think I've heard enough now. Meeting's over.'

MacLoughlin stood up sharply and the politician started, stopping just short of cowering in his seat. 'I couldn't agree more.'

Hughes sat up straight and adjusted his tie. 'Well, I'm sorry I-'

MacLoughlin was already striding out of the door.

The MP sat back and sighed heavily.

MacLoughlin reached the street, his mind a whirlwind of questions. He had no doubt Hughes was nervous, but why would he be? MacLoughlin knew that he was an imposing man, but the way the MP ridiculed him towards the end of the meeting suggested that was not why he was afraid.

No, it was something else.

He lit a cigarette and looked up and down the street. There were a few people working as they walked, holding a Device in their palm or to their ear, but he saw nothing to worry him, so he set off towards his car, which was three streets away.

He took his Device from his pocket and activated it with the chip sewn into the tip of his finger. Some people kept them in their wallet or purse, some in their pocket, some in their Device case. He had chosen the most secure method he could think of to keep his Device safe.

The more he walked, smoked and replayed the meeting in his head, the more it bothered him. Hughes' body language simply was not right. He opened his Device calendar and used his thumbprint to access the secure area.

Where to next? He had a meeting in Hull that evening, which made him smile. He could look up an old friend while he was there. Finally, something positive might come from his English mission, even if it was just for his benefit.

He circled the block twice, checking for anyone following him, more out of habit than suspicion, before getting into his blue Ford and setting off.

Trevor Layttle walked through the revolving door of the tall office building and headed for iRepair Deutsch on the 42nd floor. He passed through security and entered the elevator, pressing the 42 button and watching as other people pressed the buttons for their respective floors.

What none of them knew was that the '42' was different to every other button. It read his thumbprint as he pressed.

Next, there was a biometric scan. The imperceptible laser flashed across the entire elevator and the details of every person in there passed through a database held in a secure server on floor 42.

A specialist technician updated the database three times a day, using a carefully prepared Device manufactured only for this purpose. The information he updated it with came from every major intelligence agency in the world. The secure server was not linked to anywhere outside of floor 42. Only those working there could access it.

As the elevator ascended, The Brain, as Layttle called it, checked the details of the occupants. His Device would warn him if any of the security conditions were not met and the elevator would stop immediately. They would assess the threat and deal with it as necessary.

It had never happened, yet Layttle still felt a tingle of excitement every time he arrived at work. It would someday. Their headquarters could not possibly remain a secret forever.

The elevator pinged at 42 and he stepped off, turning immediately left and approaching the door there. He took his encoded key card from his wallet and swiped it. This led to a small antechamber, where he completed the retina and palm scan and underwent another biometric scan.

This led him through the next door, which was the main office. A woman sat at a small desk and smiled at him as he walked past. She was the security. To look at her slight frame and gentle beauty would likely mean underestimating her. That would be a significant mistake.

He walked towards his office and Vikki was already there, in her customary business suit; a light grey one today; that almost made him embarrassed to be in his scruffy beige suit, creased indigo shirt and faded red tie.

'Guten morgen, Trevor,' she smiled.

'You're even earlier than usual,' he jokingly scolded. 'Kids up early?'

Her eyes smiled. 'Not this morning. I got a delivery in the night.'

Layttle's heart jumped. He was of Anglo-French ancestry, but German was his language of choice for swearing. 'Schieße. Endlich ist es soweit.'

She laughed at the fact he had broken his own

rule. The workforce of floor 42 were highly cosmopolitan; there were forty-eight different first languages; so it was strictly English-speaking. 'Yes, it's arrived.'

He held out his hand. It was trembling slightly.

She shook her head. 'You have Mr Arnborg waiting in your office.'

His excitement vanished. Why was he here? 'Okay, afterwards.'

She nodded. 'I turned your coffee machine on. It should be ready.'

'Thanks, Vikki.'

He opened the door to his office and faked a surprised, yet pleased, smile. 'Morning, Frank.'

Frank Arnborg was an aging, rotund, bald, Swedish man, with breath issues. Even worse, the MEP was Vice-Chairman of the Security and Defence Committee. So he was Layttle's only real boss.

Layttle quickly studied himself in the window to his enclosed office. He already knew this was not a visit he was going to enjoy, simply because the blinds were drawn. His chiselled, almost stone-like, features were marred by only a few, slight battle scars gained in his forty-three years. His hazel eyes looked bright, but his face was more emaciated than usual; perhaps due to overwork. His eyes and cheeks looked sunken and his lips were nearly as pale as his skin. He ran his fingers through his short, dark grey hair and kept up the smile as he closed the door behind him. He walked over to the coffee machine on the small side table. 'Want one?'

The Swede's cold, blue eyes landed on Layttle and followed him as the German walked around to sit opposite him. The office was quite small, containing only a desk, three chairs, two filing cabinets, a side table, a coffee machine and a computer. Layttle did not even have space for a plant. 'Why don't you move upstairs to one of the larger offices? I hate this place.'

Layttle sat back in his revolving chair and smiled. 'Because I like to keep my finger on the pulse, Frank. Plus, it's not as if we have loads of space here. Three people can work in one office up there quite comfortably, rather than cramming them in somewhere else. I'm fine where I am, thanks.'

Arnborg rolled his eyes. 'Have it your way.'

Layttle crossed his legs and placed his hands in his lap. 'What's wrong, Frank? Why are you here and why did you close my blinds?'

He took a deep breath. Not a good sign from a politician. 'Do you know why we created the K6, Trevor?'

Containing his curiosity, the German answered softly. 'To investigate the threat that China posed.'

Arnborg nodded. 'And now that this threat no longer exists, what role is K6 meant to play in today's Europe?'

He shrugged his shoulders. 'To investigate any potential threat to world security.'

Arnborg's face was becoming graver and he shook his head. 'So, do you think we gathered the cream of the planet's security talent together just to spend a fortune investigating Britain?'

Layttle grinned meekly. 'That's not all we do here, Frank.'

He laughed in a scolding tone. 'You could have fooled me, Trevor. It's matter of some considerable pride to us that the K6 is the pinnacle of the intelligence community. We outperform the MI6 and all their branches, including ISI and Mossad, and we are only a quarter of the size. We are more respected than either the MSS or the FSB. These people come to *us* whenever they need anything. And you, as Director, have a responsibility to uphold that image. It's an image that strikes fear into the heart of every criminal in the world.'

The German was still smiling and shrugged his shoulders again. 'What's your point?'

Arnborg fixed his glare on the man opposite him. 'I know you understand what I'm talking about. Your constant investigations of Britain; an unproven threat; are ruining the reputation that these people worked so hard to gain. You are mostly responsible for that. Why are you so keen to undo all your work?'

'I'm doing my job, Frank, that's all. The EU

pays me a pittance to keep people safe and that's what I intend to do. I'm merely acting on intelligence.'

'If it's so little money,' Arnborg contended, 'why do you continue to work here? I'm sure a man with your multitude of talents receives many lucrative offers of work. I happen to know of several companies that would be interested in procuring your services.'

'Is that a slight nudge?' Layttle asked in a sardonic tone.

Arnborg chuckled acrimoniously. 'Not yet, Trevor. But you might get a shove if you're not careful.'

'You've never questioned my methods or my intentions before, Frank. What's changed?'

The MEP paused to open his satchel and pull out a piece of paper. 'This.' He handed it to the K6 chief.

Layttle examined it and instantly recognised a K6 requisition form. He knew exactly what this had been for and he was not about to disclose the reason why to anyone, not even a man he had worked under for almost a decade. 'I see it, Frank, but I still don't see the problem.'

Arnborg's face was turning scarlet. 'You don't see the problem? Why did you need ten million Euros in cash?'

'That's classified, I'm afraid.'

The politician slammed his fist on the desk.

'Might I remind you that my security clearance exceeds your own? What was the money for?'

He stayed calm, despite the irritation that grew inside of him. 'It's an ongoing investigation, sir. You can't expect me to compromise agents like that.'

'Where is the money now?' His tone was becoming more threatening.

Layttle sighed pensively. 'You know, as well as I do, that I can't tell anyone that information. Not even you, Frank. What you're asking me to do is incomprehensible. It's bad enough that I am forced to sit idly by as you politicians continue to restrict the liberties that the K6 are meant to enjoy, but now you are actually coming in here and demanding information of an active investigation. Every time you smell something that might cause friction with Britain, you all start to panic.'

'You are pouring resources, which we can't spare, into activities we cannot possibly condone. You're wasting them, Trevor. How can you expect us not to intervene?'

The German held his hands up. 'Do you think I'm not aware that it's a lot of money? I'm fully aware of that fact and I know the role the K6 plays in keeping the delicate balance. I'm also very aware of the underground, propaganda war that rages on between the EU, Russia, Britain and Asia and the part we play in that. As a result, I'm unlikely to simply *'waste'* precious resources, don't you think?'

Arnborg scrutinised the K6 boss. 'Well, I'm not requesting that you cease all investigations of Britain, Trevor. It's a direct order from the committee members.'

He laughed uncomfortably. 'Frank, you can give all the orders you want, but I'm the director, as you pointed out not long ago, so you'll just have to remove me if you want to stop me.'

The MEP's glare was frigid. 'I don't want to replace you, Trevor, but I will if I have to. Don't force my hand.'

Layttle paused and decided to, at least, play along. All he needed to do was buy time. The evidence was waiting for him only a few feet away. 'Okay, fine, I won't start any new investigations, but I'm going to let the current activities run their course. And there's no way on Earth I'm giving you intelligence about agents in the field. Is that satisfactory to you?'

Arnborg stood up sharply. 'I'll put it to the committee.' He started for the exit.

'Hey, Frank?'

The politician paused by the door and looked back. 'What?'

'We've worked together for a long time and you've never once questioned me before. What's going on?'

The Swede sighed. 'Pressure on budgets, Trevor, that's all. I answer to people, you know. I know you conduct yourself as if you don't, but you need to understand that people - the people - will not stand for us wasting their money any longer. Fontane is cutting budgets across the board and we need to justify what we spend. Outpost is at a critical point and we need to contribute. We can't complain, though. He promised not to raise taxes before he was elected as President of the EU, so we knew it was coming.'

'Fair enough,' Layttle replied, swallowing the lie without as much as a blink. 'See you soon, Frank.'

The MEP exited the office and strode straight to the elevator, leaving Layttle to consider his visit. Budget cuts were not the cause. Layttle had detected the lie instantly. Arnborg was under pressure from someone to stop K6's investigations.

Three dozen potential suspects entered his mind. Perhaps the package would provide answers.

He walked to the doorway and checked that Arnborg was gone. Vikki had the parcel ready and placed it into his clammy palm.

He stared at it for a few seconds, barely able to believe it was finally in his hand. 'No disturbances, Vikki,' he said, quietly. 'Not for anyone.'

'Understood.'

He closed the door to his office and sat back down behind his desk. The parcel was a small cube, a box wrapped in smooth, brown paper. He placed it on the desk and studied it for almost a minute.

This was the reason for the requisition form. Four of his agents had died to get this. It was worth more than he could possibly fathom and, if Arnborg ever found out about it, Layttle would soon be in a cell.

He slowly unwrapped the parcel and soon held a small flash drive between his thumb and forefinger. It was rectangular, black and no more than five centimetres long. If it held what it promised to, there was a sense of irony that something so small could wield such power.

He took out his Device and opened his top drawer, removing a cable. He attached it to the top of the Device and slipped the flash drive into the USB port at the other end of the cable.

The Device blinked to life and he activated the hologram setting and set it up on his desk.

There were a number of dummy files, but hidden away inside a 'Tax Forms' folder was one huge file. That was not a form.

He opened it and found the details of several banks accounts.

Imperial bank accounts.

He leaned back, smiled and let out a huge sigh of relief. They had done it.

He counted forty-three accounts in total. The British Empire obviously used far more than that, but Layttle had access to every file of every version of a tax authority in the world, including the

Imperial ones. He already knew none of these accounts would be in any of those files.

This was all the British money that 'did not exist'.

It amounted to trillions.

Layttle spent hours going through them. He knew that, although he did not have details of these accounts, he could find out where the money was going. And that was what he was interested in doing.

Large amounts made their way to known fronts of the Italian DIS, presumably for munitions. He was not surprised. Everyone was desperate for money and Italy's commitment to Outpost was causing economic stress. And the project was at the stage where failure simply wasn't an option.

There were a lot of former USSR and Balkan states receiving large sums, too, seemingly for materials, if the payees were anything to go by. It looked like they were buying all the industrial chemicals and metals they could get hold of.

Layttle cleared the whiteboard on his wall and started tracking every payee in the files. If he could find a pattern, perhaps he could guess what they were planning. If they used these accounts, then the British Empire did not want anyone finding out about it. Which meant it was probably something sinister.

There was a lot of money going to South America, he discovered, though it wasn't clear why. They weren't part of the Empire, aside from Guiana and a few Caribbean islands. The recipients were mostly legitimate service providers and charities, nothing that would worry him. Which was why it worried him. Why use these accounts unless there was something he was missing?

The whiteboard was soon full. Every beneficiary was listed, traced and catalogued. All except one.

He could not find the company or governmental body linked to the account. This was a major problem, mostly because it meant that, potentially, there were gaps in his database. Gaps meant collusion, because K6 did not allow gaps. They had access to everything.

Not only that, if he could not trace the recipient, he had no idea what the money was being used for and that worried him. It was millions; easily enough for a terrorist to make a large bomb and murder the European Parliament. Or the NPC. Or the UN.

Layttle was sitting in his chair staring at the IBAN for at least ten minutes when it occurred to him he was looking in the wrong place.

It would be a private account.

It was well concealed. The money moved from Zurich, to Seville, through the Caymans and back to Prague. It took some digging, but he unearthed a name.

Who the hell was Lillian Cheroux?

And why the hell was it familiar to him?

Layttle was in his office for the rest of the day, cogitating and searching every database in the world. Nothing.

At a little before 18.00, there was a gentle knock on the door. It opened slightly and Vikki peeked through the gap. 'Trevor?'

He continued to stare at the whiteboard. 'What's up?'

'I know you said 'no disturbances' this morning, but that was almost ten hours ago and you didn't even leave for the toilet.'

He held up a water bottle full of yellow liquid. 'I'm fine.'

'Great, but also there have been people trying to get a hold of you all day.'

'Did any of them say it was urgent?'

'All of them.'

He looked up and shrugged his shoulders. 'Do you believe any of them?'

'One of them,' she replied opening the door. 'Steffi Krane needs a word. It will only take a minute. She's been waiting two hours.'

'Okay, fine.'

'Can she come in?' she asked, eyeing the whiteboard. 'Or are you coming out here?'

'Send her in.'

She seemed relieved, smiling meekly and stepping away. She murmured something and then a tall athletic brunette appeared in the doorway. 'You okay, boss?'

'Yes, sorry, I've been busy all day.'

She walked into the office and closed the door behind her. She glanced at the whiteboard, then back at the dishevelled man in the seat opposite. 'Trev, have you eaten today?'

He pointed to the empty Haribo packs on the desk. 'What do you need, Stef?'

'Look,' she said, 'I'm not one to get involved in gossip, but I overheard something today and it's been sitting with me, so I wanted to share it with you.'

Layttle turned away from the wall for the first time. If Krane had waited two hours to tell him gossip, it was not gossip. 'That sounds ominous.'

'I was sneaking a smoke on the fire escape,' she began, noting his look of disapproval. 'Oh, shut up, it takes twenty minutes to get downstairs and back.'

He laughed. 'Go on.'

'It was mid-morning, maybe 10.30, or something. I knew it was Frank and Gustavo, I recognised their voices.'

Gustavo Pereira was a Spanish agent Layttle had been given about a year ago. By Arnborg. He seemed like a good agent, but had not really achieved much. 'Frank? You mean Arnborg?'

She nodded. 'They were in the toilets and the window was open. The only reason I noticed was because they were talking quietly. Who does that? Well, I smoke there all the time and I can tell you: nobody.'

'What did they say?'

'Something about a requisition form for ten million Euros and something about how you won't drop it.'

Layttle chuckled. '*That's* what you're so worried about?'

She held her hand up. 'No, Trev. Frank said that if you won't drop it, Gus will have to deal with you and take over as Director. I mean, you getting sacked is one thing, but he didn't *say* sacked. And his tone didn't suggest a firing, you know?'

He stood up and laughed. 'Don't worry, it's probably nothing. I'll talk to Frank again soon, I'm sure. I just pissed him off this morning, that's all, and Gus is his guy.'

She let out a heavy sigh. 'You sure?'

'Yea, yea, I'm sure. It's nothing. But thanks for telling me. And thanks for waiting. Sorry I kept you.'

She waved it away and an embarrassed smile creased her lips. 'It's nothing. I owe you a lot more than that, Trev.' She turned to leave and eyed the whiteboard. 'What's that?'

'Oh, just something I'm piecing together. When I have more I'll probably need your help with it.'

She laughed and pointed to the underlined letters spelling out 'Lillian Cheroux' in red. 'Are you also looking for Santa Claus?'

Layttle paused. She recognised it, too. 'I don't know who that is. Do you?'

She nodded. 'Sure. I was working security at the EU Annual Ball a couple of months ago and overheard Jacques Fontane talking about his kids. One of them has an imaginary friend called Lillian Cheroux, if I recall correctly.'

He stared at her, then at the name, then back at her. 'Are you sure?'

'Yea, I'm sure. Why?'

He forced a laugh. 'I guess I have the wrong name. Okay, thanks for telling me. I have to get back to it and figure out the right name.'

She gave him a puzzled look and opened the door. 'You sure you're okay?'

'Fine, Stef. Thanks again.'

She left and Layttle waited until she was gone before heading home. Vikki had already gone, so he scrubbed his white board, locked up his office and dashed home as quickly as he could get there.

The President of the EU was an office that had only been created to deal with the concerns surrounding the British Empire. And the incumbent was a British employee. It was an inspired move, he had to admit.

General Nesbitt, the driver of most European campaigns, was a brilliant man, but Layttle was surprised he had managed to get to Fontane.

Layttle reached his small house a little under

fifty minutes later. He was just there to pack a bag. He already knew this information was not safe in K6, or probably anywhere in the EU. He had to get it out.

He stuffed a few essentials in a bag and then turned all the lights off in the house. Then he sat and waited, a silenced Glock in his lap. If they did not arrive by morning, he was probably safe for another day.

They arrived shortly after 23.00. The van pulled up outside with the lights and engine already off, coasting into position in complete silence.

The standard 'Death Team' for an operation like this would usually be two people. They were highly trained specialists. It always amused him when films showed super assassins working solo for governments or large corporations. He always sent two. Always. A solo effort had a high chance of going wrong.

Not for Layttle, though. He had the honour of a four-person team. High praise indeed, he thought. That was reserved for only the most dangerous and capable of targets.

They split up and one pair moved to the back of the house, the other came to the front. Layttle was already in position and had prepared for this a long time ago. Somehow he had always suspected this day might come.

The front door opened quietly and they crept inside. There were two 'phut' sounds and they were dead before they even knew he was there. The back door opened and the other duo rushed inside. Even silenced shots were loud in such quiet darkness.

The second pair ran straight into a wall of cling film across the doorway. They had no way to see it, no way to avoid it. It would only hold them for three or four seconds, but that was all Layttle needed to take aim. Phut. Phut.

The transponder from his BMW was already on the car from the annoying neighbour to the left and, within fifteen minutes, Layttle was on his way out of Hamburg at 90 miles per hour.

There was only one person he trusted to help him with the information on the flash drive. Now all he had to do was figure out how to get to London as a hunted man?

Chapter 3

King Alfred walked into the room and the Royal Guards closed the door behind him. He took a deep breath and looked around. He was nervous. He needed a moment to compose himself.

The white walls were covered in his mother's favourite art and one piece painted by his father: a map of the British Empire. There were sculptures in the corners and Yucca plants either side of the large bulletproof window. The floor-length curtains were never drawn, except for these meetings. The room was deliberately bare of other decoration, except for the large, rectangular oak table.

Around the table were twelve oak chairs. One at the head and the others down either side. Usually there were only ten other members to support the monarch, but he had been most insistent. After all, he had two sons.

The King quickly surveyed the people around the table as he moved towards his seat. They couldn't take their seats until he did, so he reached his chair and stood for a few moments, just because he could. It was important they all knew who was in charge. There was a tornado in his stomach, but it started to settle the moment he sat down and they mirrored him.

It's normal to be nervous, he told himself. These are the most powerful people in the world. They are all brilliant, strong minds.

'Before we begin,' he declared, clearing his throat, 'I'm sure you're all wondering why we have moved the meeting back to Buckingham Palace.' He paused to study the faces before him and espied that several of them would have preferred the Whitehall office that his mother had used. He only changed it to stamp his mark on the proceedings, but they did not need to know that. 'This location is equidistant between all of you and now you all have equal travelling time and I have none. And I'm the king, so…' There was a long pause and Prime Minister Beckham hacked into his hand.

'Okay, I'm glad that's not a problem,' he continued. 'I have also asked both Leo and Chris to be here, as I want to ensure they are both involved with matters during my reign. I know the custom is that only the heir be present. I also know it's sometimes customary for the monarch's siblings to attend. I will retain their counsel outside of this meeting and they shall not attend. So, if there are any issues with my decisions, let's discuss them now.'

Everyone knew better than to argue. King Alfred was trying to pick a fight. They all sat in silence.

The King smiled. 'Excellent. I also just want to say that I'm looking forward to working with you all to help fix the many issues we have within The Empire. I know many of you only from these meetings and it's my great hope to change that. I know we have seen fifty years of relative peace, and considerable prosperity, but I think we all know the last decade has seen us sliding somewhat. My mother was not well for a long time before she died and, I have no doubt, this is the main reason. We will rectify that problem. Together. So, I now call this meeting of the Privy Council to order. Who's first?'

'Usually we go from monarch's left,' remarked Jude Astor, Chief Justice and President of the Supreme Court, a tall, wispy, grey, wrinkled woman. 'That's the official order of rank, as you know. Unless His Majesty would like to make a change to the format before we start?'

'No, I think that works well,' he replied cheerfully.

'Okay, then,' Astor continued. 'Prince Leopold is first.'

'I have some questions,' Leo announced, taking a notepad from his pocket. No Devices were allowed at this meeting. 'First, I want to discuss expansion plans.' He stared at the Imperial Minister, Sir Humphrey Harris, a short, rotund, mouse-haired, sweaty man.

Harris coughed loudly. 'What would you like to know, Leo?'

'Your Royal Highness,' Leopold retorted venomously.

'Only the monarch has rank here,' Alfred declared. 'What do you want to know, Leo?'

Chris rolled his eyes and Leo scoffed. 'What are our expansion plans?'

'Well, there aren't any,' Harris said, shrugging his shoulders. 'Your grandmother was more interested in serving her subjects, not gaining more.'

Leo looked up at the map. 'Britain controls more of the world than any other empire in history. Why don't we control all of Africa and their resources? Why aren't we getting Brazil and Venezuela, with their oil reserves, to join us?'

'Pardon me, Leo,' interrupted the head of MI6, Peter Smythe. He was an older man, on the cusp of retirement, but tiny and brilliant, his hexagonal glasses making his eyes seem huge and his loud, shrill voice piercing the room. 'It's not as if we haven't been giving them the opportunity. They voted not to join.'

'Are you saying Venezuela isn't our doing?' asked Leo, rubbing his chin. 'Looks like Imperial tactics to me.'

'You mean their economic problems?' Smythe asked with a furrowed brow. 'No, that wasn't us. Your grandmother would never condone such tactics. Those methods were pre-Elizabethan.'

'Prince Leopold,' boomed the deep voice of General Nesbitt, his thick African-Scottish accent so perfectly at odds that it was instantly obvious that his Glaswegian mother had married a Kenyan rugby superstar. He was well over six feet tall and seemed almost as wide, his uniform struggling to contain him.

'Yes, General?' Leopold's voice suddenly seemed less querulous, intimidated a little by the Commander in Chief of the Armed Forces Nesbitt.

'Your grandmother made the British Empire the most stable and prosperous coalition in the world. It was a magnificent achievement. Yes, there were some wars. But it was always the very last resort. May I ask what your expectations are?'

'I expect us to be prepared for when our enemies try to take what's ours.'

'That's why the monarch has this council, to help with that,' Beckham sneered. 'We advise and we gather information.'

Leo scoffed. 'The Privy Council failed to act in 1781. It was George III who masterminded the integration of the Rochambeau family into British nobility. That was how we won Yorktown and look where we are now. Do not underestimate the acuity of the royal family and their importance to The Empire.'

There was a brief 'silence. The Lord Chamberlain, Giles Nockle, shattered it. 'Prince Leopold, there are no secrets here. We come together only three times a year. We don't have time for theatrics and we have no interest in it. Kindly ask your questions and we will answer, or we will get you the answers. Is that clear?'

He smiled menacingly. 'Crystal. So, in short, no expansion plans, is that about right?' They all nodded. 'Okay, then. So, current threats next. What are they?'

The Foreign Secretary, a burly young woman called Florence Rami-Akhara, answered swiftly. 'Do you mean besides the EU, Russia and Asian Coalition who are always looking for ways to discredit and destabilise us?'

'Yes,' he replied. 'Besides them.'

Rami-Akhara looked across to the Home Secretary, a formidable young, slim woman called Meredith Donnelly, who assumed control of the answer. 'We have several viable terrorist threats within our borders currently. There's a particularly nasty group in Pakistan, three we're watching in North America, all up around the Toronto area and one in Nepal.'

'Nepal? That's not exactly a hotbed of

revolutionary activity normally, is it?' the king asked, suddenly intrigued.

'No, Your Majesty. That's why it caught our attention,' she replied swiftly. 'And these seem different from the usual terrorist groups. We have almost no information about them, except that they're, allegedly, a group of monks.'

'Monks?' Leopold scoffed. 'I thought they were peaceful.'

Christian suddenly spoke up. 'Can I assume we have considered the proximity to China and that they may be involved?'

Donnelly brushed her long, blonde hair out of her eyes. 'That was our first thought. When we have trouble in Hong Kong, you can guarantee Chinese involvement. But it seems not with these people. They have no online presence, no headquarters, nothing. Every few months some supplies are ambushed on their way to the Indian frontline fortifications and they disappear again. We're not even sure if they really exist.'

'Do you have a name?' the king pressed.

'The Dayak,' she replied with a shrug, 'but I couldn't even guarantee that.'

'How long have they been active?' Leo continued.

'Five or six years,' Smythe replied, giving the others a look that said he was in control now. 'We have tried tracking them, tracing them, trying to get any kind of information about them. We have the name and that's about it. If the rumours are to be believed, they have some sporadic support in Nepal but, of course, nobody can corroborate.'

Leopold was aghast. 'We have an active terrorist organisation plotting a rebellion in a country that borders China and we're not doing anything about it?'

'Well, border is a loose term,' Smythe chuckled. 'There's a good chance they move between Tibet and Nepal to stay undetected and nobody is launching an invasion through those mountains.'

'Well, if they're in Tibet, that probably means the Chinese are helping them,' Leo growled.

'Not necessarily,' Smythe snapped. 'More likely they just ignore them. The Asian Coalition would never risk a war with us by helping terrorists.'

Leopold gaped in the direction of his father, then his brother. 'How can everyone be so unconcerned by this? An active terrorist group on our borders with our most dangerous enemy, that has been functioning, unchallenged, for a number of years. Presumably they are growing, too.'

'If they were growing, we would know all about them,' Smythe retorted.

'You can't even confirm their name!' he spat. 'This should be your priority!'

'I don't think a group of mountain monks on the other side of the world is The Empire's biggest problem,' Beckham chortled.

Leopold turned to the king. 'Father? What do you think?'

Alfred ran his fingers through the thin wisps of hair on his head and sighed loudly. 'Florence, you said there were other terrorist groups, too, yes?'

'Yes, Your Majesty.'

'And how long have they been around?'

'A few weeks, maybe. I would need to check exactly.'

He waved away the notion. 'No need. My point is that terrorists are around a few weeks in the British Empire. The Dayak, if that's their real name, are no longer terrorists. Not if they have been around for several years. That's a rebellion. Rebellions cannot be allowed to gain momentum. They are a cancer that will grow and spread.'

Smythe held out his hands. 'Your Majesty, they're likely just a group of farmers and monks with fork and knives and sheep. One report I read said they were twenty-five per cent children.'

Alfred tilted his head. 'Peter, I don't doubt that they are not a serious threat to our security. I agree that those mountains are not going to be the site of an invasion. However, you must understand my position here. I am just starting my reign and to allow the first challenge to my authority, regardless of how severe, to go unpunished, well…well, what sort of precedent does that set? What does that say to others? What does it say to the dissenters in Brunei and Singapore? What does

45

it say to the people in Brisbane who have been dreaming of independence?'

'They will be too expensive to catch, Your Majesty,' Smythe replied quietly.

'You look at it in terms of money. I look at it in terms of PR, Peter. It cannot be allowed. Kill the disease before it takes a firm hold. With it being so close to China, maybe even in Tibet, then it will send a very powerful message to anyone who would oppose us.'

'Let me look at who we have with the skills we need,' Nesbitt replied pensively. 'Mountain trackers who are loyal to our cause are not exactly common. I suspect most of the best would be from that area and, therefore, might be sympathisers.'

'If they're still undetectable, that's a fair assumption,' Rami-Akhara said with a firm nod.

'I will look into it,' the general replied. 'I'll do it personally, Your Majesty, as you've made it very clear how important this is to you. This is the East India Company's area, technically, and has been since The Partition. Do you want me to get them involved?'

'Consult Sir Bista and see if he has anything and let him know you might need the Gurkhas, but oversee it yourself,' the king replied firmly. 'I want us to deal with this, not the EIC.'

'Maybe sub it out,' Smythe commented. 'In case it goes wrong. Imagine the PR if we miss.'

Alfred rubbed his head again. 'Good point.'

'The Empire doesn't miss,' Nesbitt growled. 'The SAS are the best in the world on any terrain. They can find anyone. But we only have one team I would put into that situation and they're a strike team, so they need a target first. We might want locals and maybe a blunter instrument than our very best. I'm not sure yet. Let me look into it.'

'Do it right away, General,' Leopold sneered. 'Your king has commanded it.'

Nesbitt nodded knowingly.

'Ok, that settles that that issue,' announced Alfred. 'Leo, did you have any more to say?'

He met Nesbitt with a warm smile. 'What do we know about Gloria Moss?'

'Who is that?' King Alfred asked.

Leo turned his smile towards his father. 'The newly-elected American President.'

King Alfred shrugged his shoulders. 'Why would we care about her?'

'Because America is vital to The Empire and the calls for a referendum are getting louder, Father.' He turned to Smythe. 'Do we have any cause for concern over there?'

Smythe shook his head, slowly. 'No, I don't believe so. We vetted her thoroughly before her name went on the ballot and she will serve our purpose.'

'Why do we need a president over there, anyway?' Alfred asked, rubbing his chin. 'Seems like an expensive luxury we could manage without.'

'It's important, Your Majesty,' Smythe replied quickly. 'The illusion of some level of democracy over there keeps the people satisfied. It saves us a lot more than it would to use force. There is an element of malcontent over there, but it's not more or less than any other territory. America isn't anything we need to worry about.'

Nesbitt placed his palms on the table. 'Thank you, Peter.' He looked across to the eldest prince. 'Anything else, Leo?'

'Oh yes!' he laughed. 'I'm barely even warmed up! We need to talk about Outpost.'

Chapter 4

Bayston skipped down the stairs and jumped the last four, landing in front of the huge hallway mirror. He examined himself. The white shirt was crisp and immaculate. He loved the black collar and cuffs. He had his new dress trousers and shoes on. It wasn't often they managed to get everyone together.

His father came past in a tuxedo and looked at him, humming *Cherish*, the current track from *Madonna* that played in the background. 'Slumming it, mate?'

He chuckled sarcastically at the remark and briefly examined his father, who was also now using the mirror.

William Bayston was a temple of reverence. He was tall and stocky, which had been crucial during his university rugby days. He was still handsome, despite the worn face, battered by years of political battles. He had light brown hair, in a manly crop, and penetrating, dark brown eyes.

'We can't all get the taxpayers to pay for our clothes,' the younger Bayston quipped with a grin.

'If only,' his father replied, adjusting his cufflinks. 'I once tried putting in a claim for you kids but they didn't believe three humans could cost so much.'

'But we repay it in what we brought to your life, surely?'

His mother walked in and handed her husband the JAD heart necklace her children had brought her for her fiftieth birthday. The JAD stood for Jamie, Anthony and Deborah. It was her most treasured possession and she rarely took it off, except to shower. 'Repay what? Will, are you bothering them for money again?'

They both laughed and Bayston eyed his mother. She looked beautiful tonight. A slim woman, Maggie Bayston was small, but her will, and pure, moral certitude, were unrivalled in their home. Her smile was warm and her devotion to her family was unwavering. Her bobbed, auburn hair and green eyes seem to twinkle all the time.

'Yea, Mum, he's on about that 'fathering' tax again.'

'Hey,' William joked, fiddling with the latch and finally getting the tiny hook through the miniature eye, 'I deserve some kind of payment for putting up with you lot.'

She laughed loudly. 'Because living with you is

just one delight after another, right, honey?'

'Of course.'

'I share a bathroom with you, my love. Stop lying to our children.'

Bayston laughed and his father shushed his wife.

'Anyway,' she continued firmly, 'we are waiting for you idiots.'

Bayston exchanged a knowing look with his father and they scurried away towards the dining room. Already seated were his best friend, Matt, his brother Anthony, his sister Deborah and Claire.

Bayston paused to drink her in. She was a beautiful woman, but tonight she looked incredible. She had long, golden hair that grazed her shoulder blades, deep azure eyes and a smile so perfect it looked surgical. She had thin pink lips and regally high cheekbones, with a body that carried almost no fat, making an explanation for her ample breasts impossible.

Bayston walked over and sat next to her, leaning in for a kiss. 'Hey, you. You okay?'

She smiled and nodded. 'I had a good day. Got most of that project done today, so I might be able to work from home on Friday, if you wanted to get away early.'

'Straight after I finish school, maybe?'

She took a sip of water and nodded.

He found himself gazing at her. She loved her job in the city planning department and seemed to be very good at it, but he often lamented the fact that she had provided almost all the savings they had for their future. After being together three years, he felt he should have contributed more.

He recalled the night they met; his twenty-first birthday; and how she helped him into a taxi after he had lost his friends in the nightclub. Even then, she had been assured, confident and strong. A simple text, to check he was okay, followed the next day. Three years later, here they were.

'Jamie?' Claire asked loudly, snapping him from his reverie. He gave her a bemused look, so she continued. 'Answer your mum.'

He turned to face the other side of the table. 'Your Device was buzzing.'

He looked at the dish where Maggie Bayston insisted they all place their Devices during dinner. 'May I?'

'Dinner hasn't started yet,' his mother replied. 'You have two minutes.'

He got up and rushed to the dish, locating his Device and noting that it was the professor. He left the room to answer. 'Hello?'

'Jamie?'

'Good evening, Professor. Is everything okay?'

She was panting. 'Yes, Jamie, I'm very sorry to bother you.'

'No problem. How can I help?'

'The blue folder I gave you with the class notes in, have you reviewed them?'

'Not yet.'

'I think I left next week's notes in there and I need them to prepare. Would it be okay if I called in to collect them?'

'Yes, of course. Although, you live near the university, right?'

'Yes, I do.'

'I'll be that way later tonight, so I can drop them off, if that's easier.'

She sighed happily. 'Oh, if you could, that would be wonderful. They're in the red paperclips.'

'It won't be until after ten, is that too late?'

'No, no,' she chuckled. 'If I'm not here, please just put through the letterbox.'

'Will do. Big night out planned?'

He could hear her smile down the line. 'I have a dinner with an economist.'

Bayston laughed. 'Is that going to be fun?'

'I hope so. He's driven over from Sheffield for the night.'

'Okay, well, have fun. If I don't see you later, I'll see you next week.'

'Thanks, Jamie, I really appreciate it.'

'Any time.'

He ended the call and put the Device back in the dish before sitting back at the table.

'Everything okay?' Claire asked.

'Yea, we just need to make a diversion on the way tonight. Got to drop some stuff at the professor's place.'

She did not seem impressed. 'Will that make us late?'

He shrugged. 'I doubt it, but maybe. Is that an issue?'

'Well, yes, it could be. We have to be there for the surprise,' she replied.

He shrugged his shoulders. 'It's a surprise party?'

She smiled. 'No, honey. We're giving her the baby stuff and then we have that beautiful cot. *That's* the surprise.'

'Oh, right. Well, do you want to go on ahead and I'll catch up?'

'Do you mind? I don't want to miss it.'

'I won't be far behind, but better safe than sorry.'

She kissed him on the cheek. 'Agreed.'

'Who's having a baby?' asked his father, from across the table, a note of concern in his tone.

'My sister,' Claire replied. 'We're having a little party for her tonight.'

'Like a shower?' his sister, Debbie, inquired keenly. 'How lovely.'

'Who goes in the shower?' Anthony blurted out. 'All of you? Can I come?'

Claire laughed loudly. 'As if, Tony. You think I would let Jamie come if my friends and I were drinking in a shower together?'

'It would win you that 'Girlfriend of the Year' award you've been coveting,' Bayston chortled.

She kissed him. 'I don't love you *that* much, mister.'

'Okay, okay,' his mother interrupted tersely. 'Enough of that. We're here tonight to celebrate Tony's contract.'

Bayston sat back and eyed his siblings with pride. Tony was only eighteen, and he was as bullish as his father, but his natural speed and balance meant he was a very accomplished footballer. He had signed his first professional contract with Hull City Football Club that week, after six years in their academy. He looked just like his father, with a mop of light brown hair and mocha eyes.

Debbie was already a woman, despite only being fifteen. She was smart, capable and tough and much bigger than their mother, though her temperament was exactly the same. She had already decided to become a primary school teacher, like her mother and grandmother before her. She had darker, longer hair and large, doe-like grey eyes and, though her voice was timid, like a frightened mouse, she could be a ferocious character when the situation arose.

He watched her debating Tony's claim; that Genghis, the Mongolian ruler and a key part of the Asian Coalition, was actually a former North Korean dictator; and smiled. He saw younger versions of his parents and it often amused him. They even argued the same way.

He chewed on a tender, moist slice of roast beef and looked across at his father, who was also gazing at his youngest children and grinning. William made a few jokes to cool the conversation a little, but they ignored him.

They continued to ignore the buzzes from the dish, but soon after one had finally stopped, the house Device rang. His mother stood up. Only a few, select people had the number, so it could be important.

'I'll get it, darling,' William insisted. 'You finish your dinner before it gets cold.' His plate was already empty.

He was out of the room a few minutes and then called his wife to join him. After a few more minutes, they both returned to their seats.

'What was that?' Debbie inquired in a perfunctory tone.

Their father took a sip of water. 'Oh, nothing urgent. Just some constituency business to deal with, but it can wait until after dinner.'

'Are you allowed to tell us what it's about?' Tony fired.

'Sure,' he replied, with a knowing smile. 'Are you interested in the tariffs on vegetable oil?'

'Should I be?' returned the footballer.

'Of course you should,' their father retorted jocundly. 'We all should be.'

Tony furrowed his brow. 'That's ok, I'll give this lesson a miss. I don't see how it affects a footballer.'

'It affects everyone. A footballer needs spectators and it affects your spectators, so it affects you. If they can't afford tickets, how will you be paid?' He paused a moment to let that sink in. 'So, if the EU, Russia or Asia increase the tariff we pay on exporting vegetable oil, it greatly affects our local economy because we have several large businesses, who employ a lot of local people, in that industry. If the EU increases the tariff by only one percent, then that could cost five hundred jobs. That's five hundred families that can't eat, pay their mortgage, and so on. That's five hundred people who need to retrain and find jobs, which is no small task. We have unemployment of 3.4 percent in this area, so jobs aren't easy to come by. Do you see why it affects all of us?'

Tony nodded slowly. 'Yea, that makes sense.'

Their mother stood up sharply. 'Enough shop talk, guys. Nobody is influencing the tariffs on anything until after we eat dessert. Is that clear?' They all murmured their assent before she chose a topic of conversation that she approved of. 'So, Matthew, did I hear correctly that Bradley was chosen for the Outpost programme?'

Matt Trevistan; a rotund, short ginger-haired man the same age as Jamie; had been unusually quiet throughout the meal and nodded weakly. 'He goes next month. Mum's not too keen, though.'

'Why? What's involved with it?'

'He's away for ten months of the year and then, if he's chosen, he'll be gone for ten to twelve years.' He pointed to the ceiling. 'Up there.'

She smiled tenderly. 'I can certainly understand why she would be against that.'

Matt was always at their family events. He and Jamie had been friends since nursery and the Bayston family treated him as one of their own. Matt's father had been the victim of a terrorist attack whilst serving in Africa as a UN peacekeeper. His mother had struggled to support and raise Matt and his brother, Brad, even when working two jobs. Matt had even lived with them for a time, and Maggie had insisted on feeding both boys every evening throughout their teenage years, the only offer of help that their mother, Diane, had ever agreed to accept.

'Where will he be based?' William asked curiously, as he swallowed a mouthful of chocolate truffle cake splashed with cream.

'Initially I think he trains in Aldershot for three months and then he goes to either Texas, Bucharest or Beijing, it depends what he specialises in.'

'Beijing?' Tony seemed surprised. 'Not Ulan Bator?'

He shook his head. 'No, they left Outpost in China. It made no economic sense to move it, especially when all the people were already in place.'

'And how is your job going?' asked their

mother, who had always taken a special interest in his education and career, presumably because she knew his own mother did not have the time to do it.

'Great, I finish training in May and, hopefully, I'll get a formal job offer here.'

'You will make a fine journalist,' William declared proudly. 'You always had a good sense of right and wrong. I always admired that about you.'

'Thanks, Bill.'

'Do you ever read his stuff? It's brilliant,' Claire announced enthusiastically.

'I read everything he has published,' William replied matter-of-factly. 'And I totally agree. He's an exceptional writer.'

Matt was blushing. 'Okay, okay, move on to someone else now.'

They laughed loudly and William stood up. 'I'm sorry to scoff and go, but I should attend to this matter.' He leaned over and kissed his wife on the cheek. 'Thank you, honey. It was marvellous.' He turned to the others. 'Thanks for coming. Well done, Tony. See you all later.'

Bayston watched his father leave and listened to his mother, girlfriend and his sister complaining about men to Matt, who they all suspected was homosexual. None of them were about to ask, as it was as illegal not to report someone for that crime as it was to actually be gay, so they simply set about ensuring he had the information. They all expected him to move to the EU at some point to pursue that side of himself, though nobody was about to bring up such an awkward topic.

When the taxi arrived for them, he and Claire thanked his mother and said their farewells. Bayston arranged for the driver to leave him as close to Ulinov's house as was possible on his route and gave Claire a long kiss as he got out of the car.

'Don't be too long,' she said with a smile. 'If you leave me alone, I'll get too drunk and then I won't be any good for anything later.'

'Oh, got some ideas for later, do you?'

She winked and laughed. 'I have several.'

'Then I won't be long.' He leaned in and kissed her. 'See you soon.'

The taxi drove away and he tightened his scarf. The frigid breeze swept down the dark street, which seemed to funnel it perfectly. He looked both ways and saw no vehicles or people, so he crossed the road and headed down the alleyway towards Ulinov's house.

It was only a four-minute walk, but he could already feel the chill in his bones by the time he arrived there. The street was quiet and dark, with the fog slightly thicker here, it seemed, than the adjacent streets, but he located the house quickly. It was a semi-detached townhouse, with large green bay windows and beige brick. There was a tall fence around the property and a few, small birch trees around the edge of the garden.

He examined the house, discerning that there was a light visible through the upstairs window and another light emanating from the front door, recessed in a brick, open porch. The gate was already unlatched, so he opened it with a loud creak and walked up the pathway towards the front door.

The light was quite bright and he paused to look through the small window of tempered glass at head height in the front door. He didn't see any movement inside, so he gently pressed the button on the panel next to the uPVC door. A pleasant melody sounded.

After a few moments, he thought he heard someone, or something, moving around upstairs, but nobody came to the door. He watched the light through the small window closely, waiting for a silhouette to block it, but that did not happen, either. He pressed the button again, listening to Pachelbel echoing around inside the house.

There was a faint thud from upstairs somewhere, but it could have been next door, or Ulinov could have a pet. He had no idea. He stood there for a couple of minutes, pressing his eye up against the door and peeking in through the bottom bay window, before he decided it was far too cold to wait around outside any longer.

He pulled the papers from his inner jacket pocket and folded them up. As he stepped forwards to feed them through the letterbox, he placed his hand on the door to steady himself. It opened slightly.

He stepped back, surprised and unsure what to do next. Had she gone out and left the door unlocked? Was she home and about to leave? He chose to slip the papers through the gap and pull the door closed, but then he saw the silhouette of Ulinov through the window.

He pushed the door open to greet her, but found the figure of a man there instead. Presumably her date, he thought.

Their eyes met and Bayston smiled. He held out the papers. 'Hi, I'm just dropping these off for the professor.' The man's reaction was not at all what he expected. It was somewhere between confusion and surprise, but the eyes seemed calculating, as if analysing the visitor on the doorstep. 'She needs them for class next week.'

The man said nothing, he simply stood there, staring in the darkness. At that point Bayston noticed a foot protruding from the corner. Then he noticed a wire dangling from the man's hand and, what seemed to be, blood dripping from it to form a small pool on the floor.

Bayston looked at the foot, then the blood, then at the man. The eyes looking back at him were no longer confused or surprised. They were cold. They were dangerous. They were the eyes of a killer.

Chapter 5

He felt the chill of terror in his bones. The paralysing horror seemed to grip his limbs as his heartbeat became louder and faster. Yet all his senses seemed to be working in slow motion. The killer smiled, but his lips appeared to move frame-by-frame.

Bayston heard a car pass on the road behind him, a door slam shut in the distance. His senses restored themselves slowly. The swirling thoughts in his mind started to settle down. He was standing face-to-face with a murderer and he knew nothing about the reasons why. He only knew that he was next.

The two men remained in their impasse for twenty seconds. Besides the car and the door, the only sounds were the deep breaths the killer heaved into his lungs. The light was behind him, so Bayston could barely distinguish his features at all; just the menacing grey eyes, the cold smile of thin lips and crooked, white teeth.

Bayston felt the composure washing over him. The numbness in his fingertips faded and he started to think more clearly. The distance between them was easily four metres. He was fast, very fast, and this man was tired after tackling a tiny little woman like Ulinov. Granted, he had never garrotted anyone, but he imagined she was quite weak and Bayston was not.

He could feel the blood rushing back to his extremities and washing the fear away. His brain suddenly felt stripped of the torpor that was smothering it only a few moments before. He was analysing, he was calculating. He did not understand how he was able to process what had happened, and what might yet happen, but he knew a little about adrenaline and suspected it was a factor.

As his head churned through all the scenarios, only one fact became very clear to him. The longer he stood there, the more time the assassin had to recover from his exertions. If he was going to move, he needed to go now.

Bayston turned and bolted. He leapt down the steps, sprinted down the path and vaulted the gate. He turned left and sped down the street as fast as he could. He tried to think of a safe place to aim for. He needed somewhere to hide.

He headed back towards where the taxi had dropped him off and he heard the clunk of boots behind him. As he zoomed down the alley way, he stole a glance behind him and descried that the killer had already lost a lot of ground. He was, perhaps, ten or eleven metres behind Bayston.

Turning right out of the alleyway, Bayston raced down the street. His thighs were starting to burn, but he tried to ignore it. His arms pumped at his side and his heart hammered against his breastbone, so loudly it made it difficult to concentrate on a destination.

His Device was in his inner pocket, but there was no way he could get to it without slowing down and his slender lead would be gone quickly if he did that. He could not even use the voice control because it needed his chip first to activate it. That was in his wallet, in his front trouser pocket.

He reached the end of the street and veered left again, then took an immediate right. He powered down the middle of the road, trying to train his ears to locate his pursuer, but his own footsteps were too loud. He peeked back and saw the man turning into the street as he turned the corner. That was thirteen or fourteen seconds, maybe more. He was gaining ground.

Questions kept leaping into his brain without invitation. Who was this guy? Why Ulinov? Was that her date? Was she involved in something more sinister? He forced them back out of his mind. He had to focus on finding a safe place.

He heard some voices up ahead and turned left

65

towards where they were coming from. Maybe they could help him. As he got closer, however, it became clear it was an open window and a television that teased him.

There was a short thudding noise and a shower of sparks on a lamppost ahead. What was that? A bullet? Bayston was not going to wait to find out.

He vaguely recognised the area he was in, but he did not know it well enough to be able to navigate it to safety. He knew that it was quite close to the city centre, though. And people.

He would surely be safer with more people around.

He dashed down the next street and turned again, this time leaping over a fence and pounding down the pathway through a small park. He veered from the path and burst through a copse, aiming to try and confuse the assassin. He could hear the gate hinges rattle behind him and it echoed through the darkness.

The grass cushioned his footsteps and Bayston thought that would give him an advantage. However, the lack of ambient sound and lack of footfalls told the killer what he had done. As Bayston peered over his shoulders, he saw the dark figure cutting across a flowerbed. When he reached the gate and leapt over the fence, Bayston realised he had lost most of his lead. The man followed him out of the park only five or six seconds later.

He powered down the next street, willing his legs and arms to move faster as he saw the lights of the city centre ahead. He could hear the music from a couple of bars and there were cars crossing at the junction up ahead. It was only a few hundred metres. He was sure he was far enough ahead. All he had to do was keep going.

He looked behind again and saw the gap was growing. As he turned to face forwards, though, he noticed the raised pavement too late. He tried to adjust, but the tip of his shoe clipped it and he stumbled. He strained every sinew to remain upright; the long, inelegant giraffe steps that followed were all he could manage to avoid tumbling to the ground.

He stayed up and, within a few seconds, was back into a run again. He did not dare look back to see how close the killer was. He just needed to concentrate on reaching full speed again. Once he got his momentum back, the man would never catch him. As long as he avoided another mishap.

As his legs started to get back to a run, the assassin crashed into him with a desperate diving leap. The pursuer aimed for Bayston's waist and missed, but managed to impact his shoulder into Bayston's thigh, sending both men careering to the ground.

Bayston fell sideways, bouncing off a fence and landing in a heap. The assassin landed on his front with a loud grunt, but was straight back up. He was over to Bayston in a flash.

The first kick made Bayston scream, the second made stars appear in his eyes. He fell backwards, but managed to roll back over his head and come to a halt on his knees. He knew this was a fight for his life. He could not give in to the pain.

The murderer aimed another kick at his head, but he was ready. He held his arms up to absorb the impact and then sprung upwards with his fist outstretched. The manoeuvre seemed to catch the assassin by surprise, as Bayston's propelled fist crashed into his jaw.

Bayston regained his feet and took several deep breaths as his adversary stumbled backwards slightly. They examined each other. Bayston was a little physically larger than his opponent and he felt confident after striking a blow. This was not over, not by a long way. He was not dead yet.

The man danced in and Bayston did not even see the fist coming. It cracked him on the side of the temple. It blurred his vision instantly and then he felt the knuckles in his kidney, with such power that it forced Bayston to his knees.

His confidence gone, Bayston let out a pained wail and, by the time his eyes recovered enough to see his enemy, he was looking up at a gun. His heart seemed to stop beating. He stopped breathing. Every drop of blood in his veins froze as he stared and waited for death to come for him.

The man smiled, that same smile Bayston had

seen in Ulinov's house. He seemed to be savouring the moment. Then, suddenly, a blur and a crunch.

A shadow came out of the darkness and grabbed the assassin's head, smashing it into a wall. It moved with such ferocity and speed that Bayston simply cowered as Ulinov's murderer slumped to the ground, his face pummelled into a squidgy mess of blood and bone.

The hulking shadow walked over and stood before him, proffering a hand. 'You okay, kid?'

Bayston was trembling, too afraid to move or speak.

The shadow continued. 'You're safe now, kid, but you should probably come with me so we can keep you that way.'

Bayston timidly took the hand and it yanked him to his feet. He stared at the macabre scene on the ground.

'Don't worry about him,' the shadow said gruffly. 'He wasn't worried about you.'

'W-w-w-ho was he?' Bayston stammered quietly.

'An Imperial assassin,' he replied. 'What's your name, kid?'

'Jamie.' He felt the shock starting to leave his body. 'Thank you so much, sir.'

He held out a hand, which Bayston shook lightly. 'Well, I'm just sorry I was nearly too late, Jamie. My name's Ed. Ed MacLoughlin.'

Letitia Pearl took a deep breath and opened her eyes. The warmth of the afternoon sun kissed her skin and she looked at the side of the mountain and smiled.

Most of the mountains in this range had peaks constantly hidden by cloud, but this was one was her favourite because she could always see the summit. There were traces of snow remaining from winter, but spring had arrived early, so the meltwater formed small waterfalls and streams that meandered to the river at the bottom of the nearby valley.

The side of this particular mountain was quite rugged. Craggy outcrops of rock dominated the higher slopes, with only a few, more resilient, trees, bushes and shrubs finding a way to survive. A blanket of birch, junipers, firs, blue pines and bamboo trees began about halfway down and swept all the way down to the foothills. Rain fell every day, so the vegetation was unseasonably verdant and the fresh, crisp scent of water and blooming flowers filled the air.

The local wildlife was also becoming much more active in the sunshine. Birds created a melody, interspersed with the occasional shrill of a langur monkey. Over two dozen types of butterfly fluttered around the lower slopes of the mountain, along with many brightly coloured birds. If one had the patience and discipline to wait for a sighting, they would find hares, yaks, deer, foxes, tigers, martens, snow leopards, red pandas and black bears here. Pearl had never seen any of them.

The forest blanketed the lowlands all the way to the horizon in every direction, with only a few small clearings, most of which were ponds or lakes. She was laying on the grass of the only man-made clearing she knew of for many miles.

She heard a shout and looked over towards an especially thick area of forest. There were two old, thick Banjh oak trees growing there, flanking a small cave entrance. Their outstretched branches and thick leaves almost completely concealed it, to the degree where you could not even see the cave until a few metres away.

The man shouted again and beckoned her. Whilst a lot of her companions looked very similar from a distance; all Asian men draped in orange-brown robes, with shaven heads; Krayak seemed somehow more withered. She did not know how old he was, but he looked about eighty, although she doubted anyone as sprightly and bright could be that age.

She stood up and caught her reflection in the stream next to her. Her Sioux ancestry blessed her with high cheekbones, thin lips and emerald eyes. She had shoulder-length, dark hair that glowed in the sunshine. Her slim frame was athletic, inherited from her Canadian father, who was an Olympic sprinter in his youth. Her olive skin seemed even darker today than yesterday and she wondered if young women all over the world would ever believe how great they could feel if they replaced their cosmetics with the herbal concoctions that the monks provided for her. She smiled as she briefly considered the irony of her situation: she was in the best shape of her life; she was not thirty until next year; but none of her compatriots were romantically interested in her.

She strode over towards Krayak, who waited patiently with one hand clasping the other behind his back. She smiled as she reached the cave entrance, eyeing the small wisps of smoke coming from the fires near the entrance, almost totally concealed by the leaves of the Banjhs.

'I'm sorry to disturb you, Letitia.'

'It's no problem. Is something up?'

'We need your help with something, if you might have a moment.'

'Of course,' she replied, following as he turned and shuffled towards the cave.

Pearl knew what to expect from the cave, yet it still left her awestruck each time she entered.

From the entrance, the cave expanded in all directions to form an enormous cavern. A small waterfall trickled from a crack in the wall near the entrance inside the cave, high up in the impermeable darkness, and carved a small creek in the downwards slope, leading down to a large pool. Beyond the pool was a rocky plain that stretched back for almost four hundred metres. She estimated that the cave was eight or nine hundred metres wide.

She followed Krayak past the charred remains of several fires and down the slope. There were small lanterns to guide the way, since the natural light did not even reach the bottom of the slope, and they led to the small village that The Dayak had constructed of rocks, wood and fabric. There were dozens of huts and tents, all lined up against the end of the cave, which was a sheer rock wall.

Many were occupied by families, but there were twenty-three on the far left that belonged to the monks. Most of them had ten to twelve occupants, but she had her own tent, right in the centre of the encampment. It had a single maple leaf drawn on the side.

This was the military arm of The Dayak.

'May I ask you a personal question, Letitia?'

She paused for a moment, a little surprised. It was not in The Dayak's nature to ask about her private life. 'Sure you can.'

'Did you meet the Groundbreaker who killed your father?'

She stopped walking and took a deep breath, completely blindsided by the question. 'Erm, no. No, I didn't.'

His eyes filled with remorse. 'I'm very sorry.

This is not my business.'

'It's fine,' she replied with an affable chuckle. 'We never really talked about it, even after so many years. You have questions?'

'Only if you're sure it's okay,' he said softly.

'Ask away, my friend.'

He continued walking slowly. 'I was curious about how The Empire convinces people to be Groundbreakers. I don't believe anyone would ever aspire to that.'

'They don't,' she explained softly. 'The Groundbreaker programme specifically targets vulnerable people. Sometimes they're used in Imperial territories, like Canada, to gain information on rogue elements. Usually they're used, though, when they target a country. They recruit a number of young, poor, easily-manipulated minds then send them into their target country without funding, resources or recognised affiliation. All they have is their love of Britain. They're brainwashed, incapable of operating with a free mind, like you and I. With no education, or way to provide for themselves, they often turn to crime. It's better to think of them as victims, too, like children who were turned into weapons.'

'May I ask exactly what happened with your father? How old were you?'

'Thirteen,' she replied, choking on the memory. 'We were living just outside Montreal. He transferred to the police department there after my mother died of cancer the year before, as the city was supposedly safer than Toronto and Dad wanted me to grow up in safer environment, away from the memories of Mum's illness.' She gulped and sighed. 'Anyway, he got a call to go to a car theft in progress, but he wasn't expecting a silenced Sig Sauer. He hadn't even drawn his weapon.'

'What did you do?'

'I bounced around foster homes for a couple of years, ended up working with reformed Groundbreakers at a care centre. There are a lot of them in Canada, sent on missions by The Empire and then abandoned. It was there I came across the guy who got me involved with you.'

'Mr MacLoughlin?'

'That's the one. He thought we would be a good match.'

Krayak laughed. 'In his words, you were angry and we were backwards.'

She smiled. 'And not much has changed.'

He led her to the largest tent in their shanty town. Inside were a few logs for seats and, in the very centre, was a stump that they used as a table. On it sat a laptop, over which dangled a lantern. The soft, golden light gave the laptop the look of a treasure of some kind and the monks all treated it as such.

Pearl was accustomed to being called to the laptop. It was the only one The Dayak had ever owned and they struggled with it. 'What do you need, my friend?'

Krayak indicated the blank screen. 'We are expecting an electronicised mail from a contact in India, but we don't seem able to get it on to the Device.'

'It's not a Device, it's a laptop, Krayak. We're going to try and get a Device for you at some point, but they use personal chips to work and that can be tracked.'

'Sorry,' he replied with an awkward smile. 'I meant laptop.'

'No problem,' she chuckled. 'Let's just get it on and have a look. Do you know how much battery it had? We didn't charge it for a while.'

'They took it for charging last week.'

'Good.' She turned it on and waited for it to blink to life. Then she picked it up and started walking out of the tent.

'Erm, Letitia, sorry, but can we please keep it in here? The contents may be sensitive.'

She shook her head. 'The dongle won't work this far in the cave. You need to be at the entrance.'

'Ah, I see.'

She laughed. 'I'm guessing we just fixed the problem. Since I'm looking at it already, you want me to check on it?'

'If you don't mind.'

'Of course I don't.'

She strode up the incline and to the cave

entrance, sitting by one of the Banjhs, legs crossed. The dongle connected to the Russian satellite, which the British could not trace, and the emails started to appear. She scrolled up and down.

Krayak eyed the screen. 'We have anything from Delta Blue?'

She nodded. 'You want me to read it?' He nodded, so she continued. 'Dear Krayak, blah, blah, blah.'

'Blah, blah, blah? What does that mean?'

'It's just my way of skimming, it doesn't actually say that,' she laughed loudly, her eyes darting across the screen. She fell silent and her face dropped.

'What's wrong?'

'The British have started a new programme and it will bring them this way.'

'Where?'

'The next valley, maybe. Delta isn't sure.'

'What do we do if they're so close?' he sighed.

'Hide, maybe.'

'And if they discover us? They will spare nobody, not even the children.'

She met his worried expression with a shiver. 'Then we might need to get to them before they get to us.'

Chapter 6

The motorway above drowned out the frenzied cries of the bloodthirsty crowd. The men and women formed a circle, in which there were two men. Two very large men.

On the right was Daniel Vermotelli. Six feet, four inches and one hundred and fifty kilograms of raw aggression, he shaved his head to hide the grey, but the scars gave away the fact he was getting older. He could not maintain the taut muscles of his youth, but he knew he could lose an inch or two from his waist and not lose any power. Even though he was past his best, he had not lost a fight in over two years and that was why he was the current champion of the EU. He was the strong favourite.

The crowd knew him well and loved him. This was his home city and over two hundred people had been allowed to come and watch. Normally the organisers only allowed fifty, but the police had requested that they relax these rules and let more officers attend. The extra security, and huge pile of Devices next to the entrance, suggested the precautions were for a good reason.

The reason was the man on the left. Robert Royce dwarfed the Italian, being only a fraction under seven feet tall. His immense brawn made clothes difficult to come by and he had taken to making his own, a skill learnt as a boy in Australia. The dark skin of his Aboriginal ancestry was becoming increasingly pale with each new scar. His face was broad and muscular, though dented, with a crooked nose and enormous eye sockets which appeared far too large for his brown eyes. He had caves for nostrils and his huge forehead sloped backwards to a shaven skull.

He rubbed the tattoos on his arms and eyed the crowd. It was the same as most bouts. A few people looked like they might stab him for drug money, but mostly they were here for the blood. They loved it. He could tell by the froth in the corners of their mouths.

The referee declared that the match had begun and Vermotelli rushed in with a flurry of punches. The crowd roared with excitement. Royce ducked the first, dodged the second and slapped away the third. He pivoted and moved away, giving himself a little space to study his foe. He could see the Italian was already panting. After three punches.

This was going to be easier than he thought.

Vermotelli came again. Jab, jab, swing. The swing was slow and lazy. Royce blocked it, bent his knees and then returned with an uppercut that he jumped into. He was close enough to watch Vermotelli's eyes roll back into their sockets as the giant Italian flopped to the ground.

Royce kept walking towards the table where the organiser was sitting. 'Get him a medic,' he growled. The crowd fell into a stunned silence as Royce grabbed his money, towel and bag, striding away towards his car. They parted as he waded through them quietly. He did not even look back at the supine Italian as the first aid staff rushed towards him.

He put his shirt back on as he reached his old Jeep and started counting his money. He doubted that, having watched the fight, Mr Rossini was likely to underpay him, but the Mafia had become less trustworthy lately. Satisfied that it was the correct amount, he was stuffing it into his pocket when he heard a familiar voice behind him.

'That looked a bit too easy, Bob.'

He smiled as he turned around. 'Cap!' he cried, grabbing the man in a bear hug.

Nesbitt laughed and tried to free himself, but couldn't. 'Alright, alright, brother!' Royce put him down. 'Actually, it's General now.'

Royce smiled. 'I read about it. Congratulations, bro.'

'Thanks, man.'

The Australian noted his former commander's lack of formal wear and frowned. 'You're not here for work? You came to watch me fight?'

'Well,' he began, shrugging his shoulders, 'I wanted to check you hadn't lost a step since the SAS, mate.'

'You have a fight for me?'

He shook his head. 'No, no, no, nothing like that. I just wanted to see if The Tracker was interested in coming out of retirement for a job that I have. It's specialist. I don't trust anyone else to get it done and keep it clean.'

'Clean?'

'Yes, brother,' Nesbitt replied firmly. 'Information tends to leak a lot in that part of the world and, if that happens, we will lose the target.'

Royce rubbed the back of his thick neck. He could see Vermotelli uneasily getting to his feet. He was pleased he had not hurt his opponent too much. 'What part of the world's that, then?'

Nesbitt wagged his finger with a chuckle. 'That's confidential, mate, sorry. Can't tell you that until you agree and then I will tell you everything.'

'I'm not Brit forces any more, mate,' he replied. 'Don't you have anyone in that massive army who can do it?'

'I do, Bob,' he nodded, 'but nobody as good. Plus, if you fuck it up, I have deniability. Could be sensitive from a PR POV, you know?'

'Since when do I fuck it up?' Royce returned, his voice low and deadly.

'When did you last run a tracking mission?'

He took a deep breath. 'I dunno. Maybe five or six years ago.'

'Exactly. I need to cover myself and The Empire, mate. Nothing personal.'

'Fair enough. Can I enlist on the quiet?'

'No, mate, that would mess up your pension,' Nesbitt said, grinning. 'I was thinking a one-off consultancy fee. Maybe a hundred grand?'

Royce looked at his car and his clothes. 'I could use that.'

'I figured,' the general laughed. 'That mean you're in?'

'Of course. So, what's the job?'

Nesbitt leaned in and whispered. 'You ever heard of a terrorist group called The Dayak?'

WINDSOR, ENGLAND

Leopold powered into the room and looked at the couple with interest. Every time he met them, they seemed more in love than ever. It was rare that couples were successful in these jobs, but somehow these two were able to juggle the pressures of the espionage industry and maintain a healthy relationship. Leo and his wife were nowhere near as happy as these two.

'Good morning to both of you,' he declared in a jocund tone. 'How are you both today?'

'Very good, thanks,' replied Maximilian. 'Nice new place.'

'Yes, I like it here a lot,' the prince replied. He looked around the office, filled with Devices, screens and satellite images, and smiled. He would do it all from here. He walked over to the side table. 'Do either of you want a drink?'

They both declined and he used the time to survey them quickly. It was something he liked to do whenever he had not seen someone for a while, just to see if he could ascertain any changes in their persona or appearance that should make him wary.

Maximilian was tiny and wiry, with sleek, black hair in a ponytail that reached halfway down his back. He had a black beard and moustache that were immaculately trimmed and dark brown eyes that hid a keen, calculating mind. He was from Vienna originally, but his slender, long fingers had helped him become an accomplished pianist, so his work had taken him all over the world. There were only four people in the world who knew his real profession and three of them were in this room.

Maximilian's partner, Gugano, could not have been a more stark contrast. He was enormous, a two hundred kilogramme mass of sinew and silence. He also had long black hair, also in a ponytail, but it was shorter, only reaching the base of his neck. His clothes were tatty, his hair clammy, his face unshaven, his fingernails dirty.

Almost everyone who learned the truth about this couple could barely comprehend how they were so in love, but Leopold had never seen two people more devoted to each other. Even as they sat here, they held hands.

One of the first things Leo planned to change was to legalise homosexuality. To him, it was a crime that these two had to hide to hold hands.

The other mistake people made, when they met this couple, was to assume that Maximilian was the smart one. Max did most of the talking, that much was true, but Leopold knew what most people did not: Gugano was one of the finest minds anywhere on the planet.

Leopold sat down and looked at Max first, then met Gugano's cold, grey eyes with a warm smile. 'I assume you have questions, but first you should give me an update.'

Gugano grunted and Max shifted uncomfortably in his seat. 'Your grandmother didn't pay attention to what we were doing. Is that about to change?'

He took a sip of water. 'Where are we in Venezuela, gentlemen?'

Recognising he would not yet get an answer to his question, Max chortled. 'The same place we have been for a couple of years now. It's ready. It will never be weaker than it is now.'

'Yet they have not applied, nor did the referendum succeed.'

'The referendum was poorly managed from an Imperial point of view. We were not committed and, to be candid, we were complacent.'

The prince rubbed his chin. 'I agree. I fear there are too many that do not really want expansion. They did not challenge my grandmother and it has been that way for so long, they don't really know how to expand. So, what do you recommend?'

'The country is so weak that a military invasion would lead to overthrowing the government in, we estimate, seven to nine days. There would be some resistance beyond that but, to be honest, if you give food to these people, and a little stability, they will line up with Union Jacks.'

Leopold looked at Gugano. 'I assume you concur?' He grunted and nodded. 'Right, so we tried to get them to join using persuasion, but you're convinced this isn't going to work. Could we make the economy even worse and try another referendum, maybe?'

Max shook his head. 'I don't think so. I think we missed that chance. If we make them even poorer then we will see our enemies gaining more support. There are already two other groups over there that are making noise and they're both anti-Imperial. I'm afraid we can no longer use democracy here. It needs to be more direct.'

He took a large gulp of water and scratched his

head. 'We need a reason, though. We can't just march in there.'

'We believe that we can get the two parties to turn on the government and each other. Then we can go in there to establish and keep the peace. But, before we do that, we will try using the opposition and legitimising them. Then we won't leave until we have all our people in place and the next election is ours, the next referendum shortly after.'

'That sounds like the best way forward. Wonderful work, gentlemen.'

Max sat back in his chair and sneered. 'We have worked together a long time, Leo. We have done some incredible work already, but there's much more to be done. In all that time, I don't recall you ever deliberately dodging any questions we had.' He turned to his lover. 'Do you, darling?'

'No,' he replied with a guttural growl.

The prince held up his hands. 'I wasn't dodging the question, Max. But the answer depended on your update.'

Max stroked his beard pensively. 'So, what's the answer?'

'I highly doubt Father is suddenly going to show an interest in what I get up to. He's already old and he knows my plans for the future. I don't imagine he will want to interfere. He's only really interested in Outpost, not much else.'

'So, you haven't spoken to him about it yet?'

'I don't see the need,' the prince replied sternly.

'If it alerts him to what we're doing, he might take an interest. It's not worth the risk.'

'We don't agree,' Max retorted venomously. 'He remains the monarch and, as long as he is on the throne, he will decide and steer the course of The Empire. Even if his reign is only a decade, then he could set you back.'

'He won't,' Leo assured them.

'If he lives as long as your grandmother, then he could delay our plans too long. Asia is getting stronger and Russia are poised to join the EU.'

The prince gasped and leaned forwards. 'Is that confirmed?'

'Not confirmed, but enough for me to consider it a serious threat to your plans.'

'*Our plans*,' he corrected.

'They're your plans, Leo. You're the visionary. We are the architects of your vision, nothing more.'

The prince smiled and sighed. 'You think, if I go to Father and explain everything, that he might back us?'

'Maybe,' Max replied, shrugging his shoulders. 'Alfred is never quite as predictable as I would like, except where his wife is concerned. I worry she will be influencing him more than we could.'

'You might be right.'

'I would prefer not to take the risk, Leo.'

'Agreed. We worked too long and hard to chance it on that old witch.'

'There are credible threats coming from the Asian Coalition. Some general called Genghis is gaining a lot of support. And if Russia joins the EU, then you can be sure that will not benefit us.'

'If they turn on Asia, that would be perfect.'

'I hear that this Genghis has a lot of friends and connections in Russia. I even hear that he's the one influencing the Russians to consider EU membership.'

Leopold's face suddenly became grave. 'You think they will join forces?'

'Eventually, yes. But not if they can't get the oil to grow. Which is why we need control of Venezuela and, after that, Brazil.'

The prince paused and studied the faces of the couple before him. He raised his eyebrows. 'I'm sure you didn't raise this issue without a suggestion about how to deal with it.'

Max smiled and took his Device from his pocket. 'Of course not, Leo. We have a way for you to get King Alfred to do as you want. But you're not going to like it.'

'Why not?'

'It's going to upset you.'

'I highly doubt that. Father and I aren't especially close.'

Max opened his Device and started flicking through the files. 'Even so, we apologise in advance. If there was another way, we would have taken it.'

Leo paused, now feeling a little anxious. 'What on Earth is going on? What do you have?'

He walked over and placed his hand on the prince's shoulder, adopting his most sensitive tone. 'Well, Leo, I'm afraid it involves the death of your mother.'

Chapter 7

Trevor Layttle watched the last few people enter the club and checked his watch. In seven hours there had been fifty-eight in and thirty-four out. Still too many. He wanted it down below ten, but he could not wait much longer. Fontane and Arnborg would not be far behind him. He had changed cars three times, but that would only slow them down. He doubted they would take much more than a few hours to find him.

An hour later, with six more in and none leaving, he opened the centre console of the Peugeot he had taken from the parking structure in Namur and took out his Glock. Checking that the silencer was still firmly attached, he released the ammunition clip and double-checked it was full. The club did not close until 04.00 and he could not afford to wait another six hours.

Layttle had quickly checked the rear of the

building before parking up and there was a way in. He would have preferred a safer, more professional approach, but his options were narrowing with each passing hour.

He placed the weapon into the holster under his jacket, pressed his moustache to ensure it was firmly stuck to his top lip and slipped on a PSG cap. He checked in the mirror that he would be able to pass a camera without being recognised and then got out of the car. It was chilly, so he pulled up his collar and crossed the road, walking past the single-door entrance and seeing if he could espy anything useful from a walk-by.

He stole a cursory, sideways glance at the entrance as he idled past. The door was closed, but there was a small window that told him there were two large doormen just inside, but nothing else of use. He continued past the next four buildings to the corner, turned right and then into the first alleyway to the right.

He surveyed the area. It smelt of fried chicken and rice. It was dark and wet, with steam billowing from the grills on the ground. He counted the gates and the fifth one along had a lot of padlocks on it for a gate that was only six feet high. He listened for a few moments and, hearing nothing the other side, he leapt over the fourth one.

There was a small courtyard with several cameras aimed at the locked gate and the back door. He waited for a few moments, to see if anyone was watching the cameras, even though the shop was closed. After half a minute, he guessed not, so he shimmied up the drainpipe until he had a good view over the wall to the club next door. He could see cameras and a guard sitting on a lawn chair, smoking a cigarette, with a Beretta in his lap.

Layttle looked up and saw that the fire exits from all the buildings in this row converged into a single runway up near the roof. It didn't look to be guarded, but his view was obscured by guttering and darkness.

Placing his feet flat on the wall, he clasped either side of the pipe and climbed. He sped up and grabbed a window ledge. Pushing himself from the pipe, he scampered up and across the ledge, jumping and bounding from the wall to grab the underside of the iron fire exit.

He was hanging from it for a few moments as he looked across at the rear of the club and checked the only window with a light on. It looked like the office. It was the third to the left and on the top floor, so should be easy enough to find.

Swinging up onto the rail, he pulled himself up and trod softly, but swiftly, across to the roof access of the club. The door was locked, but soon gave way to his skill with a pick and a tension wrench. Silently, he opened the door and stepped inside.

He closed the door behind him quietly and locked it again, standing in the darkness and listening intently. After a few seconds, satisfied there were no voices or footsteps nearby, he made his way down the staircase and towards the only light he could see.

He had no idea if this was an inspired move, or an idiotic one, but he was about to find out.

Sebastian LeCourte examined himself in the mirror. Tall and broad, with green eyes and short, spiky blonde hair, he liked the symmetry of his face. He had a small, aquiline nose and high cheekbones, but the dimple in his chin was his favourite. It was a perfect circle.

He felt it happen and she gulped it down gleefully. She lifted her head up and smiled. He pushed her off him and zipped up his trousers.

'You took a while tonight,' she remarked.

'You get paid for end product, not for time,' he snorted and tossed her a handful of Euro notes.

'True. Same time again tomorrow?'

He looked at her voluptuous curves, bursting from the front of her dress. Her curly, long blonde hair bounced around as she got up and adjusted her dress to cover almost half of her thighs and breasts. 'Maybe. I'll let you know.'

'Ok, no problem.' She moved towards the exit.

'Hey, no!' he commanded sternly. 'That's my office.' He indicated a door on the opposite side of the room. 'You can go back to the club.'

She smiled and obeyed.

LeCourte picked his jacket up and looked briefly around his parlour. It was probably more lavish than necessary, with a bed, two sofas, a dining set and a bathroom, but he liked to be comfortable when his needs were being attended to. The cinnamon incense covered the scent of the drugs his team smoked nearby and the low light kept it comfortable and warm.

He tucked his navy shirt in and slipped his cream jacket back on, striding back through to his office. He stopped as he found a man at his desk pointing a gun at him. With his list of enemies, he was almost not even surprised.

LeCourte waited for the gunshot, but it did not come. He paused and studied the man in his seat, trying to stay calm as his heart raced. 'What do you want?'

'I need your help, Sebastian.'

He knew the voice. As soon as he saw through the thin disguise, it was obvious. 'Trevor, is that you?'

He took off the cap. 'I knew I should have dyed my hair.'

LeCourte smiled and moved towards the drinks cabinet next to his desk. 'Why are you here with a gun?'

'Can I put it down?'

'Of course. I can't believe you brought it.'

'You're a very dangerous criminal, Seb. Why

wouldn't I?'

LeCourte chuckled. 'After all these years, why would I cross you now?'

'How much am I worth now?'

The Frenchman allowed himself a wry smile. 'You think I would sell you out for money?'

'No,' Layttle laughed. 'But I bet my successor isn't going to give you such generous terms.'

LeCourte poured himself a glass of Hoop cola. 'You might be right. Time will tell. Do you want a drink?'

The German shook his head. 'That's not healthy, you know.'

'As opposed to the whiskey and cognac my friends are always drinking,' he scoffed. He sat down opposite his guest and took a deep breath. 'What did you do for there to be a two million Euro price on you?'

Layttle studied LeCourte. He had already decided the Frenchman was his best chance and saw nothing in his behaviour to suggest that had changed. LeCourte might have been the most powerful criminal in Northern Europe, but he did not touch anything to do with children or families and anyone who did, in this part of the world, would pay the price for it. It might not have been a big thing to most, but that small difference between LeCourte and his counterparts proved that the man had boundaries. He might have been the last honourable thief in Northern Europe.

He could see his guest hesitating and took a sip of Hoop. 'You are in big trouble, Trevor, yes? How big?'

Layttle eyed the French paraphernalia all over the walls, dating back a couple of hundred years. He knew LeCourte was famously anti-Imperial, but he was uncertain how far that would stretch. 'You know my boss?'

He frowned and nodded. 'The ugly Swedish man?'

'That's the one. You know who Jacques Fontane is, I assume?'

'Of course, oui. You came here with a gun to ask me stupid questions?'

Layttle put the safety back on his Glock and returned it to the holster. 'Right, sorry about that.'

LeCourte shrugged his shoulders. 'Occupational hazard. Although I will be expecting you to explain to my security team about how you got in so it can be fixed for the future.'

He laughed. 'Of course, no problem. But let's stay on topic. I discovered a bank account, owned by Fontane, that has been receiving payments from The Empire. And Arnborg tried to kill me for it.'

LeCourte gasped in mock surprise. 'Well, that wasn't very nice of him. I suggest you make a complaint.'

'Don't be glib, Seb.'

He held up his hands and cleared his throat. 'Apologies, but I have been telling you for years that the politicians and bureaucrats are worse than the criminals.'

'That may be so, but it doesn't really help me, does it?'

'You haven't really explained why this is my problem, Trevor.'

Layttle growled. 'If this is The Empire's way into Europe, do you honestly think they're going to let you operate? They will come for you as soon as I'm in the ground. We need to get this out there.'

'What can I do? Nobody is going to listen to me and, even if they did, it would just put a target on my back, too. I'm not putting it on my socials, if that's your plan.'

'No, not that. The Empire has spent a lot of time and money convincing the world they are not a threat. This would prove otherwise. I need to get this information to someone who can use it.'

LeCourte downed his Hoop and placed the glass on the table. 'You have someone in mind?'

'There are those in Britain who don't like their empire. They think countries should be independent, that Britain would be best served letting them all leave. There are those who would help it crumble from within, if they had the right ammunition to launch an attack.'

He smiled. 'You have someone in Britain, right? You're not going to tell me who, are you?'

Layttle smiled. 'I need to go there.'

'Where?'

'London.'

'Into the belly of the beast?' he scoffed. 'There is more surveillance there than any other city in the world.'

'I know, Seb,' he replied with a shrug. 'But this isn't something I can trust to a courier. I need to deliver it personally.'

'I can get you the passports and identities sorted, no problem, Trevor. But I advise against it. I have people who make runs into London all the time. Let one of them do it for you.'

'I can't, Seb,' he replied firmly. 'It's too important.'

'Are you going to tell me who you want to go and see?'

'I would rather not.'

LeCourte stood up, smiling, and moved towards a map of France. He pulled it from the wall, opened the safe behind it and took a telephone from it. 'This only has my emergency number in it. I'm the only person who can contact it. Take it and tell me who you are going to see. I will watch them and tell you where they are the moment you get there.'

Layttle apprehensively took the telephone. It was old-fashioned. Almost nobody used them anymore. 'How about this? When I need you, I will call and tell you.'

'Fair enough,' he replied softly. 'I wouldn't trust anyone else, either.'

'Don't take it personally, Seb.'

'I'm not,' he chuckled. 'I do think that you are asking a lot, though. You break into my office, point a gun at me and then refuse to trust me. Does that seem like reasonable behaviour to you? Maybe you're not quite telling me everything.'

'I'm definitely not, Seb.'

He rubbed his chin. 'They're going to follow you here, yes?'

'No, don't worry. I will lead them away from here, to someone else.'

His broad smile covered his face. 'Ah, there we have it. You're going to let me choose, aren't you?'

Layttle chuckled. His instincts about LeCourte had always been positive and he was pleased he had trusted them. 'Indeed. You need something to compensate you for your help.'

'And you also want me to see what they will do to them, so I can understand how serious this is, I guess.'

'You know me too well, Seb.'

LeCourte paused and his face suddenly became grave. 'How serious is this, Trevor? Do I need to get my mother out?'

'I don't know yet.'

'There are always people talking about The Empire trying to take over Europe, but they aren't normally the absconding leaders of intelligence agencies.'

He frowned with a sombre nod of the head. 'I don't know who is involved and how far it goes, but I'm going to find out.'

'I should get my mother out, or not?'

'I would. You have somewhere or you need some help with it?'

LeCourte nodded knowingly. 'I have somewhere for her, but she will not be happy with it. How long for?'

'I didn't get started yet. How long before I can have the passport?'

'I will call my guy in tonight. You can have it in a few hours.'

'Perfect,' he replied with a huge grin. 'If I go and leave my car near your person of choice, can you give me a clean one?'

'Of course. I can get you a new one in England, too. Also, I will get you a package, so you can leave the weapon and use the train. It's cleaner. Do you need a clean Device, too?'

'No, I have one, thanks.' Layttle stood up. 'This could go on for years, Seb. The more The Empire invests in Outpost, the more friends they make over here. You sure you're ready for this?'

The Frenchman cast a glance at the flag on the wall. 'I have been waiting for it for a long time. I saw it coming years ago. I know you didn't, so I'm sorry I was right.'

'We don't know what the money is for yet, Seb. Let's not get ahead of ourselves.'

He waved the remark away. 'No, no, no, Trevor. I disagree. I think now is the time to prepare for war.'

LeCourte's Device started to flash. He opened it up and chuckled, turning it around to show his guest. 'We have visitors.'

Layttle leaned in and studied the grainy, dark footage. It was the camera covering the main entrance. There were two men in suits flashing badges to the door security. 'Fuck, they're closer than I thought.'

'They're locals, I know them both. I can buy you a bit of time.'

'Imperial?'

The Frenchman nodded. 'Low level, though. If they knew you were here, they would have sent heavier hitters than these two. They're just scouting for information, I guess.'

He stood up. 'I guess I better get moving. Where do you want me to leave the car?'

'Renard Trellier's house, please. You need the address?'

Layttle smiled. Trellier was one of the more despicable rising stars in Paris and a direct threat to LeCourte's dominance. 'Not unless he moved in the past few months.'

'He did not. There is a white Citroen parked opposite. The key is on a magnet under the near-side front wheel arch.'

'And the passport?'

'I will call the 'phone.'

'Okay, I better go.' LeCourte gave him a look

that suggested he had forgotten something and it took a moment to click. 'I'll talk you through your security another day, ok? I seem to have run out of time tonight.'

'Fair enough.'

'Thanks, Seb.'

He nodded. 'Thanks for coming to me. You know this is a fight I've been waiting for.'

Layttle smiled and walked away. He had an ally. It was a good start.

Chapter 8

HULL, ENGLAND

Bayston sat and stared at the lamp. It hummed soothingly and the scarlet lampshade stopped the light from hurting his eyes. He was hoping that the tornado of thoughts in his mind would settle down so he could concentrate on one. He had no idea how long he had been sitting like this, but the thoughts continued to whip past and he couldn't seem to grab hold of any of them.

MacLoughlin came out of the bathroom with a towel around his waist and looked around his hotel room. It weas cheap and dour, yellow paint on the walls, orange and red décor everywhere else. He looked at his guest. The boy had not moved for four hours.

'Hey, kid.'

Bayston finally turned away from the lamp, studying his saviour. His was a big man, covered with muscles and scars in similar quantities. There was a wisp of chest hair and a couple of army-looking tattoos, plus one he recognised that read 'Who Dares Wins' below a small skull with a dagger through it.

He didn't reply, so MacLoughlin tried again. 'I see that you're struggling, kid, but we need to talk about what nearly happened to you. I wish I could leave you to deal with it at your own pace, but every lost hour affects my ability to react to it.'

'I'm sorry,' he replied with a croak, fighting back the tears.

'Why were you at Ulinov's house? That *was* you I saw running from there, right?'

Bayston stood up and winced as his inactive muscles protested. He stretched and took tiny steps towards the jug of water on the side. 'I was dropping off something for work. I work with her.'

MacLoughlin got dressed into his only change of clothes, aware that his others were starting to stink after almost two weeks of use. 'You're a teacher?'

He poured some water and took a sip. 'Trainee.'

The American knew all the local assets and this young man was not one of them. 'Bit late at night to be dropping stuff off for work, isn't it?'

'She called me and asked me to drop them off. I was going to a party with my-' His eyes widened as he suddenly remembered. 'Shit, I need to call Claire!'

'Who's Claire?'

'My girlfriend,' he replied, hurriedly taking his Device from his pocket. 'He had a lot of missed calls.'

MacLoughlin strode over and snatched it from Bayston. 'No, kid.'

'Hey!' he shrieked. 'I need to tell them I'm okay. My girlfriend, mum and dad have all tried to call me.'

'You don't understand,' he replied softly. 'You need to turn this off and not turn it back on again. Ever.'

Bayston glowered at him. 'What the fuck are you talking about?'

'Sit down, kid.'

'No!' he spat, reaching for the Device. 'I need to call them now. I should have done it hours ago. They'll be panicking.'

MacLoughlin held it in the air, away from the increasingly desperate owner. 'Yes, they will and that's exactly what you want.'

He reached again, but was not tall enough to take it. 'What are you talking about?'

'The only time I will give this back to you is to turn it off. We will do that, grab a couple of hours sleep and then leave.'

Bayston was getting angrier. 'Give me my Device, please.'

MacLoughlin sighed. 'Do you want them all to die?' he snapped.

He froze, glaring at the American as the fear

gripped him again. 'W-w-w-what?'

'Sit down and I will explain it to you.'

Bayston shuffled obsequiously back to his chair and dropped into it. 'What's going on here?'

MacLoughlin held the Device out. 'Turn it off now, please.'

He did so, tossed it on the floor and buried his face in his hands. 'This is insane.'

He sat on the bed opposite the young man. 'I think it's important you acknowledge what happened to you tonight. You need to understand and accept it quickly. Your life just changed.'

'I'm sorry. I should be more grateful to you.'

'You're just lucky I was in town. Let's say I believe that you worked with her-'

Bayston contemplated the remark for a moment and held up his hand. 'Hold on. What?'

'I will be checking, don't worry.'

'You don't believe me?'

'Yea, I do at the moment.'

'Are you serious?' he gasped incredulously.

MacLoughlin nodded sombrely. 'I have learned to be very careful, kid. You would be horrified at the lengths The Empire will go to when they want to keep a secret or eliminate a threat.'

He shrugged his shoulders. 'The Empire? What do they have to do with anything?'

'That's who just tried to kill you. Make no mistake, they will go for your family, and anyone you care about, unless you do what I say right now.

Do I have your attention yet?'

Bayston nodded slowly. This was madness. He felt numb. 'I'm sorry.'

'Stop apologising, kid,' he said in a softer tone. 'You didn't do anything wrong, by the sound of it. You're just unlucky. But I need you to answer some questions so I can figure out what to do with you.'

'What to *do* with me?'

'Yea. Before we get to that, let me explain to you what just happened. I'm about to tell you some sensitive stuff. You cannot breathe a word of it to anyone else. Ever. Is that clear?'

'Crystal.'

'Good.' MacLoughlin heaved some air into his lungs. 'Ulinov used to work with me and the focus of what we were doing was subjugating The British Empire. The man you saw was called Harry Driscoll and he is a professional assassin. He works for a guy called Nesbitt. You know who that is?'

'General Nesbitt?'

'That's the one. Well, his social profile might suggest he likes to help puppies and kids, and he probably does, but what he doesn't like is dissenters. They are threats.'

'But I'm not a dissenter.'

'No, but Ulinov was. You're a witness. Unfortunate it might well be, that won't save you. Driscoll was going to kill you and, probably, set it up so it looked like she did it.'

'Why would anybody ever believe that?' he spat angrily.

MacLoughlin kept his voice low and even. 'You will be surprised what people are prepared to believe, kid.'

He scoffed. 'This is absurd!'

MacLoughlin put his finger to his lips. 'Not so loud, please. There will be people looking for us really soon and we don't want to draw any attention to ourselves.'

'But what you're saying is utter bollocks!'

He met the young man with a fierce glare. 'You have literally just seen them at work. Or do you have other ideas about why she was killed?'

'Maybe.'

'So, let's hear them.' There was no response after a few seconds, so he continued. 'Come on, please, regale me with your theories.'

'It could have been a burglary,' Bayston offered weakly.

'Okay,' he replied, frowning thoughtfully. 'Let's play that out, shall we? Let's look at the reasons that may not be true.' He lifted one finger. 'First, I already told you who he was and what he does. You think people like that are in the habit of robbing terraced houses in crap little cities?'

Bayston looked at the speckled beige carpet. 'No, probably not.'

'Do I need to offer more counter points to dispel

that theory?'

'No, I get it.'

He stood up sharply, startling the young man a little. 'There is a concept you need to get your mind around, kid, and quickly. The Empire wanted to kill Ulinov because she was working at undermining them, finding and supporting those who would see the whole thing broken up and allow each member state to choose independence.'

'It just seems so surreal.'

'Yet it's what happened. Trust me, they don't send Driscoll after just anybody. He was a professional. Someone was on to her, which means they're on to me. If they had evidence, they would have arrested her and put her on trial for espionage. They love to be able to showcase anything that shows the skill of The Empire and the despicable nature of their enemies. You honestly think that, if they had a Russian spy they could parade around in front of the media and their citizens, then they wouldn't have used it? Their propaganda machine chews up stories like that and spits out more followers.'

'Well, yes, they wouldn't have kept it quiet. They shouldn't have needed to,' he conceded, reluctantly.

'So,' MacLoughlin continued, his lips curling upwards in either corner, 'do we agree that The Empire killed our friend?'

He shrugged his shoulders. 'I don't know who

Driscoll was. I don't know that's his name. I just have what you have told me.'

He laughed loudly. 'Saving your life doesn't gain your trust?'

'I guess, sort of…'

'Wow, you're a tough crowd,' he chuckled. 'Even if you don't believe who, let's talk about the situation, because the 'who' doesn't really matter. Now, can you at least concede that you're in danger from having witnessed it? Can you accept that the killers will try to get to you?'

He nodded once. 'Yes, probably.'

'Do you, therefore, concede that these people, who use professional assassins, are likely to have skills you don't possess and access to resources that you don't?'

'Yea, that's pretty likely, too.'

'So, do we agree that, no matter who wanted Ulinov dead, you're in danger?'

'Yes,' he replied quietly. 'Yes, that's probably true.' A tear formed in the corner of his eye.

'To expand upon that, do you see how, if you contact your loved ones, that these people may not know what you have said to them, only that you've contacted them? They will assume the worst and think that you have told your family and/or friends about Ulinov's murder and who carried it out, do you understand?'

'I suppose,' he replied uncertainly.

'If you were that person, or people, carrying out

an unthinkable crime, that nobody could ever find out about, would you take the chance that someone knew about it? Or would you eliminate all, and any, potential threats so this could never, ever come back to haunt you in the future?'

'I don't know. I wouldn't do something like that to start with.'

MacLoughlin smiled softly. 'I wish I could tell you these people were as decent as you are, kid. I really do. But they're not. They're cold and ruthless. They don't hesitate or regret. They will slaughter you, and everyone you care about, to protect what they love. And they don't love their family or friends. They love only The Empire.'

'I love The Empire, too. We all do.'

'Yes, you do. But you wouldn't kill innocent people to protect the secrets of others.'

'Of course not,' he spat, disgusted. 'And nor could The Empire.'

He could see Bayston was struggling with this. 'It's important you understand that these people believe they're doing the right thing. They believe in their cause and that any sacrifice is worth it to protect what they care about. They think differently to you, kid.'

He took a deep breath. It was starting to make more sense to him now. What was unthinkable a few hours ago now seemed plausible. 'I'm not sure.'

'Watch and pay attention. I will prove it to you.'

'So, if they have their cause, you must have yours, right?'

'Of course,' he nodded. 'I'll get you to safety and show you what that means, if you're interested. We always need smart people to help us.'

'You want me to join *your* cause?'

'Why not? You showed great fight back there, kid. We need people like that. There are too few.'

'Is that the price for saving my life?'

He laughed. 'Not at all. You can help us or go off on your own. I'll try my best to help you, no matter what you choose. But, at least, learn a bit about us first. Then make your decision.'

'So, what's this cause you want me involved in?'

MacLoughlin grinned wryly. 'Have you ever heard of The Dayak?'

Chapter 9

Bob Royce rarely lamented being so huge. It was useful and, in his chosen profession, ensured he commanded respect from his peers. As he got older, though, he realised it was not the sort of respect that he craved. It was respect based on fear, not love.

He sat next to the lake, looking at the reflections of the trees and mountains in the clear surface, and sipped on coffee. There was a sweet scent in the air, blowing in from some trees across the water, and he could hear the rumble of traffic and the birdsong in intermittent periods, as if they were taking it in turns in a conversation with each other.

He had only been in the city a day and he could already see that the East India Company were failing to honour their obligations to the crown. There were buildings falling apart and roads with huge holes in. He suspected the area was not of much commercial value and the EIC cared more about profit margins than their Imperial responsibilities, but he would be mentioning it to Nesbitt when he saw him.

The mug was like a child's toy in his giant hand. He indicated to the waitress that he wanted another and she dutifully scurried over and poured it into the mug as he put it on the small table.

He smiled at her, but she eyed him suspiciously and rushed away again. He was a big man wherever he went, but he seemed even bigger in this part of the world. His skin was a similar colour to the locals, but he was clearly not one of them. They regarded him with mistrust and they were right to. He would snap one of them in half to get the information he wanted.

Royce had come to learn that he would never fit in anywhere. He was lonely a lot of the time, but every time he trusted someone, every time he thought someone finally saw him as a man, not a colossus, he ended up being disappointed. They always had some kind of devious ulterior motive that, inevitably, led him into trouble. Nesbitt might not have been any different, but at least he was honest about it.

He lifted the mug to his lips, blew the steam away and took a small sip. It was still too hot to drink, so he placed it back down and continued to stare into the distance. He needed to maintain focus.

Royce knew better than to start asking questions about The Dayak. The locals already treated him with suspicion and, he guessed, the terrorists would be heroes to them. He needed to find another way.

The local economy depended on the vibrant tourist industry, which focused on regional hiking and camping trips. Royce figured that was his best way to move around the area without causing alarm. They might have been suspicious of him, but that wasn't because they knew his reason for being there. It was because he could crush any of them with his bare hands.

He picked up the mug, sipped the coffee again and saw the waitress looking in his direction. She was a tiny woman, young and pale, with jet black hair and a tiny frame. He suspected she weighed about as much as one of his hands. He beckoned her over. 'Excuse me, miss. You speak English?' He knew she did. Nepal was in The Empire and it was mandatory in every Imperial school to teach the main language. But it was polite not to assume, his mother had taught him.

She walked slowly towards him. 'Yes, of course. Is there anything else I can get you?'

'You have any cake?'

'We have some fresh jeri, just made this morning.'

'That would be wonderful,' he replied.

She went through to the kitchen and emerged

with two interwoven pretzel-style pastries dipped in syrup. She walked over and put the plate on the table.

'Thanks,' he said, trying to smile.

She seemed keen to get away. 'Is that all?'

'Well, maybe you can help me with some information.' She seemed horrified by the idea, so he moved to assuage her fears, whatever they were. 'I'm here for hiking and wild camping, but I think I left my map in the bus. I don't want to use my Device, because the battery will die and I won't be able to charge it out there. Is there anywhere around here I can buy a map?'

The relief washed over her face. 'Oh, yes, there is a camping store just down the street. When you leave I will point it out to you.'

'That's very kind,' he replied, taking a bite of his jeri. 'Mmmm-hmmm. That's incredible. Did you make that?'

She nodded enthusiastically. 'It's a family recipe. My mother only shared it with me when I turned eighteen last year.'

He took the rest in one bite and gulped it down. 'It's incredible. No wonder she's protective of it.' He indicated the mountains on the horizon. 'Are there any places you recommend out there?'

'It depends what you want to see,' she replied, now seemingly at ease with him.

'I have enough supplies for about a month and I would love to see a tiger, if that's possible.'

She eyed him curiously. 'They won't come anywhere near any settlements, most are in the foothills. But most people avoid them and have weapons to protect them from tigers. They're very dangerous.'

Royce laughed and indicated his torso. 'I don't really have to worry about that. There would need to be a few of them to bother me.'

She examined him briefly and nodded with a chuckle. 'Yes, I see what you mean. You are a very large man. But a tiger can take a buffalo, so you should still be careful. Do you have any weapon?'

He indicated the bayonet in a sheath on his belt. 'Can't be too careful, right?'

'Do you see that flat peak?' she said, pointing across the lake and gazing into the distance.

He peered over to the horizon. 'You mean to the right of the jagged one that looks like a spear tip?'

She was nodding as she turned back towards him. 'Yes, that one. That is said to be where most tigers live and most tourists are told to stay away from it. There are many other dangerous animals, too, such as snakes, crocodiles and spiders. I doubt you will go high enough to worry about leopards.'

'You're right, I will stay in the foothills, I believe.'

'Do you need a guide?'

'No, I think I'll be fine. I just need a map.'

She scowled. 'That's dangerous country. The tour guides don't go there, but I know one that will, for the right price. I would advise not going there alone. You don't know this country and your muscles won't help against a cobra.'

Royce laughed loudly, making her jump. 'You're right. Of course you're right. Where is this guide?'

She seemed pleased, presumably because it was going to cost a lot and one of her friends would benefit from it. 'I will take you when you are finished. They live nearby. And they will give you a free map.'

'Great!' he grinned. Of course, nothing was free and he was about to be conned. But it didn't matter. The Empire had plenty of money and he knew where to go and had someone to take him there.

Because if that was the dangerous country the locals advised tourists to avoid, then that was exactly where he wanted to be.

LONDON, ENGLAND

The room smelled of peaches and garlic. It was an odd combination, Leopold thought, but intriguing. He looked around his father's private office. He knew it had been completely redecorated, but he could not remember what it looked like before, so he noticed no differences. There was a lot of beige, he noted.

It was a big room, much larger than a monarch needed. It was only a little smaller than one of the reception rooms on the other side of the palace. The large oak desk was at one end, the table and chairs at the other end, a good twenty-five metres away. There were oil paintings of his antecedents along both walls and a drinks cabinet about midway. The room was bare except for that.

King Alfred walked in and he stood up and bowed his head slightly.

Alfred held his arms out either side of him. 'What do you think?'

'It's a bit threadbare, don't you think?' Leo replied in a perfunctory tone.

'I haven't finished choosing the décor,' his father said with a smile. 'I want to get it just right.'

Leo chortled. 'You mean *she* hasn't chosen it yet.'

'Her name is Angela,' he retorted querulously. 'You need to start respecting your stepmother.'

He watched his father sit down and did the same. 'Don't call her that, please.'

'I'm not going through this again with you, Leo. What do you want? I have a full schedule today already. I have a big meeting about Outpost with the Russians and Chinese.'

Leopold shuffled in his seat slightly. He had played this out in his head a thousand times, but he was still nervous. He was feeling uncertain for the first time. 'I appreciate you finding the time,

Father.'

'It sounded urgent. So, what is it?'

He paused, running through it all again in his mind one, last time. He briefly considered not going through with it, but pushed the idea away. This was the right thing. It was best for everyone and, especially, The Empire. Plus, he reminded himself, his father was far from innocent here. He took a deep breath. 'I would like you to rescind the British Penal Code Section 377 and amend the Sexual Offences Act of 1967.'

King Alfred studied his son for a moment, bemused. 'Do you honestly think I have any idea what that means?'

'You don't know the Sexual Offences Act?'

'Not by heart!' he laughed. 'I don't know what lewd things you want to do with Tiffany, but I'm not changing laws so a prince can be a pervert.'

Leo met his father with a stern glower. 'I want homosexuality legalised and for them to be able to marry.'

Alfred was stunned. 'Leo, are you-?'

'No, of course not! But it's wrong and unfair. It's not in keeping with the modern world at all. It's archaic and ridiculous and The British Empire should be leading the way in these things.'

The king scratched his head. 'The church disagrees with you.'

'The church would stop any kind of progress at all, if it could.'

'Okay, well, I will consult some other people and think about it.'

Leo felt his stomach turn. 'No, Father, I'm sorry, but that's not good enough.'

'Excuse me?' his face quickly started to turn crimson.

He took a small black and white photograph and slid it across the desk. 'Sorry, Father, but this needs to be done.'

Alfred looked at it for a few seconds, his face screwed up in confusion. Then, suddenly, the colour drained from his face. His blue eyes seemed opaque and afraid, moving up to meet his son's ferocious glare. 'Where did you get this?'

'At least you're not trying to deny it.'

'Leo, I-'

He held his hand up. 'Shut your mouth, Father. She was my mother and nothing you can say will ever make this ok.'

'It's not that simple, Leo.'

'You had my mother killed, didn't you?'

'That wasn't the plan, Leo.' He started sobbing, burying his face in his hands. 'She was just meant to get a scare. It all went wrong.'

'I don't give a fuck!' he spat, the anger turning his face purple and his fist slamming the desk. 'If this leaks, your siblings will instantly mount a challenge to your succession. Imagine how Auntie Matilda will react, after you left her in exile. From now on, you will do exactly as I tell you.'

The king could not fathom what was happening. 'What?'

Leo's voice was low and deadly. 'If you disobey me, even once, I will reveal all the evidence I have to every news outlet in The Empire. You will be forced to abdicate in disgrace.'

'You're not going to tell anyone?' He was confused. What was happening?

'Not if you do as I say. Starting with my request earlier. You will also direct the Privy Council as I see fit and we shall come on to the other details as we go.'

His face was screwed up in bemusement. 'What are you doing, Leo?'

'I'm saving The Empire, Father. I'm saving it from a man so inept, he couldn't even scare my mother without murdering her.'

'Leo, it was an accid-'

'Silence, Father!' he commanded. 'I'm not interested in your excuses. She died alone, in a foreign country, in pain and crying for her children.' He paused to compose himself and took a few, deep breaths. 'So, what's your answer?'

Alfred slumped in his chair. 'To what?'

'My proposal. Will you do as I say, or do I need to use this?'

'I'll do it, Leo. Of course, I will.'

He stood up sharply. 'That's what I thought you would do.'

'Leo, just let me explain.'

'Go fuck yourself, Father,' he sneered, turning on his heels and walking away. He had just told the ruler of The British Empire to go fuck himself. He smiled.

'Leo! Don't go. Not like this.'

He kept walking and did not look back. His smile widened.

'Leo! Leo, please come back! Let me explain. It's not as simple as you think. You don't know the whole story.'

He reached the door and paused, eying the portrait of his grandmother on the wall. She would have done the same. The Empire needed him to be ruthless now.

'Leo! Please! Don't go!'

Leopold walked out and grinned. He was now the most powerful person in the world.

Chapter 10

UNKNOWN LOCATION, NEPAL

Letitia Pearl sat on the rock and stared through the Stabiscope she had stolen from an Imperial outpost a few months ago. She examined the valley patrol with dismay. They were a little less than ten miles from the cave.

There was a perfume in the air from the nearby wildflowers and she took a deep breath, squinting to get a clear view in the glaring sunshine. There was a large truck and ten soldiers, sitting around, smoking and talking.

Krayak sat on her left, Lindo on her right. 'Are they coming or going, Miss Pearl?'

She turned to Lindo, the youngest of the Dayak warriors. He was short and broad, with a head shaped like melon. 'I think they're leaving, but I'm not sure.'

'Which way are they walking?'

'They're not walking, they're in trucks. But

they're having a break, or something.'

'Can I see, please?'

She handed the Stabiscope to Lindo and looked around them. They were high up and it was sunny, but they were hidden in the bushes and this equipment had dulled lenses to avoid reflecting the sun. There was no risk of anyone spotting them.

Krayak looked grave. 'It's too close, Miss Pearl. What do we do?'

She smiled tenderly. 'It's not *that* close.'

'They are moving more and more in this direction. Do you know where they're from?'

She nodded. 'I'm pretty sure they're from the base at Anbu Khaireni, but they're a long way from home for a standard patrol. They're looking for something, I think.'

'Us?'

'Could be. Seems unlikely they would be looking for anyone else.'

He pondered her words for a few seconds. 'Should we move the people?'

She shook her head. 'They're still a long way from the cave and, even if they come right next to it, they won't see it from the valley floor in trucks. I don't know if they could even get trucks into the valley near the cave, anyway.'

'They could walk,' he replied thoughtfully. 'It's less than a day's walk from here.'

'Think it through, Krayak. If you're an infantry soldier stationed at a crappy Imperial outpost like that, on the very edge of The Empire, why would you care enough to walk through forests and over mountains in search of anything? Never mind some ghost stories about monks with guns. They wouldn't care. Why should they?'

'It's their duty, isn't it?' Lindo suddenly asked.

She placed her hand on his shoulder. 'For most Imperial soldiers, they are in the army because they need a job. The very worst of them are sent to outposts like the Anbu camp. They're not going to care enough to find us. And, even if they did, there's a good chance they could walk past the cave without even noticing it. It's high up and the view is obscured from the valley floor.'

'If we were quiet and still, that might happen,' Krayak said, his lips curling upwards.

'I'm not concerned about these guys at all. I would be more worried about scouts or operatives of some kind than some random patrol. These soldiers are just lazy. They wouldn't even bother to search properly.'

'Let's say they do find us, there're no more than 300 soldiers at Anbu. We could handle that, anyway.'

'Better to avoid conflict, Miss Pearl.'

She turned to Lindo. 'I totally agree, but it might be the best form of defence.'

'What might be?'

'Attack.'

Krayak shook his head ruefully. 'You're not

126

suggesting we attack them, are you?'

'I'm saying that we shouldn't discount it as an option. Maybe it's time. We can't hide forever.'

'That is not our way,' the elder monk replied. 'We could never do that.'

She smiled, knowing that already. She took the Stabiscope and put it to her eyes. 'They're leaving, anyway.'

'Good. Shall we leave now?'

She shook her head. 'Not yet. Let's make sure there's nobody else around that we need to watch and let's get some more scouts organised.'

'Okay, good idea.'

They sat and watched the patrol leave and ate some fruit as they watched the sun set. There was no way to navigate these lands in the dark, so they set up a small, makeshift bivouac in the trees and settled down for the night. It was too risky to have a fire, so they wrapped themselves in blankets and rested.

It was as her eyes were starting to close that Pearl saw a faint light in the distance. She sat up slowly and looked across at the monks. Both were fast asleep.

She stood up, as she plucked the Stabiscope from the branch it hung on. Putting it to her eyes, she peered through them keenly in the direction of the light. It was a small fire.

It was a long way in the distance, and her view was obscured, but it looked like just one person

127

was camping there. She watched for over an hour but, seeing nothing, decided it was best to sleep. It was much too far away to be a threat tonight. Not even The Dayak could navigate this land in the dark.

The monks arose with the first rays of sun and were soon ready to return to the cave. 'Are you ready, Miss Pearl?'

She had decided not to mention the camper. Krayak was already jittery and that would soon spread to the other elders if he took it back with him. 'It's going to take two days to get a scout back here, right?'

Lindo nodded. 'Yes, Why?'

'I'm not comfortable leaving this area unwatched when there are Imperial patrols nearby.'

'You're right,' Krayak replied. 'Lindo can stay.'

She spun on him quickly. 'No, no. I want to stay.'

The elder monk exhaled loudly. 'I don't think that's a good idea, Miss Pearl.'

'Why not?' She tapped the Sig Sauer in her belt holster and the bayonet in her thigh sheath. 'You think I can't take care of myself?'

He shook his head. 'I know you can, but I don't like to leave you exposed.'

She laughed. 'Look, no offence, but I wouldn't mind a couple of days by myself. I don't get much alone time.'

Lindo smiled. 'Yes, there are many of us in that cave.'

She met Krayak's uncertain gaze. 'I'll be fine. You go straight back and send a scout here. I'll wait and watch until they get here, then head back myself. You can then discuss this with the council.'

He pondered the idea for a few moments. 'Okay, Letitia.' He handed her the Stabiscope. 'You will need these. Please do not go closer than this ledge.'

'I won't need to,' she said with a firm nod.

Krayak turned to Lindo. 'We must go. The sooner we are back, the sooner Letitia can be relieved.'

The younger monk grinned. 'Stay safe, Miss Pearl.' He then strode away through the bushes.

Krayak placed his hand on her shoulder. 'Please be careful.'

'Of course. See you in a couple of days.'

He bowed slightly and then was gone into the undergrowth.

She sat for almost two hours, watching the area where she had seen the fire. The fire was out and there was no sign of a tent, or anything like that. They must have moved on. But in which direction?

She surveyed the valley many times, but saw no sign of anyone. She was just about to leave the ledge, and head down to the valley floor, when she saw a movement in the distance. It was at the bottom of the valley floor, on the left-hand side.

She scoured the whole valley. It was easily a mile wide and probably six or seven miles long, so they were still a long way away. But they were closer than the fire, she guessed. Not much, but they seemed to be heading in her direction. Even so, it was a full day of hiking to get to her position, so would have plenty of time to move.

She examined the camper. It was a man. He looked local, almost, but for his size. He was either really big, or the wildflowers he was walking through were unusually small.

Pearl stayed hidden and watched, intrigued. Nobody ever camped wild out here. He was either really brave, really stupid or he was looking for something. She decided to stay where she was and observe. Something did not feel right and she was eager to know what it was.

LINCOLN, ENGLAND

Bayston sighed loudly as he stared out of the window. It was raining hard and the melody of the water hitting the glass seemed to soothe him.

MacLoughlin was sitting on one of the beds, on his Device. He scrolled though several articles, replied to a few messages, then turned it off and watched the young man for a few minutes.

'You ok, kid?' he asked, finally. The boy had

not yet conceded that his own country would try to kill him.

'Why are we here?'

'I have to go out later to a meeting. I have another one in Milton Keynes tomorrow night and then we can head to London.'

'What are you doing in these meetings?'

'I will explain more later, but there are some Outpost anomalies we're tracking. You need to focus on what we do when we get to London.'

Bayston wiped his red eyes. 'And what happens then?'

'We get you some documents and get you out of the country.'

He turned on the American viciously. 'You told me that part already. What do *I* do?'

MacLoughlin smiled weakly. 'Look, Jamie, I know it's not easy for you. I promise you, this is what's best for everyone you care about.'

'I'm sure it is,' he scoffed. 'I understand that. I just don't see what point there is in me living without them.'

He furrowed his brow. 'Oh, so you want to let them get away with ruining your life, do you?'

'Well, no,' he gulped.

'They want you dead or gone. You want to give them that? Let them succeed?'

He looked at the floor. 'Well, no. But everyone I know will think I'm dead, won't they?'

'Probably. It's better for them to think that. The

more they know, the more danger they're in.'

He moved and sat in the armchair. 'It's just so surreal. I mean, The Empire doesn't just turn on their own citizens. Britain is the good guy.'

MacLoughlin sensed an opportunity and picked up the TV remote, turning on BBC News. 'Let's see, shall we? If they have nothing to hide, then it will be all over the news.'

Bayston frowned slightly. 'You think so?'

He shrugged his shoulders. 'Sure. Why not? If they're on the level, then why wouldn't they be appealing to the public for witnesses or reporting the crime? They would, right?'

'Yea,' he replied uncertainly. 'I guess so.'

They watched a story about a British company buying a Brazilian company and read as the headlines scrolled across at the bottom of the screen. After a few minutes the words started to repeat themselves.

'See? Nothing on the news.' the American declared triumphantly.

'That doesn't mean anything. Maybe it was on already and is old news now.'

He laughed and checked his watch. 'After fourteen hours?'

'Yea, you're right,' he conceded. 'Maybe the bodies weren't discovered yet.'

'Ulinov's front door was left wide open and I crushed his skull about half a mile, maybe less, from the city centre. It would have been found last night. Maybe the Ulinov story would have made it until this morning.'

Bayston searched for other possibilities. 'Maybe it's just not a big enough story.'

MacLoughlin looked at the TV and they were switching to a story about a travelling carnival that was in the area. 'No, good point. It does appear to be a big news day all around.'

Bayston narrowed his eyes. 'You know, they say sarcasm is the lowest form of wit.'

'Fuck that,' he said with a grin. 'That's only what stupid people say.'

'There must be an explanation.'

'There is,' he retorted. 'You just don't want to hear it.'

'Let's say I do.'

MacLoughlin took a deep breath. 'Okay, I will tell you what I think happened. Driscoll was meant to check in last night to confirm that his mission was complete. You interrupted him before he was able to. They will have sent another operative to Ulinov's house and found her. They would have cleaned that scene immediately.'

He paused to sip water from a glass on the sideboard and Bayston gulped. 'Go on.'

He swallowed and hacked into his hand. 'Once they knew something had gone wrong, they would have started searching the area. Maybe they found his body first, maybe they checked the cameras first, I don't know. Doesn't matter. They would

133

have cleaned that up, too. Wouldn't have been too hard at the time of night, assuming nobody else found it first.'

'And if they did?'

'Then probably they would have been lied to. Maybe given a reward and a thanks for reporting it. Maybe told it was a confidential matter and given a NDA to sign to get their reward. That's a common Imperial tactic. Works really well because the person gets a financial incentive and the chance to help contribute towards The Empire. British people like that a lot.'

Bayston nodded. 'That's very true.'

'Next, they identify you. Now, the place where I caught him wasn't covered by cameras, so they won't be sure if you did it, or not. They have no footage of you and I together, or anything that can identify me. So, you're their prime suspect. But they can't use media or socials to appeal to anyone without raising too many questions. It's much better for them if they find you quietly and make you vanish.'

'What about Ulinov? Her students will soon notice she's missing.'

MacLoughlin waved it away. 'Oh, that's easy. Take her suitcase, passport, some clothes and tell everyone she *was* a spy after all, as they suspected. I bet nobody even questions it.'

'And me? What about me? My family, friends and girlfriend know I would never disappear like that.'

'There are literally dozens of ways to explain it. The last place you were known to be was Ulinov's. If it were me, I would be telling your family that Ulinov was a spy and they suspect you found out and that's why she got rid of you and fled.'

Bayston's jaw dropped. 'Holy shit. You're right.'

'I know. I do that a lot.'

The young Englishman stared at the American, without blinking, for almost half a minute. 'That makes perfect sense.'

'Now spend a few minutes thinking about news stories you heard over the years. You'll start noticing some similarities to your predicament.'

Bayston met him with a cold glare. 'I can already think of five or six, just from the last couple of years.'

'And there you have it.'

He sat back in the chair and slumped as the realisation hit him. 'I can't believe it. It can't be right. There has to be another explanation.'

'You already know there isn't,' MacLoughlin said softly. 'They've been lying to you since you were born, kid. Britain this, Britain that. Let me tell you: the things I have seen Britain do in the name of their empire is horrific.'

Bayston felt his stomach churn. He darted to the bathroom and managed to vomit into the toilet. He retched until there was nothing left. MacLoughlin stood at the door, waited for him to finish and then handed him a glass of water. He took a sip and then sat on the floor, leaning back on the bath, head in his hands. 'This can't be happening. It can't be.'

MacLoughlin flushed the toilet, put the lid down and sat on it. 'It is. I wish it weren't, Jamie, but it is. The Empire is a ruthless machine that will stop at nothing to protect itself.'

'But they're so altruistic,' he wheezed.

MacLoughlin patted Bayston's back. 'Many parts of The Empire are good, kid. The Queen spent a lifetime trying to make it what it could be. Her father, the same. Her uncle, before his drama, not so much. Each monarch is slightly different, but you need to realise that they can only do so much. Their influence is tremendous, but they don't run everything single-handed. There are loads of people, in high positions, that will protect The Empire by any means necessary and the monarch will never know about it. They need to protect what they have.'

'But she's dead now.'

'Alfred is weak sauce, kid, believe me. He's going to do fuck all until he dies. But, Leopold, well, that's a very different matter. That boy is formidable, smart and ruthless. From what I hear, he's focused on expansion.'

'So, what are you actually trying to achieve?'

'It's not just me. There's a whole bunch of us. There are movements in almost every country.'

'With what goal?'

'To get independence for our countries.'

Bayston peered up through his hands. 'You would need a referendum granted by both Parliament *and* the monarch.'

'I know that!' MacLoughlin replied querulously. 'We have done a bit of research, you know.'

'Right, sorry,' he said with a weak smile. 'So, what's your long-term objective? Surely independent nations can only mean one thing, right?'

MacLoughlin nodded enthusiastically. 'That's right. The end of the British Empire.'

Chapter 11

Trevor Layttle slowly and carefully steered the small Citroen into the parking structure, switching off the radio that blared out *AC/DC's Thunderstruck*. He drove it down two levels, as LeCourte had asked him to, located B6 and then stopped inside the large blue rectangle painted on the floor.

He looked around and quickly reached the conclusion that LeCourte was correct: this space was out of view of any cameras. He put his cap and moustache back on and waited for the other motorists to vanish towards the elevator at the far side of the structure.

He took the Glock out of his pocket. There should be a weapon waiting for him in London, but he still felt trepidation as he removed the cartridge and bullet, before slipping it into the holster attached by Velcro to the underside of the seat. He felt a bit naked now.

He took the passport and wallet from his inner jacket pocket. He would be Dieter Helman for the next few days, at least. The passport might have been a forgery, but it was an excellent one. He had credit and bank cards, over five thousand Euros and a few hundred pounds. He was not concerned about getting through immigration control. His only concern was that a camera would capture his image and they would track him later, but he would try his best to avoid them, if he could. Even if he could not avoid them all, nobody was going to be watching that exact screen at the exact time he went through. His thin disguise would be enough to stymie the limited facial recognition technology used at train stations.

All he had to do was get to the car in London, in a car park near King's Cross, which was only over the road from St Pancras. After that, he just needed make contact.

That part should be easy, but he knew better than to make any assumptions.

He took out his Device and checked the messages and emails, waiting that extra minute to run the encryption software first. Nothing. If he got no reply, he did not know where he could make contact, as he did not have access to any itineraries, which would all have been on the K6 server. The impenetrable K6 server.

Drumming his fingers on the steering wheel, he

pondered it for a few moments, snapping himself from his reverie when he noticed a pair of black 4x4s drive past him and park near the elevator. He watched them, waiting to see who got out. Not many people drove identical vehicles on a day out, so he was curious. As he half-expected, it was not a couple of families looking to catch the train. Nobody got out at all. He looked at the licence plates. Interpol, he guessed. Maybe at the behest of The Empire, maybe by Arnborg. They were not on his tail, he was sure of that. They would already be arresting him, if that were the case. No, they were probably watching the train station, just in case he showed up.

He did not understand why they were sitting in their vehicles, though. They could see the elevator from there, but not much else. He craned his neck to look around and he saw another black 4x4 parked on the far side of the garage, next to the path that led to the rear of the station.

He felt his heart start beating a bit harder and sweat formed on his brow. If there were three, then there might be several vehicles parked around the site. Why would they send so many here? He could understand sending some people to watch on the off chance he appeared, but to send several teams suggested they knew he would leave via this station. There were dozens of ways to enter Britain and he doubted they would be covering all of them with so many people.

Had LeCourte betrayed him? He doubted it very much. There was no long-term gain for him and he did not need the reward money. Layttle searched his brain for any way they could know he was here. He checked his every movement since Paris. He was sure he had not made any mistakes.

He was never going to make it on to a train unnoticed with so many eyes here. He was about to start the car and leave when the elevator opened and Arnborg walked out of it.

Layttle's jaw dropped, but he suddenly felt calmer. They were not here for him.

The doors to the 4x4s opened and agents stepped out of them. But they weren't K6 agents. He did not know where they were from, maybe DGSE. He watched the agents scouring the area robotically. They were a security detail, that was clear immediately.

Layttle had known Arnborg for many years and he travelled with one bodyguard. Never a huge team like this. He whipped out his Device and checked the arrivals in the past ten minutes. London, Brussels, Nice and Amsterdam trains had all arrived in that time. He was pretty sure Arnborg had come from one of those. It certainly was not Hamburg.

If Arnborg was travelling with such an entourage, he was carrying something valuable. This could be serendipity. The evidence he carried was certainly useful, but maybe there was something more compelling with Arnborg right now. Layttle was not one for believing in fate, but even he had to concede this seemed too fortunate to be coincidence.

Arnborg was here for a sinister reason, he could sense it. Why else would he travel with so much security? There should be no need. And that made Layttle very curious. This seemed to be an opportunity that had fallen right into his lap. He needed to get to London. But to have something more concrete to use against The Empire would make the job of convincing his allies so much easier.

The 4x4s started to pull out of the parking structure and he looked at the elevator. London was waiting, with allies and a chance to really cause The Empire some damage. He looked at the convoy leaving and sighed. It was too good a chance to pass up.

He started the Citroen's engine and drove after them.

TWELVE MILES NORTH-EAST OF POKHARA, NEPAL

Bob Royce laid on his back and listened to the melody of birds waking up. The sun barely peeked over the horizon, and it was close to freezing, but the valley was alive with birdsong. He found it relaxing and peaceful. Indeed, he could not recall the last time he had felt such peace. He pulled his sleeping bag up to cover his nose and smiled. The air was frigid, but there was very little breeze and it surprised him that the flora remained so fragrant even at night. He had spent many a night in jungles, deserts, forests and tundra all over the world, but nowhere was quite like this.

He looked at the silhouettes of trees around him and took a lungful of fresh, crisp air. The thought of absconding crossed his mind briefly, but he dispelled it swiftly. He wanted to stretch the assignment out, but knew that option was gone now he had set things in motion.

His guide had turned back when Royce 'ran out of money' three nights before. He wanted privacy. He sensed he was close.

He checked the ridge where he had undoubtedly seen the shape of a person last night. That was the third time he had seen someone, or so he thought. They kept their distance and hid. Usually, he would not be alerted by that. Plenty of people gave him a wide berth.

However, both the previous times he had reached the spot where he had seen them to find no traces of them at all and no tracks indicating where they went. If not for that, he might have dismissed it as locals who were afraid of him. Had he only seen them once, he might have ignored it as a trick of the light. But he was certain that someone was watching him. The fact they were so expert at covering their tracks meant he was getting closer.

He waited for the sun to rise and then lit his fire. He made a pot of coffee and poured a cup as he took chunks of bread from the loaf in his bag and chewed them slowly, holding the mug with both hands as often as he could to warm his hands. He peered towards the ridge regularly, but whoever was there did not show themselves again. He finished his breakfast and packed his things.

It was a six-hour hike to the ridge and, when he got there, he found exactly what he expected: nothing. He sat and drank some water, looking back over the valley and wondering.

Why would anyone so skilled at hiding their tracks be careless enough for Royce to see them three times? He ruminated over the paradox for a while as he enjoyed the warmth of the sun on his face. Eventually, he realised the answer was obvious.

They wouldn't be so careless. Nobody who could so expertly vanish would ever been seen by anyone.

Not unless they wanted to be seen.

Royce chuckled to himself. 'Clever,' he said to a butterfly that fluttered past.

They were leading him away from something. And, if they were trying to do that, then he was closer than he thought. So much for dragging out the assignment to stay here longer, he thought to himself ruefully.

Royce stood up, stretched and yawned loudly. He looked back the way he had come. Valleys, mountains, forests and a lake in the distance. He had seen nothing that even looked like a cabin and certainly nothing that might be hiding an entire army.

Nesbitt did not have much information about The Dayak, but his intelligence suggested they must be a large army hidden in several locations. Otherwise, how had they proven so difficult for The Empire to defeat?

Royce was now suspecting something he was sure Nesbitt had not even considered. The Empire couldn't find The Dayak because the group was so small. It made hiding much easier.

He spent several minutes in silence, carefully studying everything around him to ensure nobody was anywhere nearby, watching or listening. Finally satisfied that he was totally alone, he reached into his bag and pulled out the SatDevice Nesbitt had given him. It was an encrypted, single-use SatDevice that could make a single call to a single number. After that, it would fry itself.

He pressed the button, lifted it to his ear and waited as it made the call. He sighed and looked around him, saddened by the fact it would soon be over. He liked this place so much.

'Bob?'

'Sir.'

'I take it you have something for me?'

'Yes, sir.'

'You found them?'

Royce rubbed his shaven scalp. 'Not exactly, sir.'

'Don't tell me The Tracker can't find some farmers,' he quipped, his thick Scottish accent resting on the word 'farmers' for emphasis.

'Perhaps, sir. You need to make a decision, though.'

Nesbitt paused and took a deep breath. 'Well, now you have piqued my interest. Go on.'

'I'm ninety per cent certain I know where they are.'

'That's great. Give me the coordinates.'

'Wait, sir,' he replied apprehensively. 'I don't know exactly, but I have a very good idea of the region they're hiding in.'

'Have you seen them?'

'Maybe. I can't be sure.'

'But you saw tracks?'

'No, sir, they don't leave any tracks. They're like ghosts.'

'So how the hell do you know where they are?' Nesbitt snapped querulously.

'Because someone is trying to lead me away from them, I think, by trying to make me think I'm tracking them.'

'Hold on,' the general replied with a confused tone. 'You're saying you know where they are because they're leading you to where they aren't?'

'I think so, sir. In fact, I'm sure of it.'

'So, just go back to where they're not leading you, Bob. It seems pretty simple. Indeed, now you've wasted the call for this, how will you tell me when you do actually find them?'

Royce chuckled. 'Sorry, sir, but I don't think you really want me to do that.'

'Why the fuck not?' His patience was clearly wearing thin.

'If I do that, they will know that they didn't fool me. If I pretend to be led away, they will think they have succeeded and won't be aware that I have a very good idea where they are. Not exactly, but close enough, I think.'

Nesbitt paused and his smile was so wide it could be heard even over the poor connection. 'You're a bloody genius.'

He laughed. 'I have my moments, I will admit.'

'And then you return with the battalion from the nearest base?'

'They won't have time to escape, even if they do see us coming. The worst that happens is they see and/or hear us coming and we flush them out. Either way, we find them.'

'Any way to trap them?'

'I have a couple of ideas about that, sir. Do you think you can get a number of platoons from different bases in here without anyone knowing? Or, even better, a battalion or two?'

'I can't move battalions without anyone knowing, but I could probably get you four or five platoons within a couple of days. What's closest to you? Anbu?'

'Yes, sir.'

'How long before you get back there?'

'Two to three days, maximum, sir.'

'I will issue orders that you have temporary command of the base. The local is a man called Captain Tenchi. He's lazy and won't care at all about being supplanted.' Nesbitt was elated, his voice almost high-pitched. 'I knew The Tracker wouldn't let me down.'

'What do you want me to do with them when we find them?'

'We'll make an example of them, Bob. I want everyone to know what happens when you defy The Empire. I'll find some people to help with that.'

'Consider it done, sir.'

'Great job, Bob. Really, really amazing work.'

'Thanks, sir.'

The line went dead and Royce put the SatDevice back in his bag. He looked around at the scenery and sighed. It would be a shame to cover it in blood, but he had orders.

He stood up and made his way in the direction the shadows were leading him. When he returned, it would be very different.

Chapter 12

The House of Commons fell quiet as King Alfred burst in. The room was dusty and stale, a thick stench of sweat lingering in the air. The lights were always dim, making the fading sun of late afternoon seem even darker.

Every person in the room rose from their seat as King Alfred powered down towards his throne, closely followed by both his sons. Leopold hurried eagerly behind his father, but Christian was more curious than he was zealous. It was not often his father demanded his sons be with him and even more out-of-character for him to storm into Parliament with such verve.

Christian briefly tried to remember when he had ever seen his father display such purpose. He did not think he had ever seen it before.

Alfred strode up to the throne and indicated that someone should come and clean it. The throne was always there for the monarch to use, but nobody had spontaneously sat in it for at least four decades.

The usher rushed over and wiped the dust from it swiftly, bowing and backing away. The king took his seat, his sons standing either side of him.

There were a few uncertain and uncomfortable moments of silence, as the MPs all exchanged glances and waited to see what would happen next.

King Alfred looked around and eventually his eyes rested on The Speaker, a small, rotund man with thinning black hair and a face like a giraffe. 'What do I do now, Vincent?'

'Erm, w-w-w-w-well, sire, I'm not exactly s-s-s-s-sure,' he stammered.

'Do I need to hold a staff or sceptre or something?'

'No, Your Majesty. I'm sorry, I don't know the protocol for this circumstance.' He looked around the room to see if anyone else did.

'I'll just say what I came to say, then,' Alfred boomed.

'If you'll forgive me, sire, this is highly unusual,' squeaked a Liberal Party MP from the front row.

The king turned on him sharply. It was Travis Beane, one of the few MPs even older than him and the regular dissenting voice in the room. 'Why's that, Mr Beane?'

He visibly shrank. 'Well, erm, well...your mother never-'

'Maybe she should have done!' he barked. 'This

is my right, as head of the British Empire, and I have chosen to exercise it. Do you have a problem with that?'

Beane seemed to be an inch tall. 'Of course not, sire.'

'Good! Anyway, Travis, shut up and listen. You will like this.'

'Very good, Your Majesty,' he replied quietly, bowing his head.

The monarch held his arms out and motioned for everyone to sit down, waiting for them to obey, before he stood up. 'I'm not here to put a bill to you today. I'm not here to listen to you or talk to you. I'm here to tell you that I'm going to use the power of Royal Executive to pass a law. Does everyone understand what that means?' The entire room suddenly seemed to be in a fog of confusion. Alfred turned to The Speaker. 'Do you know, Vincent?'

'I think it means you can pass a law without the Commons or Lords voting on it, Your Majesty.'

'Correct.' He paused to let that sink in and watched their faces as they started to understand. 'I know this is unconventional, but I can assure you it's entirely legal. So, today, I'm going to change the law.'

'Which law, sire?' asked a woman at the back of the room.

The king looked first at Leopold, who nodded, and then at Christian, who gave him an encouraging smile. 'I want to revoke Section 377 of the British Penal Code and amend the Sexual Offences Act of 1967. We're going to make homosexuality legal today, ladies and gentlemen.'

There were whispers and murmurs, but nobody dissented. There seemed to be a few begrudging expressions, but not a single word spoken.

Beane stood up slowly, looking around him with a beaming smile. He started to clap.

Soon, others joined him. Within a minute, all but a few MPs were on their feet, whooping and cheering. The sounds of the rapturous applause bounced down the halls and spilled out the windows.

Leopold took a deep, happy breath and puffed out his chest. Barely even a mumble of discontent.

Christian leaned into his father. 'Amazing work, Father.' He had never been so proud of him, stepping out of her shadow and righting one of the biggest wrongs within their beloved British Empire.

King Alfred smiled at his youngest son. 'It was your brother's idea.'

Christian looked over at Leopold. 'Yea?'

Leo smiled back. 'There were some fights that Nan just never got around to. She was tired the last few years, I guess.'

'Good work, brother. Really, really good,' Christian remarked happily.

'Thanks, Chris.'

Christian looked around the room, the adoration flowing towards his father, and he grinned to himself. After their first Privy Council meeting, he had been a little concerned about the energy in the room, especially his brother's plans for expansion. But he felt hopeful now. The team his father and brother were forming seemed to be ready to take the British Empire in to the modern world.

He loved the British Empire with his whole heart, but their grandmother had not been in good health for the last twelve, or more, years of her reign, so they had fallen behind the other powers of the world in many things. Plus, their grandmother had a very conservative mindset that allowed the politicians to ignore blatant human's right violations and call it 'tradition' without her ever challenging it.

His father had just told the world he was not going to continue that. He was going to change things for the better.

King Alfred's reign had well and truly begun.

MARACAIBO, VENEZUELA

The wind swept in fiercely from the Gulf of Venezuela and swirled across Lake Maracaibo, before disappearing inland towards the jungle. The Urdaneta Bridge towered over the small fishing boats that chuntered under it, making their way over to the markets at Cabimas, back home along the coast, or back out to sea to make a living.

Gugano sat quietly in his seat, half-listening to the conversation, half-looking out at the view of the city. To his left, he could see the Villa del Rosario, blindingly white in the midday sunshine, and even the airport in the distance. To his right, he could see the lake and in front of him the ocean glistened all the way to the northern tip of Colombia. He could also see all the half-finished construction projects and the buildings left to fall into disrepair. There were dozens of them.

Max stopped talking for a while and looked over to his partner. He knew a rooftop garden restaurant would keep Gugano relaxed and happy. It made him smile and he admired the colossus for a few moments. His hair was tangled, but he had showered and was wearing a new, crisp, white shirt and grey shorts. They were the first new clothes he had worn for a few weeks. Max knew he even had new underwear on. That showed how important this meeting was to him.

He caught a glimpse of his reflection in the window of the entrance to the building and he liked what he saw. He was wearing the same thing as his lover and, here, out of the British Empire, they were free to do such things. He knew that they would soon be able to be open when back home, too, though, and that pleased him greatly.

He looked over at the people opposite him. They were both wearing casual, smart shirts and trousers, loose-fitting and comfortable. The heat here was almost unbearable, although at least, up here, there was breeze and shade.

'So, Max, how do we proceed?'

The question was from General Florenz, a ruthless and calculating woman, who was almost as round as she was tall, with dark hair tied in a bun and a huge scar on her left cheek.

Hernando Otero, leader of the opposition, continued. He was a tall, wiry man, with thick, silver hair in a crew cut and a nose so long it might have qualified as a beak. 'We need assurances of support before we can do anything.'

Max laughed and sipped his ice coffee. 'I have given you assurances already. The next move is yours. We cannot weaken your economy any more than we already have. The people are never going to be more discontent than they are now. We have flown directly from London to this meeting to show our support.'

Florenz sighed and cleared her throat. 'If we do this and you don't honour your promise, we are both dead.' She indicated herself and Otero.

'We're very aware of that,' Max replied, making a calming gesture with his hands. 'We're also very aware that the National Republic and the Free Alliance are gathering momentum. We want to act before they gain traction. Do we have your

assurances they will be dealt with as a priority?'
Both nodded. 'Good. Their anti-British sentiments
need to be silenced if our support is going to mean
anything in the next election.'

'When will your troops get here?'

'They're in Guiana now. We have been
sneaking more and more into the country over the
past, few weeks. How many troops do you control,
General?'

She paused to consider it. 'Probably half, so
about sixty thousand troops.'

'Which regions?'

She smiled. 'All of them around here. Don't
worry, when we do this, we will control the oil and
that's what matters in this country.'

'Agreed,' Max replied pensively. 'When they
come, and they will, then we will have the reason
to intervene. How long can you hold the bridge?'

'Indefinitely, but they will come from the south.
There's only one road in that will allow for mass
troop movement and we think we can hold that,
and the bridge, for a month.'

'That's plenty of time,' he replied confidently.
'We will be in Caracas, we believe, in about a
week. Where is President Herrera now?'

Otero grinned. 'In his private residence, about
six kilometres north of here. He is hosting your
ambassador tonight, I believe.'

'It's important you take her, too. And then return
her to us unharmed immediately, you understand?

And publicly. We need the support of the British public.'

'Yes,' Florenz said with a firm nod. 'We have a good idea how to do that. Do you want to hear it?'

He shook his head. 'No need. I trust your judgement. You have your statement ready and it's all about fixing the country and bringing stability, removing corruption and feeding the people, yes?' They both nodded. 'Excellent. So, I think everything is in place.' He touched Gugano's arm. 'Anything else you can think of? Did we miss anything?'

The giant snapped himself from his trance. 'We have a good plan.' He met Florenz and Otero with a deathly cold glower. 'You take Herrera, you return our ambassador, you give the speech, you defend the city and Britain will rescue you. We have a four-star general from Germany ready to ratify your ascension treaty. Our own General Nesbitt will do the same and then we can occupy to preserve your new government. It's all easy now. The hard work has been done.'

'What hard work?' Otero scoffed.

Gugano sat up and growled. 'Getting the country into a position where a man like *you* appeals to them.' They all sat in silence for a few moments as the viciousness of his remark landed. He pressed his point. 'We will hold an election in three months, a referendum next year and Venezuela will join The Empire. Then we will get the Department of Missionary Services to despatch people here and start importing British values, ideals and teachings. They will bring the food with them.'

'What happens to Herrera and his government?'

Max answered. 'The ones who join you can stay, everyone else goes to Anglesey the day you become British. Any other questions?'

'Even Herrera?'

'Especially Herrera. He will be a war criminal and, under British law, he goes to Anglesey to await an Execution Trial before the Supreme Court.'

They all smiled, except Gugano, who had returned to admiring the view. Florenz stood up and bid them farewell, Otero did the same only a few minutes later, both being reminded to follow the plan by the gargantuan opposite them.

Once they had gone, Max took his partner's hand and squeezed it. 'We're nearly there, honey.'

Gugano smiled back, flashing his grey and black teeth. 'Shall we stay here?'

He looked at the lake and the ocean and took a deep breath. 'That would be nice, but you know we can't. We have to go home in a few hours, my love.'

'At least we won't be illegal there any longer.'

'True.'

'Where do you want to go next?'

Max paused and exhaled loudly. 'I don't know.

I haven't thought about it yet. Let's see what Leo thinks.' Gugano nodded and turned back to the view. Max did the same, but grinned as he did so. 'So begins the invasion of South America.'

Chapter 13

Bayston sipped his cola and kept watching the street. It was cold and dark. He adjusted his hood again, although MacLoughlin had assured him there were no cameras anywhere near him. His job was to watch the street and report if anything suspicious came down it.

He had no idea what suspicious looked like, but was hoping he would know it if he saw it.

MacLoughlin was in the building behind him, meeting with someone from local government, that Bayston had never heard of, but was somehow involved with The Dayak.

Bayston had thought long and hard about MacLoughlin's proposition. The more Bayston thought about it, the more likely the truth was that The Empire was behind Ulinov's death and that the best thing he could do was disappear.

MacLoughlin certainly made a very compelling

case. He seemed to know exactly which moves The Empire would make and why, suggesting he was more involved with them than he had, so far, admitted.

It felt too fantastic to be possible. That, somehow, the country he had grown up in, and loved for as long as he could remember, was murdering people. Not only that, but they would also murder him, if they found him. And his entire family, if he contacted them.

Bayston had done nothing but think about it, playing that night over and over in his head, like a live-action snuff film. And he could not find anything to disprove MacLoughlin's claims. As much as he did not want to believe it, there seemed to be no other explanation.

He could hear the blood dripping from the wire. He could feel those eyes staring through him, their latest target. He could still hear the pounding footsteps behind him. It felt fuzzy and ethereal, like a nightmare, but he knew it was not. It had happened. It had brought him here, outside a closed pub in Milton Keynes at three in the morning, sipping a can of coke and watching a dark, deserted street.

He tried to imagine how he could live without his family and Claire. It made him want to cry. How could he have a life without them? He knew they would be crushed, hurt, maybe even angry, but he also knew he had no choice.

Even if MacLoughlin was wrong about The Empire, he was right that *someone* had killed Ulinov and *someone* knew Bayston had witnessed everything. He was not safe to go back home. To even contact them was to put them all in danger. If he went back, it would be selfish. He had to protect them. His life might be ruined, but there was no reason theirs needed to be, too. They would get over his disappearance and move on, eventually. They could not do that if they were all dead.

There was a sudden gust of frigid air and it made him shiver. He spent a few minutes trying to think of any explanation for the past, few days, that would counter MacLoughlin's, but nothing came to him. He had already spent hours ruminating on the subject and had reached the same conclusion every time.

MacLoughlin was his best chance to survive, as he seemed to know something about this life.

This life.

The phrase almost seemed to mock him. What sort of life could he possibly have now? A life of nothing. It hardly seemed worth the effort.

Yet something inside of him drove him on. He was not sure what it was, exactly. His emotions were all over the place and was struggling to pinpoint them. To start with he had felt numb, which his American saviour said was shock. After that had passed, there was melancholy, a chasm so deep he felt like he would suffocate in it. But there was something in that chasm to keep him warm, that was keeping him alive in the cold darkness. It was deep inside him and grew more powerful with each passing hour.

It was anger.

He could sense the white-hot sensation in his gut and it was spreading. He wanted revenge. They had taken everything from him and he wanted them to pay for it.

That seemed to be all that was driving him at the moment, his only reason for living.

That was fine by him. It certainly felt better than the emptiness.

He craned his neck and looked back at the pub. It was completely dark inside. He knew MacLoughlin and his colleague were back there somewhere. He turned back to the road. It was four lanes wide, with tall buildings either side of it, interspersed with trees and parking spaces everywhere. On one side of the road was an enormous shopping centre, while the other side seemed to be all office buildings.

It was eerily quiet, but that was hardly a huge shock in the middle of the night. He saw headlights approaching and watched them carefully, but a van drove past and turned the corner behind him. Once the sound of the engine had faded, the silence resumed.

Another few minutes went by and he finished his cola. He saw a green bin just a few metres away and walked over to throw it in. As he tossed it through the gap, he caught some movement in his peripheral vision. There was a van, with no lights, coming down the street. He could not hear the engine, either, suggesting it was coasting. If not for the reflection from the shopping centre lights, he would never have noticed it. It was still a couple of hundred metres away from him.

He knew something was not right instantly. Why would anyone be driving around like that? Maybe they were here to rob one of the shops or offices, but it seemed too much of a coincidence. The trees hid him from view at this distance, but that would not last much longer. When they got close, they would see him easily.

Bayston felt the adrenalin surge again. He did not seem to panic. His thoughts felt crisp and clear. He had two options: run or hide.

If they knew he was there, hiding seemed futile. However, if they did not know exactly where he was, then it was a better option than running. He eyed the distance to the corner and looked back at the van, trying to judge if he could make it. He doubted he was fast enough, but he might be.

He decided not to take the chance. He sprinted towards the pub and dove behind a small decorative bush in a half-metre tall, wooden grow box. He landed with a thud and almost wailed, but he managed to keep it in. He could not see the van from this position, so he stayed quiet, tried to control his breathing and listened.

Once it got closer, he could hear the tyres on the road. It was very slight, but the sound of rubber on the tarmac was just audible over the pounding in his chest and throbbing in his head. He waited for it to roll past and heard the engine start. There were a few low revs and then it drove away.

Bayston peeked out from behind the wooden box. He could hear the van turning the corner and getting further away. He took a deep breath, but shuffled out on his hands and knees, his head spinning and eyes flicking around, scanning every shadow for any sign of danger.

Content there was no threat nearby, he sat on the floor and peered towards the dark pub. What should he do now? Should he warn MacLoughlin? Would that help? They obviously did not know where he was, or they would have gone in. Maybe they weren't here for him, or Bayston, anyway. Maybe it was nothing.

But something did not feel right about that van. This was exactly what MacLoughlin had told him to watch for, he was certain of it. He had better try and warn his saviour while he could. They could reappear at any moment.

He stood up and slowly walked over towards the glass door of the pub, surveying everything as he moved. He cupped his hands either side of his head and peered inside. There was nothing. He had no idea where the American was now.

He gently rapped his knuckles on the glass and waited. Still nothing. He knocked harder, then harder and then harder again.

'Hey,' came a voice behind him. He spun around, his heart leaping out of his mouth, to see MacLoughlin behind him. 'What you doing?'

Bayston closed his eyes and sighed as the relief washed over him. 'There was a van.'

He shrugged his shoulders. 'I'm sure there are many vans around here.'

'No, Ed,' Bayston replied firmly. 'There was something about this one. It had no lights and was coasting past.'

He suddenly stood up straight and looked around. 'Are you sure?'

'Yes, I'm sure. I hid.'

'Okay, let's get the fuck out of here, kid.' He took Bayston's arm and started leading him away, towards where the car was parked.

Suddenly, there was a commotion in the distance. The sounds of something crashing and some loud voices.

'Go!' MacLoughlin shouted and broke into a run.

Bayston did not need telling twice. He darted after the American, sprinting across the four lanes of road and vaulting the bushes the other side. The car was just behind the next building.

They ran past the office block and turned the corner. Bayston was quickest and was there first.

As he turned the corner, the sight before him made him skid to a halt and freeze in terror.

There were four armed soldiers next to their car.

They were only a few metres away, so there was no way they would not see or hear him. He could not hope to avoid them. They started to raise their weapons in his direction.

As Bayston became a statue, MacLoughlin came around the corner. He was not as fast as Bayston, but he was still quick. Unlike the young Englishman, however, the American did not stop. He sped up. As the nearest soldier was starting to aim, MacLoughlin reached him, pushing the rifle to the side. The bullets hit another soldier in the side of the head, spraying blood up in the air. He screamed and fell.

MacLoughlin kept going. The rifle had a strap and he kept running into the third soldier, kicking him so hard he fell forwards onto the floor. Simultaneously, the American yanked the weapon and pulled the attached soldier from his feet.

The fourth soldier had been aiming at Bayston, but quickly realised where the immediate threat was coming from. He moved to target MacLoughlin, but the American was already on him, punching him in the stomach. He grunted and the American grabbed the back of his head and smashed it into the car bonnet with such force that his teeth flew in every direction.

Number three was starting to get back up, but

MacLoughlin aimed a running kick at his ribs. The force lifted the soldier from the ground and he fell back into a heap with a wail of agony. The American still held the rifle and he twisted it so that the soldier who was still wearing it bent over. MacLoughlin snatched a pistol from the holster on his hip and fired three quick shots at the three nearby targets. All of them dropped to the ground, blood leaking from their faces.

He looked up at Bayston. 'You can drive, right?'

Bayston nodded, open-mouthed and wide-eyed.

MacLaughlin tossed him the car keys. 'We need to change vehicle, but we need to get out of here first.'

Bayston caught them, but just stared at the four corpses in front of him.

'Jamie! Get the fucking car started. They will have heard that.' He still did not move.

MacLoughlin detached the rifle from the strap and grabbed the Englishman, shaking him hard. 'Jamie, if you don't get that car started, we are dead!'

The word 'dead' seemed to resonate with him and he suddenly blinked a few times, then ran over to the car. He could hear the engines of the van behind them. The others were coming.

MacLoughlin was already running towards the sound. Bayston started the car and reversed it over two of the lifeless soldiers, spinning around in time to see the American drop to one knee. The gunshots clacked off the office buildings around them, reverberating down the street.

Bayston could see the van windscreen crack as holes appeared in it and, presumably, whoever was driving it. The van veered off and crashed into a tree. Within moments, MacLoughlin was next to it, emptying the entire ammunition clip into the windscreen. When that ran out, he released and switched the clip in a split-second, emptying that into the vehicle, also.

When that was empty, he paused and, seemingly satisfied, turned back towards where Bayston had the car idling. He strode over, dropping the rifle to the floor as he got into the passenger seat. He pulled the pistol out from the holster under his jacket and kept his eyes on the van. Bayston pulled away and sped down the road. 'Where we going?'

'Just put as much distance between us and them as you can, as quickly as possible. We will switch the car when we're a bit further away.'

'Who were they?' panted Bayston.

'Imperial agents,' he retorted brusquely, turning to face the Englishman. 'You still think I'm exaggerating about what The Empire will do? That was a double Imperial kill team, kid. They really, really want you dead.'

Bayston stifled a cry. 'What do we do now?'

'We get out of this car and get somewhere to lay low and rest for a few hours. We need to get to London, but I need to make some arrangements first.'

'Arrangements for what?'

'We need to go in quietly and we can't be seen. I need to contact a couple of people first. It's not safe for them. Anyone we go near seems to be dead soon after.'

'Because of me?' Bayston sobbed.

MacLoughlin did not answer the question. He did not need to.

Chapter 14

MOISSAC, FRANCE

Layttle watched the convoy of 4x4s stop outside the huge abbey, so pulled up down the street. He grabbed his bottle of water and took a gulp, before stuffing more sandwich into his mouth. He cricked his neck and yawned.

The sun had only been up a couple of hours and he had not slept well in the car, but it had allowed him a good view of the hotel that Arnborg and his entourage had stayed in. If not, he would not have been ready when they left before dawn this morning.

He eyed the abbey. It looked almost orange in the morning sunshine and the scent of the local fishmonger drifted around this part of the town. There was a restaurant spilling out on to the plaza and the outdoor seating meant the convoy had to park fifty metres from the abbey. It had a large entrance, with a tympanum portico over it, sculptures down either side and a pointed tower high above. The abbey itself was mostly hidden by other buildings, as it stretched away to the right, down a narrow alleyway.

He watched Arnborg walk over towards the entrance, escorted by four armed guards, and disappear inside. The guards all waited outside. He clearly wanted privacy.

Layttle sensed this was his best chance to find out what was going on. He had already gone over a day out of his way and needed to get London soon. The longer he delayed, the more likely someone would find out what he knew about Lillian Cheroux.

He got out of the car and walked away from the abbey, finding the railway that ran adjacent to the rear wall. He checked that nobody was watching and darted down the wall, hiding under a pair of trees, behind a bush. He waited a few moments and surveyed the area. There was a public footbridge over the railway, maybe thirty metres down the track. He would need to get over the wall without anyone seeing him. His best chance, he knew, was also by far the most dangerous.

He needed a train to come.

He waited for the people on the bridge to walk over and then sprinted across the track. There was a small recess in the wall and he hid next to it. Nobody from the bridge would be able to see him if he crouched, but he needed a train to hide him as he scaled the wall. It had chunks of bricks missing and random pieces of protruding stone, so it would be easy to get up. He just needed to wait.

It was around six minutes before he felt the rumble under his feet, then heard the distinctive clacking. He got ready.

As soon as the train engine passed the bridge, he jumped and scrambled over. He only had a few seconds to get up the five-metre wall and on to the roof. There did not seem to be anyone below, so he jumped, landing on a perfectly verdant cloister. It was soft and muffled the sound of his drop. He eyed the covered walkway around the courtyard and ran to the nearest one, leaping over the waist-high wall and hiding behind it. The ornate pillars around the walkway obscured his view across the grass, but they also helped hide him. He was, however, in an exposed walkway with no cover. He needed to move and hide. He had seen a couple of tourists entering before Arnborg and there were monks in residence, he suspected.

He found the nearest door and pressed himself up against it. He could not hear anything inside, so he cautiously opened it and entered. Closing it quietly behind him, he found a small kitchen, with another doorway on the far side.

He snatched the fire evacuation plan from the wall and studied it for a few moments. The other doorway led to the refectory, which had a warming room the other side of it. That seemed to be unnecessary in the age of central heating, so he would see what it was being used for now.

He carefully opened the far door and peeked into the refectory. There were two long benches and seats either side of them both, but nobody was still eating breakfast, so he sped across it and to the next doorway. Taking a moment to press his ear against the wood, he discerned no voices, so he went inside.

It was a large room, with several empty baths and a lit fireplace on the far wall. It seemed it was still used to warm the monks, but there was no danger of that being necessary this early in the day, he thought. He could spare a few moments to try and figure out where Arnborg would be.

He eyed the evacuation plan and saw a couple of staircases. Above him there seemed to be an office, which was a good possibility. He needed to hurry. Whatever Arnborg was up to might only take minutes and he would miss it all if he was not quick.

The warming room led back out to the cloister walkway, which then led to the staircase. He heard some footsteps and voices at the far side of the cloister, but he was swift and used the pillars to hide as he moved.

He reached the staircase, ready to rush up them, but stopped as he saw they also went down. It was not on the plan because it was not a route to take in the event of a fire. He paused for a moment, then dashed down them silently. That was where he would go.

He was only a few steps down when he heard the voices beneath him. They seemed to be raised, so he was able to approach on tiptoes, but faster than he usually would. As he got closer, he realised there were two distinct voices. He needed to pause and listen intently to identify Arnborg, but he did not know the other one. It sounded Dutch or German, maybe Belgian.

He slowed down his descent and looked around him. They were in a crypt and it was long and dark, with very low lights dotted down either side of it. It curved to make the shape of a banana, so he could not see the end. There were dozens of recessed tombs carved into the wall on both sides, each one housing a dim, exposed light bulb.

He noted that he could not see any way out, other than the staircase he was at the bottom of. The two men he was looking for were about halfway down, where the curve began, hidden by shadow. Layttle managed to dart across the crypt to a recess holding the grave of a monk from 1865. He reached up and unscrewed the bulb in the hanging light above him, putting him in a dark shadow. He waited to see if either man noticed, but they were too busy arguing, it seemed.

Layttle managed to squeeze himself between the stone tomb, in the shape of a man, and the cold wall. It was tight and uncomfortable, with a rock buried in the base of his spine, but it concealed him quite well. He could not see the men from this position, so he closed his eyes and tried to train his ears.

'I know what we said, but that was before this situation.' Layttle's breathing was too loud, making it difficult for him to hear.

He recognised Arnborg's voice immediately. 'This changes nothing. It's an inconvenience, nothing more. And we can use it.'

He tried to heave a couple of breaths into his lungs when there was a pause. They were probably sixty or seventy metres away, which would usually be too far to hear their conversation, but the crypt was quiet and had excellent acoustics. He stayed still and listened as intently as he could.

'We need to find them.'

'No, we don't. Layttle will and we follow him.'

'Do we know where Layttle is?'

'Last seen in Paris, so we suspect he will try to get over to England.'

'Can we stop that?'

'Probably not. Trevor is exceptional. The only way to find and stop him will be to find his contact.'

The mystery voice growled. 'Do we know what he has yet?'

'Not yet,' Arnborg replied. 'I told you before: he's a genius. He knew better than to share it with anyone. Besides, we don't need to know. We just need to know who he gives it to.'

'The tracker is active already, though?'

'Not yet. Not until he downloads the files to a non-K6 computer.'

'You're sure he doesn't know about it?'

'I didn't tell anyone. Not even Gus.'

'Good. This is our only way to find the leak.'

Arnborg sighed loudly. 'My meeting went well. I'm heading back to Hamburg soon, to finalise the details and await the tracer.'

There was a long pause and Layttle could hear the rip of Velcro. 'We waited a long time for this.'

'It has all of them on. Every single one. We're on there, too.'

'And it's the only copy?'

'Yes.'

'Excellent.' Lyttle knew the voice, but could not place it. 'How many of us are there?'

'Over two hundred active participants.'

'And the orders for each person is on there?'

'Yes, but it needs to go to the chairman and they will be disseminated from there. There is a year's worth of assignments on it.'

'Directly from him?'

'He put it in my hand himself.'

'How did he look?'

'Ready.'

'He's waited a long time.'

'We all have.'

'And they're agreed on Outpost?'

'Apparently King Alfred has sanctioned it

himself.'

'Wow. He's braver than I thought. The Russians and the Asian Coalition, too?'

'Yes. It's just us that need to sign the accord now, then we can announce.'

There was a shuffle near the staircase and they fell silent for a few moments, waiting for the sounds to pass. Arnborg continued. 'Okay, I need to get back. My meeting in Marseilles is tonight and I can't be late, then I need to get back.'

'I will have this to the chairman by tonight.'

'Good. Speak to you next week.'

The footsteps approached and Layttle bowed his head to hide. He recognised the sound of the gait as Arnborg. He guessed the Dutch/French/Belgian man would wait a few minutes before leaving, so they would not be spotted together.

He spent the time considering what he had just heard. The data he had was a trap, but that wasn't a huge concern for him. Now he knew about it, the trap would be easy to circumvent. What Arnborg did not understand was that he would have assumed the data was not safe once downloaded, anyway. It was a basic K6 safety protocol. The fact Arnborg, and probably Gus, did not know that suggested they were too distracted doing other things to be paying attention to the details.

Layttle had always found the details to be the difference between success and failure, victory or defeat.

Nothing he had heard was helpful, except one thing.

Fontane was being called the chairman of something. Chairman of what? No doubt the leader of The Empire's European campaign. The one they repeatedly denied existed.

They seemed to be Imperial agents and were responsible for the management of a couple of hundred agents within Europe. Or that was how Layttle perceived it.

He suddenly heard footsteps coming his way and bowed his head again. As soon as they started disappearing up the stairs, he screwed the bulb back into the fixture and leapt out from behind the tomb, stifling the groans from allowing blood back into some of his pained muscles.

He needed a few moments to stretch out his limbs and he felt the pins and needles evaporating under his skin. He made his way back up the stairs and caught a glimpse of the mystery voice as they turned the corner of the walkway around the cloister. He tried to see who it was from a distance, but the pillars obscured his view.

He sprinted to the corner, but was not fast enough. They turned before he could get a good look. Layttle followed them into the church, but they were exiting the building and he was too far behind. There were tourists there now, and a couple of monks, but he sprinted across the nave, leaping over the pews and landing in a roll. He arrived at the doorway and peeked outside just in time to see the mystery voice getting into a black sedan.

His jaw dropped as he watched Jacques Fontane being driven away. He was just a delivery boy.

But if Fontane was in the car, then who was The Chairman? Who was running the European campaign?

He ran to his Citroen and raced after Fontane. Whatever Arnborg had given the politician suddenly seemed even more valuable than ever.

It took him a few minutes to get the car turned around and he sped down the little streets, dodging cyclists, honking his horn to warn pedestrians and slamming his brakes on to skid around every corner. He got to the crossroads at the main road, coming out of the town centre, and looked both ways. No sign of the sedan. He had a decision to make. And quickly.

Straight over was the small road he was already on, which he quickly discounted. Dissecting it was a main road and he guessed right, the direction that most likely led to Brussels, Paris or even Switzerland.

The wheels screamed, leaving black rubber marks on the road, as he tore away, pulling out in front of a bus that needed to screech to a halt. His foot was trying to push the accelerator through the bottom of the car. He shoved it up through the gears, swerving around the cars in front and finding an open stretch of road. He sped up. There was a roundabout ahead and he zoomed around it, narrowly missing a truck. The car wailed as he dropped a gear and raced away.

He was only a few minutes behind, but he knew he needed to be careful. If he caught up and they saw him, which was likely the way he was driving, then they would be suspicious straight away. He needed to slow down the moment he spotted the sedan.

He undertook a Winnebago and kept going. Surely, they would not be far ahead. There was no way they would be driving at anything like the speeds he was managing in this small car.

He saw another turn coming up, this time it was another main road leading off to the right. He decided to keep going. The engine protested so much he was starting to worry that it might explode, but he kept his eyes on the road ahead, waiting for the sedan to come into view.

A few minutes later, he took his foot off the accelerator and sighed, as the road straightened enough for him to see far ahead. No black sedan anywhere. He should have caught up with them by now.

He had gone the wrong way.

Pearl watched Tepo come jogging up the slope with a huge smile on his face. The other monks came around the cave entrance and they were all chattering excitedly.

'Did it work?' she demanded tersely, striding over amongst them.

'It appeared to,' Tepo replied through the glow of success that he had in his eyes.

'Do we know who he was?' asked one the junior monks.

'He seemed to be a wild camper,' Lindo answered.

'He wasn't a tourist,' she spat. 'He was looking for us.' She had deliberated for a long time about telling them. Their reaction had surprised her. They seemed intent on action, something she had argued for a long time. Somehow, though, this did not feel quite right. It felt off.

'We led him away, as the council decreed,' Krayak assured her soothingly. 'There is no sign that he was a threat.'

'Why did he follow the shadows if he wasn't looking for us?' she returned, venomously. 'We need to move out.'

'He probably thought there were other campers he could socialise with,' said one voice in the crowd.

'Or maybe he was afraid of the wilderness,' another suggested.

'His vacation could have been over.'

'Maybe the ground was too rough for carrying a heavy bag.'

She chortled sardonically. 'He was looking for us and we bought ourselves some time, nothing more. You led him away, but he will be back, probably with a patrol, or two.'

Krayak touched her arm gently. 'It is a tremendous effort to pack up everything and move, Miss Pearl. We have many weak here who will not be able to journey far. We would need to leave them behind. And what of the families? The children will be slow and noisy and will attract attention when we pass through villages.'

'The local villages will protect us. The families can stay with them.'

'Letitia,' the senior monk continued gently, 'you have been the most vocal advocate for standing our ground and fighting, if we need to.'

'That was against average Imperial troops, my friend. Something feels different about this. I can't put my finger what exactly, but I don't think the families should stay here.'

He paused a few moments. 'We can tell them what happened and offer them the choice. If they wish to leave, we will get them to a village. There is one about two days' walk away from here that would help us, I believe.'

'We should all go,' she insisted.

'And go where?' Lindo asked, softly. 'We do not have anywhere to hide. We cannot keep moving around. We have been moving from village to village for years. It's time to make a home for ourselves. Even if we think it's unsafe, The Dayak needs a home. We left ours behind when The Empire took it for a training camp, but we are not nomads. We need roots, Miss Pearl.'

'He's right,' Krayak continued. 'The elder council has discussed this at length. We are all tired. The people are tired. We do not have the energy to move again. We have finally found a place where we all feel happy and safe. We do not wish to leave it.'

'And if they come?' she enquired in an acerbic tone.

'We will defend it.'

She met the elder monk with a steely glare and pointed to the cave. 'There are civilians in there. Families.'

He smiled. 'We will tell them what we know and give them all a choice.'

'What if they choose to stay and The Empire comes?'

'Then we will protect them.'

She scowled. 'Are you kidding? If they come with a couple of battalions, we don't stand a chance.'

Krayak looked out over the ridge they were on

and the slope leading down to the valley below. 'It is very narrow topography here, Miss Pearl, and we have the high ground. I don't think they could sneak so many soldiers up there.'

Pearl exhaled sharply and massaged her scalp. He had a point. 'I think it's an unnecessary risk.'

'We don't believe we are in danger, Miss Pearl,' Tepo said with a broad grin.

'I know, I know. You led him away.'

'Exactly, Miss Pearl. We have scouts out all over the area to watch for any sign of further intrusions. If anyone comes, we will see them and act accordingly.'

'Act accordingly?' she repeated. 'What does that mean?'

'It means, if we see a threat, we will react to it.'

'In what way?'

'It depends on the threat, Letitia,' Krayak interjected.

For the first time since she had been here, in the mountains with the monks, she felt as if there was something she didn't know. 'What does that mean? Be more specific, please.'

'Whether we react defensively or offensively.'

She frowned, confounded. 'You have discussed attack plans?'

'If we feel that we are under threat, we have some ideas about how to protect ourselves. Sometimes attack is the best form of defence.'

'Sometimes...what are you talking about,

Krayak?'

'Letitia, we're not worried about the families being in danger. We don't intend to let Imperial troops get anywhere near them. The council has an idea about that.'

'And what's the idea?'

'We're going to ambush them.'

Chapter 15

The night seemed somehow darker than usual. The thick clouds hid the moon and the fog drowned out any artificial light. Leopold flicked his cigarette on the ground and walked back inside.

He looked around the reception room. There was gold and silver everywhere, thick carpets and warm colours. There were aerial photos of all their homes on the wall and one family portrait. It always smelt of lavender in here and he hated lavender, but he knew better than to protest. It was not an argument worth having with his wife.

His father and stepmother sat at the table, helping his children complete a jigsaw puzzle. Joseph and Victoria were twins, and they looked almost identical. Both had blonde hair and blue eyes and, although they were only five years old, they were prodigious.

He looked at his stepmother, Angela, who

appeared every moment of her seventy-six years. She had short grey hair, dark brown eyes and saggy, wizened cheeks. Leopold had accepted her presence for his father's sake, but he hated her. She was dull, but she loved the children and they loved her.

A hand touched his shoulder. 'Leo.'

He turned to face his wife, Tiffany. She was short, thin and so beautiful that she still took his breath away. She was a year younger than he was, only thirty-six, but she aged much more elegantly, her dark brown hair and blue eyes always making his heart skip a beat. 'Hi, my love.'

She indicated the doorway. 'Chris and Rebecca are here.'

He smiled and looked across at his brother. His wife, Rebecca, was stunning. She had long, black hair, green eyes and a smile that glistened. She was the darling of the British press and the fact that she was American made her a dream for the Royal marketing department. Her merchandise outsold all other members of the royal household by at least three-to-one.

Chris walked over and shook his brother's hand, as Rebecca walked towards the children and gave them hugs, greeting his father and Angela with a warm smile.

'What's going on?' Chris asked, a little irritated. 'We had tickets to Chelsea tonight.'

Leo grinned, patted him on the shoulder and

walked past him. 'Thanks for coming everyone. Apologies for the short notice, but it's important. If you would like to make your way through to the dining room, dinner will be served shortly.'

They made their way through to the equally lavish dining area. It had plush furnishings, but the focal point was the eighteen-seat, oak table in the centre. He indicated that the nannies should take the children away and they obeyed swiftly. As everyone sat down, he waited for the drinks to be served and for everyone to be seated.

He remained standing, at the head of the table, and nodded to the staff. They all left immediately and closed the doors behind them.

Chris noticed them going and looked around, his eyes resting on his brother curiously. 'What's going on, Leo?'

'Father has something he wants to tell you,' he replied, taking his seat.

Chris turned to his father, who seemed a little solemn, even reluctant. 'What's that, Father?'

'I have made a decision,' he began, taking Angela's hand and squeezing it tightly.

Chris felt his chest tighten. He could see the nerves in the king's eyes and hear the quiver in his voice. 'Go on.'

'The British Empire is facing a set of unparalleled challenges,' Alfred explained tremulously. 'Mother, as much as we all loved her, was not especially forward-thinking. This has left us behind our main rivals at a time when the rate of progress is alarmingly fast. Indeed, maybe so fast that we may struggle to catch up. Added to this is the Outpost Programme, which I need to focus a lot of attention on at the moment. It is at a critical stage.'

'None of this is news to me, Father,' Chris scoffed.

'I realise that,' he replied softly, tightening his hold on Angela's hand. 'However, what will be news to you is how stretched I am with the joint responsibilities of The Empire's future and that of our entire species. It's only been a few months and I already know it is too much for me.'

Chris furrowed his brow, confused. 'What are you saying, Father? Are you ok?'

'My health is fine, at the moment. But I have accepted that I cannot possibly hope to concentrate on both. Not if I want them to be successful. I have decided to focus on Outpost.'

He exchanged a confounded look with Rebecca, before turning back to the monarch. 'So, you're going to ignore your duty as Head of the British Empire? Father, I must protest.'

Alfred waved the suggestion away. 'Don't be absurd, Chris. The Empire is in my blood. But it's not that simple.'

'Well then,' he retorted angrily, 'why don't you explain it to me?'

'I'm trying!' he shouted, slamming his free fist

on the table and making the silverware clatter. He took a breath and composed himself. 'If you would be kind enough to stop interrupting me, that's exactly what I intend to do.'

'Apologies, Father,' he said quietly, noting the gleeful expression on his brother's face.

'Thank you,' the king sighed, taking a sip of water. 'I had a meeting the other day with Russia and China, about the Outpost Programme. What began as an internationally agreed and funded project has fallen into disarray and is running out of time and money. There are now eight billion people on this planet and, if we cannot successfully colonise the moon or Mars for habitation, then we will need to introduce mandatory childbirth limitations. I don't want to do that. I want to be the king who tore down the restrictions and improved human rights, not the one who made everyone have only one child and punished anybody who had more. Could you even imagine how many 'accidents' that we would need to deal with? The Empire is not in the business of killing babies and it's not about to start on my watch, son.'

'That's understandable,' Chris commented sullenly.

'That's where it's heading. The natural resources of this planet cannot sustain a population so large. Russia and China have similar problems and they concur with me that Outpost is the only solution to this problem. Russia is going to join the

EU, who have fallen behind in their contributions, and they will fund the programme together. China is going to ensure Asia contributes the same. The British Empire will match their contributions. It will be one third each.'

'What about the rest of the world?'

'They are welcome to help us. If they don't, their citizens will not be eligible for resettlement when we begin colonisation.'

He nodded. 'Okay, well, that's not exactly something I like, but I understand and agree with it. Why all the fuss for that little bit of news?'

The king bowed his head and took a deep breath, before looking back in his son's eyes. 'That's not the news, Chris. We need the Asian Coalition to support the Outpost Programme, so I will be visiting them to improve diplomatic relations. After that, Angela and I are going on a tour of The Empire, to whip up the public support and understanding. It's going to be a considerable financial undertaking, which Europe and Asia can spread amongst several members. We cannot do that. I can't manage that *and* bring The Empire back up to speed in the modern world. We are too far behind. We can catch up, but I can't do both.'

'So…?'

He indicated his eldest son. 'Leo is going to assume responsibility for that while I'm away.'

'How long will you be gone?'

'Probably the rest of my life.'

Chris fell back in his seat, stunned. 'What are you saying? You're not that old, Father.'

He shook his head. 'I'm an old man and Leo is not. I won't be able to come back and take over this vital and, frankly, very difficult task.'

'I-I-I- don't understand. Are you saying you're never coming back?'

Alfred chuckled uncomfortably. 'Of course I will. But Leo will remain here and do everything else for me. He won't be Prince Regent, either. He will be King Regent, so that everyone understands that his authority in my name is absolute.' He could see that his youngest son was upset, so he pressed on before an argument could ensue. 'I have been thinking about this since before Mother died and everything I have seen in my reign, so far, has convinced me this is the right thing to do. It's not what I want, but it's right, Chris. It's what's best for the people of our empire and our planet. And that's my first duty.'

Leo's expression had become grave. 'Can I count on you for your support, brother? I will need you now, more than ever. I can't do this alone.'

Chris eyed him with suspicion, but he did appear genuine. 'Of course, brother. I will help in any way I can.' He turned back to his father. 'So, how does this work? Are you abdicating?'

'No, no, there's no need for that. I will still be the Head of The British Empire. My face will still be on the money. I will still hold rank, but I won't use it. I trust your brother to deliver what I have asked of him. It's his duty.'

He looked at his father with admiration. What an incredible man he was. 'I don't really know what to say, Father. Such a sacrifice, for the good of the people…well, I imagine it will go down in history as the most altruistic thing any monarch has ever done.'

King Alfred smiled. 'I'm so pleased you understand, Chris.'

He raised his glass. 'To King Alfred! Long live the king!'

They all raised their glasses, toasted and cheered.

But Leo's satisfied smirk did not go unnoticed by his younger brother.

ANBU KHAIRENI, NEPAL

Royce sat alone at the picnic table and sipped water from his canteen, his eyes glued to the television on the wall. He watched the images of British troops storming through Caracas on the news. Britain had not invaded another country for over half a century. The last occupation had been Angola, who had invited the British in to push the Portuguese out in the early 1970's.

He rubbed his chin pensively. This did not

surprise him too much. What did surprise him was that this was not even the biggest news of the day. King Alfred's speech was the lead story.

Royce watched the new Venezuelan government return the rescued British ambassador as he pondered the events of the past two days. He had not even been gone that long but, somehow, The Empire he knew had changed to The Empire he was watching.

King Regent Leopold. It did not sound right.

As much as it bothered him, being a devout Successionist, he had to admit King Alfred seemed to be making the best decision he could. To hear the monarch speak so passionately about sacrifice and duty had caused horripilation all over his body. Royce had not much respected Alfred as a leader before today, but he could see that he was wrong. Perhaps his judgement was not quite as assured as he had always thought.

The man had put the needs of everyone ahead of himself. Royce was a cynic, though. He wondered if it was just a PR stunt to make The Empire's rivals look bad. If that was the case, it was smart. Russia, Asia and the EU would need to recommit to Outpost now.

King Alfred had made the situation very clear: the future of the entire planet was at stake.

With Britain being the first to sacrifice something and devote themselves to Outpost, it was they who were now taking the lead in saving their species.

Royce did not know Aflred. He had no idea if it was a trick or if it was genuine. But he did know King Alfred had just secured his place in the Hall of Heroes and even his mother was not in there.

He sipped more water and looked around the base. It was nothing more than a few crumbling buildings and huts, of which he was now the unwilling commander. There were three-hundred and ninety-five soldiers based here, most of whom had barely completed basic training. He did not know how many The Dayak numbered, but he knew that the local forces would not be enough.

Nesbitt had delivered, though. Five platoons of special forces had arrived already and he expected another one later that day. Those eighty-three professionals would be able to turn this rabble into an army.

The men and women scurried around, preparing the equipment and vehicles. He wanted them ready to go at a moment's notice, just in case. He did not know a lot about The Dayak, but he knew they moved a lot and they could not risk missing them. They had seen him. There was a good chance they would move.

He heard some noise at the gate. He looked over as the security checked the clearance codes and let them pass, turning away as the minibus drove through the lowered bollards. He continued watching the news for a few moments, when there was roar behind him. He turned to see a pair of young soldiers circling each other, both with daggers drawn.

Standing up, he walked towards them slowly, keen to see if either of them would see sense, or if any of their senior officers would intervene. But they did not. It seemed they were keen for any kind of action.

A crowd had gathered around the duo; a man and a woman; and the man lunged forwards. Royce scoffed at their ineptitude, but the slow, and painfully telegraphed, attack sliced the arm of the woman. She screamed, and he was about to follow up, when Royce charged in. He barged five spectators out of his path like they were feathers and grabbed the man's wrist as it swung through the air.

He picked the man up off the ground effortlessly and squeezed his wrist, forcing him to drop the dagger. The crowd fell silent, gasping as Royce grabbed the man's neck with his free hand and pulled his face close. 'Save it for the enemy!' he roared, tossing the man to the ground.

The young man wailed, landing in a heap. The woman whimpered and started to thank him.

Royce had no idea what she was saying and he did not care. 'Get to the infirmary now,' he ordered and she scurried away.

He was about to punish the attacker when there was a gentle, Irish voice from behind him. 'Cabin fever.'

He turned around to find a tall, muscular soldier, standing with a group of ten others, grinning at him. They all looked completely different to the locals and the platoons he had seen so far. They were the only non-Nepalese or Indian soldiers he had seen here.

'Who are you?' he growled.

'Captain Dermot Monaghan reporting for duty.'

Royce paused and the corners of his mouth creased upwards slightly. 'The Monaghan Marauders?'

He laughed loudly, his brown eyes sparkling, his white teeth gleaming and his long, brown hair bouncing around. 'Nice that you've heard of us.'

'Nesbitt didn't tell me you were coming.'

'He flew us in this morning,' he replied.

The Australian was pleased. This was one of Nesbitt's best teams. 'It's nice to have some real soldiers here. Were you in the region?'

'Not even close. He pulled us off another job to be here. Said this was more important.'

Royce indicated the dispersing crowd. 'You see what I have to work with.'

'They just need to see some combat, Royce. That's all. We see it all the time in the outer territories.'

'They're not warriors. They're fodder. The command here is a joke.'

Monaghan hooked his hair behind his ears.

'That's normal out here. They're lucky you're here.'

'I'm not a commander. I'm a tracker.'

'*The* Tracker, so they tell me.'

He narrowed his eyes. 'I see we have both heard of each other. But I don't see how I can lead this rabble.'

'Not to worry. That's why we're here.'

'You're taking over?' Royce inquired, uncertainly.

'Like you said, you're the tracker.'

He rubbed his scalp, not entirely sure how he felt about his latest development. 'So, you're leading the op?'

He nodded, beaming a brilliant smile. 'That's affirmative, soldier. I will command, my team will lead the troops. That ok with you?'

'Yea, that's great. I can leave now.'

'Leave?' Monaghan laughed. 'What are you talking about? You can't go.'

Royce aimed a cold glower at the Irishman. 'The fuck I can't. You're here now.'

'The general told me you were contracted to find the enemy. Do you have their exact coordinates?'

'Not exact, no.'

'Then your contract isn't fulfilled, as far as I can tell.'

Royce growled and briefly considered crushing Monaghan's skull, but took a deep, soothing breath instead. 'You want me to come with you, then?'

'Of course. We don't know where they are and The Tracker has other talents, so they tell me.'

He looked at the soldiers behind Monaghan. They all looked like professionals. He was not sure what he had expected, but he was relieved that he did not have to lead the mission. At the same time, though, he felt uneasy about it. He could not quite fathom why. 'You sure you want to annoy me and find out what they are?'

The Irishman's laugh was soft and melodious. 'Not personally, no. I have seen the footage. I would like to think my team could protect me, but I don't doubt most of us would fall first. No, no, Bob. Do you mind if I call you Bob?' He did not wait for an answer. 'Wonderful. We need you to lead us there and a warrior of your repute will be a huge asset, I'm sure of it. The general was very keen that I tell you how pleased he is with your work and wanted you to know there will be a hefty bonus in it for you if we can eliminate the terrorist threat.'

'I don't know how much of a threat they are. I didn't hear much about them, but I get the impression they're a bunch of farmers and monks.'

'Then they should be quite easy to subdue, no? I also hear that you have a strong stomach. You'll need it.'

Royce's interior alarm suddenly went off. He was remembering more about this team. They were dangerous and merciless. 'Why?'

'My orders are to make an example of these people, Bob. And I take my work very seriously.'

'Good to know,' he replied curtly. 'Can I go now?'

'Not just yet, Bob. When can they be ready to leave?'

'Probably tonight, if you want.'

'I'm going to delay that by three days.'

He shrugged. 'Okay, if you want.'

'Don't you want to know why?'

'Not really.'

'Well, I'm going to tell you, anyway.'

Royce grunted. 'Of course you are.'

'I want to, Bob. I'm a bit like that. You'll see. Anyway, I'm waiting for the specialist mountain platoon to get here. I have a plan that will only work with them.'

He furrowed his brow. 'You're waiting for The Scots?'

'Affirmative, soldier.'

'Is McNeary with them?'

'It's The Haggis that I especially need.'

Royce raised his eyebrows. The Haggis was so called because he was, possibly, the ugliest man in The Empire. He even made Royce look like a supermodel. But he was also probably the finest warrior in mountain terrain anywhere in the world. 'Should increase our odds. Can I go now?'

'Of course,' he said with a grin. 'Rest up, we will have a long trek ahead. Should be fun, though.

You're dismissed.'

Royce harrumphed, turned around and strode away. He felt his stomach turn a little as he realised why he had heard of this team. The Monaghan Marauders were also known by a different nickname.

They were also called British Butchers.

Because they liked to skin their enemies alive.

Chapter 16

Bayston walked out of the bathroom and made his way to the small kitchenette, where MacLoughlin had just finished making some sandwiches.

'Eat up,' he commanded, pushing the plate of stale bread and questionable ham across the breakfast counter.

Bayston looked around at the caravan and shivered. At night he could pretend it was less disgusting, but the sun had been up a few hours, so there was no hiding from it now.

There was mould on almost every wall, cobwebs in every corner and stains on the shorn carpet. It reeked of mildew and the small heater barely managed to pierce the winter air that swept in through the holes randomly strewn about the roof and windows.

They were about two miles outside some tiny

village he had never heard of, in a caravan once used by people who worked at nearby Whipsnade Zoo. They had clearly abandoned it years ago and, when MacLoughlin had driven down the track in their stolen Jeep, Bayston had not imagined it was to find something like this. The American had treated it as if he had discovered lost treasure.

'You want a coffee?'

He shook his head. 'Got any tea?'

'Why would I have tea?'

'You don't like tea?'

MacLoughlin laughed. 'I know the Missionaries push tea on all the colonies, but it's actually not especially tasty.'

He shrugged. 'Well, I like it.'

'Of course you do. I don't have any, though. Do you want a coffee, or not?'

He nodded and sat down on the dirty stool. 'How long are we staying here? It's been two days.'

'I know it's not very pleasant here, but it's safe and I need to wait for a response from my contact.'

'Why? I thought we were leaving the country.'

He smiled. 'We can't get you out without their help, kid. You need new documents. They'll be watching the airports, ferry ports and train stations. We need to wait a little while, get you the right documents and then get out. I can't stay any more, either. After Milton Keynes, they know you're not alone and they know I'm involved. They'll be looking for me, too.'

'Can't we just steal a boat and go to France?'

He took a bite of his sandwich and chewed as he nodded. 'If we don't hear back soon, we might have to. But the winter weather in The Channel is pretty dangerous and they patrol that area heavily. Besides, they will assume that we're going to run. A couple of days have already passed, and they'll be wondering if they missed us.'

Bayston frowned disbelievingly. 'Really?'

'The biggest weakness The Empire has is arrogance. They don't believe that there is anyone in Britain who would help us, and they don't think there's anywhere for us to hide. Especially in the Mother Country.'

'So, who is this contact?'

'A guy I used to work with, a long time ago. We can trust him, don't worry. He'll get you clean documents and get us a safe way to Europe. I can get us anywhere from over there, no problems.'

'What's his name?'

'You don't know him.'

'Why not tell me then?'

MacLoughlin scoffed. 'I don't know you that well, yet.'

Bayston paused eating and studied his saviour. 'Seriously?'

'Seriously.'

An idea suddenly struck him. 'Are you getting him to check on me?'

He laughed loudly. 'No, I'm not, but I like the way you think. This life might actually suit you.'

This life. The phrase made images of his friends and family flood his mind, but he pushed them back out. 'I can't believe you don't trust me.'

He held up his hands in a gesture of surrender. 'You will soon learn that there's no such thing as over-cautious.'

'Is this guy in The Dayak, too?'

MacLoughlin finished his sandwich and wiped the crumbs from the desktop on to the floor. 'No, he's not, but he's a sympathiser, I guess you would say.'

'How come I've never heard of The Dayak until I met you? I mean, if they're such a force, surely they would have been on the news, or something.'

'It doesn't work like that,' he replied, blowing the steam from his coffee and taking a sip. 'The Empire doesn't like people to know about anyone who resists their oppression. They keep it out of the news, suppressing the stories of resistance. The Dayak aren't the only ones. There are about a dozen I know of that exist right now and have been easily a hundred since I started paying attention. The Empires figures that allowing news of them to spread might inspire others. All you will hear about is when they're defeated, so Britain can promulgate their own version of events, usually the terrorist stories. History is written by the victor, after all.'

'Are you saying The Dayak are terrorists?'

He sipped his coffee and paused to consider his answer. 'They're not a big organisation, but they have support all over the world. They resist the British rule and the imposition of British values over their own. They don't adopt British cultures, either. They have their own. They don't go randomly murdering people. They don't blow up churches or schools. They don't attack military targets. They will defend themselves when threatened, but all they really want is to be able to choose how to live their life. Would you call that a terrorist organisation?'

'Well, no, I guess not.'

'Yet, I can promise you, if they're defeated, there will be some kind of attack on a civilian target and The Dayak will get the blame. The story in the news will be about how The Dayak attacked some innocent people in the name of their 'cause' and the British saved the people and vanquished the threat.'

Bayston scowled. 'Are you saying that all these terrorists I saw in the news weren't actually terrorists at all?'

He shook his head fervently. 'Oh, no, no. Definitely not. Some of these organisations are horrific and I totally support Britain for wiping them off the face of the planet. Fuck, I would help them, if I could. I *have* helped them. I was SAS for a long time.'

'I guessed you were ex-service.'

'But, Jamie, when you see it up close, you start to realise that it's not always as black and white as The Empire would have you believe. Sometimes it is. I remember an organisation called Black Fury, in Kenya. They just wanted to kill any white folk they could find. It was madness. Make no mistake, there is evil on both sides of the fence. These people were so angry they had totally lost control of their faculties. They went from town to town just murdering anybody with white skin.'

'They teach us about them at school.'

'Yea,' he replied sullenly, the plague of memories suddenly in his mind's eye. 'It was before your time, kid. But it was horrific. Just awful. I can't even tell you how bad. My platoon got there about three days after it started and we were despatched to intercept them at a farming village.

We got there in the early evening and it was already underway. The worst part was that the locals had joined the killing. They had worked for the farmers, living with them, eating with them, for years. Their kids played together, for fuck's sake. And, here they were, hacking their kids' friends to pieces. I just couldn't fathom it.'

Bayston fell silent for a few moments. 'What did you do?'

MacLoughlin was staring into his mug, as if in a trance. 'We killed them all. Even some of the children.'

He could see the tears forming in the eyes of his saviour. 'The children, too?'

'The ones that were hacking up their friends, yea. We rounded up any that were hiding, which was a lot of them, and sent them to state facilities, but there were too many small kids with guns, hacksaws and blades. It never made any sense to me. I guess their parents must have made them do it, but I don't know.'

'What did you do to the parents?'

He looked up and met the Englishman with a cold, angry stare. 'I promise you this: if you ever catch a grown adult hacking the legs off a baby, there is nothing inside you that can control that rage.'

'I can't imagine.'

'No, you can't. I hope you never have to.'

'So, what did you do to them?'

'Bad things,' he replied stonily. 'Very bad things.' He returned to looking into his coffee, lost in his brain, for a minute, before snapping himself away and shaking his head. 'Anyway, the point being that some terrorists are terrorists, and some are not. The Dayak are not. It infuriates me that, if they are defeated, they would be considered the same as Black Fury, when they're nothing alike.'

Bayston could see the torment in the American's face, so decided to try to change the subject. 'How did you get involved with them?'

He smiled slightly. 'Oh, a friend of a friend told me about them years ago, when I was serving out in that part of the world. I was actually on a mission to catch or kill them but, when I found them, they were nothing like what I expected. My entire team, all nine of us, spent a few weeks with them and we joined them.'

'There are nine operatives like you?'

He nodded. 'Only four of us left now. I was the only one who retired from the SAS, the others all stayed and helped me from within. Five have been killed in service, though. You heard about the Battle of Bombay?'

'Terrorists?'

'Genuine ones that time. I don't know if you remember the details, but they were protesting when the East India Company first released Devices to the public. The bomb trap they placed in the head office there killed all five of my brothers and sisters.'

'Sorry, Ed.'

His smile was a solemn one. 'Sadly, it's a part of the job.'

'So, now you do what?' Bayston asked, almost enthusiastically.

MacLoughlin grinned and finished his coffee in one, huge slurp. 'You will have plenty of time to find out, kid. There's no rush. Just know that this is a cause that's worth fighting for. These people just want to have choices. They want to be able to respect their own culture, have their own religion, teach their children the values that are important to *them*. They don't hate Britain. They hate being controlled and told what to do. That's all. The Department of Missionary Services does not allow these choices. They enforce the British culture and values on everyone in the colonies and resistance is considered hostility, when, in fact, it's not that at all. It's just a wish for something different.'

'When you say it like that, it makes complete sense.'

'That's because it *does* make sense, Jamie. You were just never told about it or taught about the options. You might like Buddhism if you tried it, but it was never presented to you as an option.'

As Bayston opened his mouth to respond, the Device on the table bleeped. They both fell silent, looked at it, then at each other.

MacLoughlin was next to it with two, large strides and opened it with his forefinger. He read for a few moments, then looked up at the Englishman. 'Finish your food and get your stuff. We have an important meeting to get to.'

Chapter 17

Leopold watched the crowds cheering and crying. They waved at the Concorde RegalJet as it vanished over the horizon. He smiled at them, kissing Tiffany on the cheek, before taking the tiny hands of Joseph and Victoria. With one child either side of him, he slowly walked back towards the George V hangar at London Airport and looked across at his brother.

Christian held Rebecca's hand tightly, the genuine tears in his eyes, even though he tried to hide them and smile for the vast collection of lenses behind the barricades.

Leo knew his brother was upset at their father leaving. He also suspected that Chris had seen through their ruse and smelt Leo's involvement in the whole thing, despite the king insisting it was his decision to go. He had considered sharing the secret about their mother with Chris, but had opted not to. Partly because he knew it would break his younger brother's heart and he never wanted to do that. But mostly because the secret gave him the power he needed to repair The Empire and that was more important to him than anything.

They all walked slowly, with other members of the royal family behind them. His uncles and aunts, cousins and second cousins all walked at the same speed that he did. He was in charge now. He set the pace.

He eyed the other people that had come today; the officials, archbishops, judges, generals, admirals, politicians and CEOs. They were all desperate to show their love for The Empire. And, he expected, to grab any crumbs that might fall from his table.

When they reached the hangar, there was a reception organised in the Monarch's Lounge. He kissed his wife again, then his children, and told them he would be along shortly. Then he approached his brother.

He nodded towards Rebecca. 'Sorry, Bec, but I need to borrow him for a little while. Is that ok?'

She smiled sweetly, knowing that it was not a question. 'As long as you return him in one piece.'

'I'll try.'

She kissed her husband and rushed to join Tiffany and the twins. Chris watched her go and turned to him, a little bemused. 'What's up?'

'We have a meeting.'

'Who with?'

He indicated Nesbitt, on the far side of the hangar, who was conversing with one of Leo's staff. The general looked up at the King Regent, nodded, and then walked away towards the back. Leo nodded back and looked back at his brother. 'You'll see. Come with me.'

He led Chris across the hangar, stopping to greet all the well-wishers they crossed paths with on the way. When they got over there, they walked through a recess and to a guarded doorway. The guard, a member of the Royal Guard, Chris noted, swiped a card and let them through.

Royal Guards were usually reserved for royal properties, he thought. He did not know any of them were stationed outside any of the palaces. Although, technically, the hangar counted as one, he supposed.

It led to a small antechamber, a cold room with sparse light and cold concrete walls and ceiling. Chris looked around curiously. He had been to this hangar several dozen times and did not even know it existed.

Leo walked over to a dark corner and Chris followed. There was a barely perceptible staircase leading down underground and they descended two floors, coming to a passageway. There were a few neon tubes lighting the way, flickering in the gloom. Leo continued, clearly knowing where he was going, and Chris walked a few paces behind, twisting and turning until they came to another antechamber and a very heavily fortified door, with a huge red light above it. The bright bulb filled the room and made the grey walls look blood-stained.

'I'll have to let you through,' Leo announced. 'You don't have clearance yet, but I will get that sorted out soon.'

Chris did not respond, he just stood there, dumbfounded. There was clearly a lot he still did not know.

Leo placed his palm on the pad next to the door and then rubbed the inside of his cheek with his forefinger, placing that on a small sensor. The red light above the door blinked a few times, changed to green and then buzzed. There was a clunk and the door slid to the side.

The King Regent motioned for his brother to enter first and he obeyed. Leo followed and the door swished shut behind them.

Chris stood at the entrance for a few moments and took in the sight. It was a cavernous room, filled with screens, computers, laptops and Devices. There were satellite images on many of the screens and the files of military personnel on the others. There were seven or eight doors leading out of this main room, he noticed.

In the middle of the room was a large rectangular table, at which sat the Privy Council.

Chris looked at his brother, who was already moving towards the head seat.

'Come on, Chris,' he beckoned, sitting down. 'We need to hurry and get to the reception before we're missed.'

He walked slowly to the seat to the left of his brother and sat down. He could see the other attendees were as confused about the meeting as him.

'Welcome, all of you,' Leo greeted chirpily. 'I know most of you didn't even know about this bunker, and it's not my intention to share royal secrets with you, but we are pressed for time and this seemed a good opportunity, since everyone was here already. I will try to make this as swift as I can.'

'We don't appreciate being herded in here like cattle,' protested Sir Humphrey Harris.

Leo grinned menacingly. 'And I don't appreciate my Imperial Minister interrupting me, so I guess we're even.'

'What's the meaning of this?' demanded Archbishop Fryer, head of the Church of England.

He scowled. 'If you would let me speak, Archbishop, then it will achieve two things: first, you will find out and, second, I won't cut off your finger for interrupting me.' The room fell deathly silent. He smiled malevolently. 'There you go, that wasn't so hard, was it? I know this is unorthodox, so you all have questions. Be quiet and I will get to the point, as I already said once, but you didn't allow me to do.'

Chris was gaping, looking across at his brother, barely able to recognise the sinister tone in his voice.

Leo noticed his younger brother glaring at him and chuckled. 'I can see some of you are hiding the shock better than others.' He reached across and patted the back of Chris' hand playfully. 'I've asked you all to come here today to establish the direction that I expect the Privy Council to take in the near future. We have an important job to do and Father has charged me with ensuring that it happens. I assure you all that I take Father's orders very seriously and he has given me the power to take absolute charge because he has faith in me to deliver. I will not disappoint our king and, perhaps even more importantly, our people. Before I go on, does anyone have any issues with Father's decree that they wish to discuss? Because this subject will not come up again, I promise you that.'

Chris looked around the table. There were clear misgivings, but nobody was brave enough. They knew Leo would make an example of them and, indeed, it seemed like that's exactly what he wanted.

'Excellent!' he cried, only waiting a few seconds. 'So, to business, shall we? Father has identified two main challenges The Empire is facing. The first, and his priority, is the Outpost Programme. You all heard his speech, and I know he spoke to many of you personally, so we don't need to dwell on that.

The second is bringing Britain back to the level of our main rivals. Russia will apply to join the EU soon and Asia has been growing in strength for the past decade, whilst we have not been. Their technological advancements are embarrassing us and it needs to stop. We can only reverse-manufacture so much. I remember it was only fifteen years ago that The Empire was at the forefront of nearly all of these advancements. Did you know that, twenty years ago, Britain was responsible for 85% of all patents registered in the world? Do you know how many it was last year? 24%. This isn't good enough.'

Lord Chamberlain Nockle held up his hand. Leo granted him permission to speak. 'Sire, your grandmother diverted funds away from R&D grants to education programmes in the poorer Imperial regions. We lost probably 50% of our most innovative scientists because they can get better grants in the EU or Asia.'

Leo held up his hand. 'I'm not blaming anyone here. I'm very aware that Nan is mostly responsible for this. It is, however, the responsibility of those here to redress this imbalance. Since you know about it, Nockle, then this is going to be your assignment. I expect monthly updates and you can brief this council about it at our quarterly meetings. Yes, they shall be four times a year from now on.'

They all exchanged worried glances. Prime Minister Beckham was the next to raise a hand and get permission to speak. 'Was Venezuela us?'

Leo chuckled. He eyed the PM. Beckham's handsome face and shaven head were annoying, but his tattoos were worse. However, the public adored him, so that could be useful. 'You see, David, there are those who suggest you're not smart enough for that job, but they're wrong. You're learning fast.'

Beckham ignored the backhanded compliment. 'So, it was?'

The King Regent stood up and placed his palms down flat on the table. 'We're going to be doing things a little differently from now on, ladies and gentlemen. We are going to be expanding the British Empire and finding ways to ensure new members contribute to our overall greatness and ensure the dynasty remains the greatest in the world for many generations to come.'

'You didn't answer the question, Your Royal Highness.'

Leo turned on the speaker, but realised it was Smythe. The MI6 Director was one man he did not want to alienate unless he had to. 'It wasn't us, Peter. It was *me*.' He let the comment sink in for a few moments. He could see it marinating in their brains. 'I did what we should have been doing together. So, if I can gain us access to the world's fourth biggest oil reserves without the Privy

Council, imagine what we can achieve together.'

General Nesbitt spoke up next, his deep, booming voice echoing around the bunker. 'Was it sanctioned?'

Leo let out a guttural growl. 'Sanctioned by whom? I'm King Regent now. You answer to me. I will worry about what is sanctioned.'

Chris watched Nesbitt shrink in his seat. He had never seen anyone do that to the general, not even their grandmother.

'Are there any other questions at this point?' Leo asked tersely. He only waited three seconds. 'Good.' He walked over to a door on the left of the room and opened it, walking back to his seat and dropping into it.

Four men came through the doorway. Chris watched them closely. Two of them were Asian and he vaguely recognised them, but he had no idea about the other two. One was small and sleek, with a ponytail, whilst the other was enormous, passing through the door sideways, and looked like he might be semi-homeless. They all moved to stand behind the King Regent.

Nesbitt's eyes were trained on the Asian men. His fear seemed to vanish at the sight of the guests. 'What the fuck is going on here?'

'What the fuck is going on here, *Your Royal Highness*? Although protocol also allows Your Majesty, if you prefer,' Leo corrected in an admonishing tone.

The general turned to his fellow council members. 'Some of you won't know who they are,' he announced, indicating the Asian men, 'but they're generals in the Asian army.' He pointed to a small, wiry man, with thick grey-black hair in a side-parting and an elegant, thin moustache that swept down either side of his mouth. He had large brown eyes and almost no eyebrows. 'This is General Nimko.' He then indicated a burly, rotund man, who had beady green eyes and black hair shaven to be only a couple of millimetres long. 'And this is General Tarnat.'

'Actually,' Leo interjected, 'they're also the top advisors to Genghis.'

Smythe narrowed his eyes. 'All due respect, sire, but what are you trying to achieve here?'

'I'm bringing the Privy Council up to speed on my plans,' he spat. 'As you can see, I've already done most of the hard work for you.'

Smythe looked across at Nesbitt, who was clearly seething and gave him a look to tell him not to say anything. 'We know all about Generals Nimko and Tarnat, sire. What we don't understand is why you would invite two of the most senior officers of our largest enemy to the most sensitive and privileged meeting in The Empire.'

Leo levelled a cold glower at the MI6 Director. 'Why would you say they're our enemy? Father is on his way to Ulan Bator right now to promote cooperation between Britain and Asia.'

'Even if they're not going to be our enemy,' Smythe continued in a calm tone, 'bringing them to this meeting breaks every protocol and value we hold dear. It's an unfathomable breach of professional etiquette, Your Royal Highness. Did King Alfred approve this?'

The King Regent's eyes flashed with anger, but he simply exhaled loudly and grinned. 'It was his idea to bring Britain and Asia closer together and he empowered me to achieve that in any way I deem appropriate. So, I'm doing what I think is right.'

'To invite people from outside our hierarchy to our most inner circle?' Smythe shot back quickly.

The room fell silent for a few moments, as Leo turned scarlet and fought to contain his rage. 'Has it occurred to you, Peter, or any of you, that they might be here to tell you something, not to learn all of our secrets?'

'They could have told us at an official meeting,' Smythe retorted. 'This is unacceptable decorum, sire. I appreciate you have been charged with a very difficult task. I'm sure I speak for everyone here when I say how grateful we all are for your devotion to The Empire. We all know how much you love our great nation. But I fear this is a huge error of judgement, sire.'

'Be careful, Peter. You're trying my patience here. Are you going to make me question your loyalty?'

Smythe sucked air through his teeth and exhaled loudly. 'I think it's very important that we establish some facts here today, Your Royal Highness. Firstly, let me say that I'm devoted to The Empire. Not you, not your father, not your grandmother before you both. My duty is to serve Britain as best I can. I work for the British people, as do you, as does your father. Your grandmother understood that very well. That being said, I acknowledge that you are senior in rank to myself, and I will follow your orders. But I will not do so blindly, and I will voice my opinion. You're not obliged to listen to it, but you will hear it all the same. It would be remiss of me, and a dereliction of my duty, not to speak out.'

The entire room looked to Leo, waiting for his reaction. His eyes were bulging and his veins were popping out of his neck.

To their collective surprise, it was the giant man with dirty clothes and long, dishevelled hair who spoke next. 'That's a very noble sentiment, Mr Smythe, and I commend you for it. You are quite correct: you do serve the British people. As does everyone at this table. The Privy Council is a noble institution that is an absolute credit to The Empire.'

'And you are…?' asked Smythe.

He ignored the question. 'But let's be clear about something else here today, ladies and gentlemen. The Privy Council has stood by and watched the great British Empire deteriorate over the past fifteen years and, I wonder, Mr Smythe, how many times did you speak out against the poor decisions that have led to that? Maybe never. Maybe every time. If it was the former, well, then, that brings into doubt your very judgement. If the latter, well, then you were summarily ignored and, clearly, your voice does not carry the weight you think it does. Either way, The Empire has been in freefall and each person at this table is culpable, except for the two, newest members of the Privy Council.'

Smythe's jaw dropped. 'Who the fuck *are* you?'

Gugano smiled sardonically. 'I'm one of the people your King Regent has asked to come and help you clean up the mess you have all made. My advice to you is that you sit there and listen.'

'And if I don't?' Smythe fired back.

He chuckled. 'Well, I could probably pull your lower jaw off with my hands, but let's not find out, what do you think? I promise we'll find out if you disrespect him again.'

Leo watched the MI6 Director fall silent and looked at Gugano, nodding his gratitude. 'Ok, now that's settled, I want to get to the reason you're all here today. I was hoping this would be quicker than this, but that wasn't to be.' He indicated a map of Brazil on the nearest screen. 'The reason our Asian allies are here today is because my father and I have agreed that we will not oppose them as they seek to gain new members of the Asian Coalition.

They are hoping to expand and we are going to help them by not getting in their way. In exchange, they will help us with our next targeted acquisition: Brazil. They are here to explain how they will help with that.'

Chris looked over to his brother. 'Leo?'

'Yes, Chris?'

'Who are the other two men?'

He laughed apologetically. 'Oh, yes! Do forgive my manners!' He pointed to them in turn. 'This is Maximilian and Gugano. They will be helping you all with a number of projects, so I suggest you get used to their faces. Now, if you will please allow our Asian friends to speak, then we can all get out of here and back to the party.'

Twenty minutes later, everyone was filing out of the door in silence. Chris was about to leave, when Leo grabbed his arm gently. 'One minute, brother.'

They waited for everyone else to leave, except for Max and Gugano, and Leo sat back down again, indicating that Chris should do the same.

'Can I count on your support, Chris?'

He nodded. 'Of course. Why would you even question that?'

'Because this could get really difficult for everyone. I'm going to force them to fix what they've broken and they will not like it.'

Chris shrugged his shoulders. 'I guess it depends on your opinion of broken. I think you're overstating how advanced our competitors are and

Peter wasn't totally out of order. You blindsided them.'

'I just wanted them out of their comfort zone.'

'Well, I think you achieved that,' he laughed.

'This new era of British-Asian relations is Father's idea. He thinks we need to be closer to them and he wants Russia in the EU to help keep them all focused on their commitments to Outpost.'

'That makes sense. We can start a new era of cooperation and that could be something truly amazing for everyone.'

Leo rubbed his hands together. 'That's one way to go. I kind of had another direction I was thinking about.'

'What do you mean?' he asked, almost reluctantly.

'I think this might create an opportunity for us.'

He furrowed his brow. 'To do what, precisely?'

He pointed to the taciturn men behind him, who stood with their hands clasped in front of them. 'Max and Gugano have worked with me for many years. You don't know them, but believe me when I tell you that they can achieve literally anything that we ask of them. They're beyond exceptional, Chris.'

He was unsure where this was leading, but he sensed it was not somewhere he would like. 'That's wonderful, but what are we asking of them? What opportunity are you talking about?'

'With Father over there building stronger diplomatic relations, and with us showing such complete trust that we invited their senior officials to a Privy Council meeting, they will drop their guard a bit.'

Chris studied his brother through narrowed eyes. He really did not like where this was leading. 'You're planning to betray them? With Father over there?'

'Not betray, exactly,' he sneered confidently. 'More like help them see why they should join The Empire.'

'Are you insane?' he yelled. 'They will execute him!'

'They will never know it was us. Father will be there to pick up the pieces for them and pave the way for us to step in and save them.'

'And how do you plan to make sure they don't find out?'

He indicated the two men behind him. 'The Asians are currently developing a weapon that we have not even thought about. It couldn't possibly be us, because we don't even know it exists. All we need to do is create a disenfranchised faction in their government and then leave the breadcrumb trail. We have already started to sow evidence of discontent within our two guests today. They're oblivious to it, of course.'

'You're going to blame Nimko and Tarnat?'

He nodded enthusiastically. 'I needed them here

to gain access to their Devices, which they had to hand over for a Privy Council meeting. We all do. Even the monarch.'

Chris sat back and sighed loudly. It was dastardly, but genius. 'But how do you topple a power as mighty as the Asian Coalition? It would need a prolonged and enormous campaign, which we can't afford if we're committing to Outpost as we have agreed.'

'Gugano has that worked out. One strike, multiple strategic targets. It would cripple their infrastructure immediately and their economy within three months.'

'Right, okay. Let's say that stands a chance. What weapon could possibly do that?'

Leo grinned so widely it covered over half his face. 'What do you know about cold fusion?'

Chapter 18

Layttle stopped the car outside the small hotel as the sun set. His eyes were so heavy he could barely keep them open. He had dared not sleep on the train, unsure who might be there. He had not even dared to stay on the train past Dover, opting to get off and make his own way up to the car LeCourte had left for him in the King's Cross parking complex.

The small VW had been easy enough to steal and would do the job he needed. But it was too small to sleep in and he was now realising he needed some rest sooner rather than later.

Once he reached London, he had no idea when he would be able to get some. Something told him he would need all his faculties to be at their sharpest. Even if he was wrong, it was better to arrive fresh and ready for anything.

This was uncharted territory, even for him.

He paid for the room in cash, showered and eagerly fell onto the bed, pondering the events of the past couple of days. He had driven around the Moissac area for several hours, but there was no sign of the black sedan.

It was probably for the best, he decided. He already had an objective and had been side-tracked for almost seventy hours. He needed to get this information out. Every hour he delayed increased the risk of something going wrong.

At the same time, though, who was The Chairman? The fact it was not Fontane seemed to make his information about Lillian Cheroux less significant. He was almost grateful he had not been able to keep up with Fontane. He had no doubt he would have pursued the lead as long as possible, and he planned to get back to it as soon as he could, but it seemed like there were some bigger pieces of the puzzle he needed to find once he concluded his business in London.

The existence of The Chairman also seemed to be a piece of information that might nicely complement the USB drive in his pocket. If he had never heard that name, in his capacity as K6 Director, then he doubted that anyone had.

He felt himself starting to drift away to sleep, so got himself up, got dressed and set the room up. He took the two spare pillows from the wardrobe and put them in the bed, adjusting it to make it appear as if he was sleeping in there. He turned off the lights and the bathroom fan, drawing the curtains to keep the streetlight out and muffle the sound of traffic. Taking two coins, he put some toothpaste between them and balanced them on the door handle.

This was a trick he had used many times. The toothpaste would hold the coins together long enough so that, if anyone used the door handle, they would fall and land together, making a distinct clang. They would fall apart immediately, as the adhesive properties of toothpaste were slim. But it was just enough for that single, unmistakable clatter. It would give him a few, precious seconds warning and was quiet enough so that anyone entering would not know he was aware of their presence.

For it to work, though, he needed to be close, so he set up the spare duvet in the wardrobe, sat inside and closed the door. Leaning against the back and side of the wardrobe, he rested his head on the cushion he took from the chair, which he perched on his shoulder, and was soon fast asleep.

The slight metallic clang woke him, resonating in the darkness. Layttle was a light sleeper, and had been for many years, so the noise woke him abruptly. He reached for the gun he always placed in his lap when sleeping in this position, but it was not there. It was still in Calais, under the seat of the Citroen.

The adrenalin hit his body and he felt his hands

shaking. He took a long, quiet, deep breath to compose himself. There was a loud squeak of the door hinges and light flooded in from the corridor.

Layttle already knew he was dealing with a professional or professionals. There had been no bleep of a key card. He would have heard it. They had opened the door with a shim, he guessed. That's what he would have done. Easy, quick and silent. But it was no easy skill to master.

He saw a shadow pass the small crack between the doors of the wardrobe and heard the door being closed quietly, telling him there were two adversaries. He knew the best time to strike was right now.

Standing up as he burst out of the wardrobe, the door cracked into the assassin closing the door and separated them. Layttle concentrated on the one closest to the bed. They already had their weapon drawn and aimed, but could not turn in time to target the man bursting from the wardrobe less than two metres way.

Layttle grabbed the wrist with one hand, pushing the muzzle of the silenced weapon away from him, as he rammed the heel of his other hand into their jaw. The balaclava dampened his strike a little, but the loud wail told him his assailant was female. He executed a hip throw, using his hold on her gun arm as a pivot. She flew into the television and landed on the sideboard with a crash, knocking cups, glasses, tea and coffee all over the floor, dropping her weapon.

Layttle had intended to snatch her gun at the same time as throwing her, using it to execute the other enemy, but she was lighter than he expected, or he was stronger than he realised. Either way, it spilled on to the floor in the darkness.

He looked up and the wardrobe door was closed. The second assassin had recovered from being smacked in the face with it. They were raising their weapon, so he needed to grab the kettle and throw it at them. It struck the gun as they fired, knocking the aim into the wall. Layttle pressed his advantage, leaping at them and covering the small distance in a flash, with his fist extended. It cracked their nose, and he could smell the tang of iron in the air as the nose exploded. The pained grunt was definitely male, so he followed it with a hard punch to the groin. The man dropped to his knees. It was only then that Layttle realised they were wearing night-vision glasses, feeling them under his fingers as he grabbed the man's head, crashing it so hard into the wall that it went through into the cavity. His arms flopped to his side and he stopped moving.

Layttle heard a shuffle behind him, turning to see that the woman was scrambling on her hands and knees. She had her weapon in her hand and was turning. He had no time to think, only his instincts. He reached over and switched the lights on.

She was blinded instantly, allowing Layttle time to get to her, smacking the gun from her hand and jabbing her in the throat. She tried to scream, but couldn't. She was on her knees now, grabbing her neck with both hands and gasping for air.

Her gun had landed near the window, so he rushed to pick it up and aim it at her. She found her breath and removed her glasses, blinking several times as her eyes adjusted to the light. By the time she was able to see clearly, he was sitting in the chair and aiming the gun at her, a half-smile creasing his lips. He also had the man's weapon on the table next to him.

'Sit on the bed, keep your hands in front of you and take that balaclava off,' he commanded.

She obeyed silently, looking over to see her colleague flopped against the wall, his head inside it. She looked back at Lyttle, resignation in her eyes. She was younger than he expected, maybe twenty-five, with a heavily split lip and blood all over her chin.

'The way I see it,' he began confidently, 'you and I have a decision to make. We can either both get what we want or neither of us can get what we want.'

'What do you want?' she asked uncertainly.

'I would ask you the same question. What you wanted a few minutes ago was to kill me and collect the reward on my head, right? Well, I think we can both agree that ship has sailed. Can we?'

She nodded. 'I thought as much. So, in light of this new situation, what do you want now?'

'To leave.'

'To leave alive you mean?'

She nodded and indicated her colleague. 'Is he alive?'

He chuckled. 'Do you care?'

She nodded again. 'He's my fiancée.'

Layttle laughed. 'Wow. What's that? Couples that kill together, stay together?'

She met him with a cold stare. 'Is he alive?'

'For now,' he replied, in a perfunctory tone. 'It seems you're negotiating for both of you. You want both of you to leave here alive, yes?'

'Ideally.'

'You can see why that might not serve my best interests, though, I assume?'

Her expression seemed assured. 'You would already have killed us if you wanted to.'

Layttle smiled widely. 'To be clear, I never wanted to kill either of you. *You* were the ones who came to kill *me*. There is still a price on my head, which I imagine you still wouldn't mind collecting. So, can you see why leaving you both alive doesn't really seem like the smart thing to do?'

'I can. Why have you?'

'Because we can help each other here. I can help you survive a huge misjudgement, and you can give me the information I need.'

'What do you want to know?'

'Who put the contract out?'

She shrugged her shoulders. 'It's an open contract.'

'With which agency?' he fired back.

'The one we work for is called Air Con Pros Ltd. It's based out of Lewisham.'

He considered it for a moment. He had heard of them, so it seemed plausible. 'Do you know which client presented the contract?'

'No, but I can guess.'

'The Empire?'

She nodded slowly. 'You knew that already, right?'

'I didn't know which agency,' he replied, quickly stealing a glance over towards the door to ensure the man had not woken up yet.

'It's an open contract, though. All the agencies will have it.'

He smiled. 'What's your name?'

'Aimee.'

'Aimee, I know what an open contract is.'

'Okay,' she replied, uncertainly. 'So, what now?'

'You told me what I asked.'

'But I didn't tell you anything you didn't already know.'

Layttle was still smiling. 'No, you didn't. But that's not all I want.'

'What else do you want?'

'How do they contact you?'

She indicated a pouch on her leg. 'Encrypted Device.'

He placed the gun in his lap, keeping his hand on it and keeping it aimed at her. He saw her eyes flicker towards it. 'You can't get to it before I kill you, Aimee.'

'I know,' she replied, almost irritated by her situation.

'Did you bother to research me before you came tonight?'

'We tried, but there's not much to find.'

'That should have told you something,' he laughed. 'Actually, how *did* you find me? I was really careful.'

'We saw you get off the train. The file said you would probably go to St Pancras, but we guessed, if we couldn't find any info, that you would be too smart for that.'

'Pretty clever,' he replied. 'Let's hope you're as clever now.'

'What do you want us to do?'

'You're going to report me dead,' he replied.

She shook her head. 'They'll kill us when they find out you're not.'

He scratched the grey stubble on his cheek. 'What makes you think they'll find out? I'll be gone in two days.'

She frowned mockingly. 'They always find out.'

He shrugged his shoulders. 'So, Aimee, I guess

you're left with a tough choice here, then. If you don't report me dead, I will kill you both, steal your Device, figure out how to open it and then report myself dead. Or, you can do it, leave here alive and go and hide somewhere. I mean, it's not what you wanted, but it's alive.'

'The Device is encrypted.'

'It's probably not something that's going to trouble me too much,' he lied. He had none of the equipment he needed and, he knew, did not have the time to get it. He would need to get moving quickly now he had been found.

She considered it for a few moments. 'You make a sound argument.'

'It's the only way you both leave here alive. The payday is gone, forget about that. But, Aimee, you seem pretty smart, so I'm guessing you have a contingency hidden away somewhere.'

Her lips curled very slightly for just a moment, giving away the fact that she did. 'And you're just going to let us go?'

'Well,' he continued, satisfied that his deception had worked, 'I'm not going to let you both just walk out of here. You will be in here, constrained, until the hotel staff wonder why I haven't paid my bill and come looking. But you will be alive and, I won't lie, probably have done some toilet on yourselves. Can you live with that, do you think?'

She nodded, almost enthusiastically. 'Yes, I can.'

Layttle indicated the unconscious man. 'Can he?'

'Yes.'

'That's good news!' he exclaimed, glancing at the clock. It was 03.15. 'So, we both have what we wanted. I'm very pleased.'

'Can I ask you something?'

'Of course.'

'They're paying a lot of money. What did you do?'

He laughed. 'I found out something they don't want people to know.'

'What?' she asked, suddenly intrigued.

'You'll see it on the news soon enough, I hope,' he replied jovially. 'But, Aimee, I'm really sorry, I don't have time to chat. Would you please send the confirmation? Then I need to get you both contained so I can leave.'

She started to reach for her leg. 'Yes, okay.'

'Slowly,' he warned, raising the gun slightly. 'I don't fully trust you yet, Aimee.'

She stopped for a moment, decided the threat was real and proceeded in slow motion. 'They will want proof.'

'And you will tell them you need a few hours to clean the scene and then you will provide it. Which, of course, only gives you a few hours head start. But it's the best I can do for you, given the situation.'

'That only buys you a few hours, too. And

239

you're being hunted by everyone.'

He smiled broadly. 'I only need a few hours, Aimee. Hopefully, in a few hours, this will all be nearly over and I will be long gone.'

Chapter 19

Chris took the seat opposite his brother and looked at Max and Gugano sitting in the chairs over at the side of the room. He looked around. He had never been in here before and he had been to his brother's home many times.

'What is this place?' The office was huge, maybe twenty metres long and ten wide. There was not much on the walls except for screens and Devices on charge, besides a few crests from various branches of their family and a large photo of Windsor in 1902.

'It's my home office,' he replied.

Chris pointed to the security panel on the nearest door. 'Taking it seriously, I see.'

'Kids break everything, brother,' he laughed. 'You'll see when you have some.'

He smiled. 'I saw yours break enough already, I think. So, what did you need, Leo?'

Leo lit a cigarette and blew the smoke above his head. 'Do you remember that summer at Sandringham?'

'Which one?'

'The one where we snuck out of the grounds and got the bus to Hunstanton?'

Chris searched his brain for a few moments. 'Oh, yea, you mean when I climbed the cliff?'

'When you *fell* from the cliff,' he corrected.

'*You* were the one who encouraged me!' he laughed.

Leo stood up and walked towards a drinks tray on the sideboard. 'Only because I made it up so easily.'

'You were a bit bigger than me back then.'

He poured himself a cognac and offered one to his brother. 'Want one?'

'No, thanks.'

'Fine.' He turned to his other guests, who both took a glass. 'And when you fell, do you remember what happened?'

'Vaguely. It was a long time ago. I couldn't have been much more than seven or eight.'

'You were eight,' he replied swiftly, moving back to his seat and flicking his ash into a small, glass ashtray in front of him. 'I can remember it like it was yesterday.'

'Really?' Chris asked, chuckling. 'I don't remember it being such a big deal.'

'Oh, fucking hell, I was so scared.'

'You would have been in deep shit,' he chortled.

Leo's face became grave and he took a lungful of smoke. 'No, not because of that. I don't think you understand how much I love you, little brother. The thought of you being badly hurt, or losing you...well, it breaks my heart.' He paused to blow the smoke out and gulp down the emotion. 'I remember the fall so clearly, even after all these years. The rock you were gripping just snapped off in your hand. You shrieked and fell on to the sand below. When I remember you falling, it's like it's in slow motion. I remember the ground. It was mostly sand, but there were rocks there and I knew, *I knew*, that if you hit your head on one of them, you were dead.'

'Brother, it wasn't that bad.'

He held up his hand. 'You don't know, Chris. You don't. I could see the rocks and you were plummeting towards them. I wanted to come and catch you, but my feet were frozen. I wouldn't have made it in time, but I should have moved, you know? But I couldn't. I was too afraid to move. It's like they say: paralysed by fear. That's exactly how it was.'

'I don't remember it being serious at all,' Chris shrugged.

'That's because you were okay,' he replied softly, sipping his drink and flicking his ash again. 'You banged your head on the sand, missing a huge rock by centimetres. Honestly, Chris, I think that was the most scared I have ever been.'

He studied The King Regent for a few moments, unsure where this was leading. 'I remember you buying me ice cream afterwards.'

Leo let out a bellowing laugh, blowing smoke from his nostrils. 'That was all you cared about! You had nearly smashed your head in, but when I asked you if you needed anything, you just said...'

'Peanut butter ice cream!' they said in unison

'I still love that,' Chris remarked.

'I know, brother. We only keep some in the freezer here in case you want it.'

'You have some? Isn't Tiffany allergic?'

He nodded as he swallowed more Remy. 'She is, but we keep it in a separate drawer on its own.'

'You keep a freezer drawer of ice cream for me, just in case?'

'Of course. You're my brother.'

Chris continued to study him. 'You like it, too, though?'

'I don't mind it,' he laughed.

Chris laughed, too, eventually pausing to ask the question bouncing around in his brain. 'What's up, Leo? You didn't call me here to talk about old adventures and ice cream flavours.'

His face dropped. He took another puff of his cigarette and stubbed it out. 'No, I haven't. I wish it was that, though. Truly.'

He was suddenly alarmed. 'What's happened?'

'We think someone on the Privy Council has

sold secrets, Chris.'

Chris gasped, sitting back in his chair. 'What? No! They're all devout Imperialists. They all love Britain.'

He wagged his finger. 'They all loved Nan, brother.'

He was shaking his head. 'I can't believe it, Leo. Do you have any evidence?'

He looked over towards Max, who stood up and took a Device from the wall. He opened it, pressed a few icons and an image of the Russia-Azerbaijan border came up. He zoomed in to a town called Khudat. 'Ever heard of this place?' Chris shook his head. 'No, I'm not shocked. Pretty much the same as everyone else. Khudat used to be an important place under Shah rule, but has been nothing for over a century. It's a small town, where people base themselves to explore the nearby beaches. Azerbaijan was the first country to vote to leave the USSR and join the EU, triggering the rush of other countries doing the same and the consequential collapse of the USSR. The EU didn't support them like the USSR did and they declined. Azerbaijan wasn't the only former-Russian state that the EU let down, but it was probably hit the hardest.'

Chris eyed the small, ponytailed man. 'I know all this, thanks. What's it got to do with a Privy Council spy?'

Max grinned. 'What you don't know is that, four years ago, the EU and Russia met in Khudat and started discussing their plans for Russia to join.'

'I still don't see your point.'

'Britain was invited. We didn't attend, but your grandmother told the Privy Council about it.'

'So?' He was starting to get frustrated.

'So, this information was sold to an organisation, a group of Russian dissidents, that tried to bomb Khudat. We traced it back to the Privy Council.'

He scoffed. 'How? There must have been two or three dozen people there. It could have been any of them.'

He was shaking his head. 'You think they wanted to die? No, Chris. The attempted bombing would have killed everyone there and there was only one invitee that did not attend: Britain.'

'You have any evidence?'

He pressed some more icons and an image of an email appeared. He read it quickly. It was a communication about the failed attack. 'We managed to trace this back to London before it was lost in dummy IP addresses and dismantled servers. The only people not in London at that time were your father and your grandmother. They were in Scotland.'

Chris eyed the time and date. 'That's Father's birthday. They would have been at Balmoral.'

He struck the air with his finger. 'And that's precisely where they were.'

He turned to his brother. 'How long have you

known about this, Leo?'

'A while.'

'Did Nan or Father know?'

He let out a cackle. 'You barely believe it, despite the evidence. Do you think either of them would have entertained this notion?'

'No, you're right. They would have probably brought it up in one of the meetings, too.'

Max continued talking. 'That was our prognosis, too. Obviously, it's important we seal this leak. We don't doubt that their reasons were to try and help The Empire, but this isn't the way to do it.'

'Agreed,' Chris commented. He looked at his brother. 'Why did you bring up the cliff story? What does that have to do with this?'

'I just want you to remember that you are one of the most important people in my life before I ask you to do something for me.'

'What's that?' he asked apprehensively.

'I want you to find the leak.'

An hour later, the King Regent watched his brother leave and looked over to his other guests. 'You don't agree yet, Max?'

'He isn't qualified.'

'He's the only one I trust completely.'

'We can find the leak.'

'You can help *him*,' he insisted, thumbing the air at the door Chris had just left through.

'What would you have us do?'

Leo sat back in his chair and finished his third drink. 'Follow them all and see if anything comes up. Just for a couple of weeks.'

'Everyone?' Gugano suddenly piped up. It was the first thing he had said all evening.

Leo turned to him. 'You don't agree with that?'

'Not Nesbitt or Smythe. They will spot it, unless we do it ourselves. We don't have the time.'

'You think they will see it? Really?' he asked, his tone sceptical.

Gugano nodded fervently. 'Nesbitt, maybe not. But Smythe definitely will. He's one of the only Imperial agents that I would say rival us in terms of ability. Either way, I would only entrust observing those two targets to myself and Max, nobody else. Imagine if they find out what you're doing. Do you want those questions at your next meeting?'

He shook his head. 'No, you're right. Okay, so just the others. If we don't find anything on them, then maybe we look at the last two. Although they're nowhere near my top suspects, anyway. Personally, I like Harris for it.' He poured himself another drink. 'So, where are we with cold fusion, gentlemen?'

'A scientist in Nampo has solved the calorimetry problem,' Gugano replied, matter-of-factly.

Leo met him with an unimpressed glare. 'Am I

meant to know what that is?'

'It's the measure of heat released, or absorbed, during a chemical reaction,' he explained. 'It tells us if the reaction is exothermic or endothermic, mostly.'

Leo shrugged his shoulders and looked at Max. 'Does that mean any more to you than it does to me?'

Max laughed. 'It means they know how to make a bomb from it.'

'But they can't use it for energy?'

Gugano shook his head. 'It's too unstable, which is why it's a useful weapon. The signature will be different when the blast area is investigated, so nobody will know what caused it. I suspect they will litter the bomb with uranium from one of our stores, or the EU or Russia's. It depends who they want to blame. That's if they even want to blame anyone at all. They may not want that.'

'This is our priority.' Leo declared. 'The intelligence is solid?'

Max nodded. 'As good as it gets.'

'And they have no idea that we know?'

'None at all.'

'Do I want to know how you got it?'

Max shrugged. 'I wouldn't ask if I were you.'

'Then I won't,' he laughed. 'Can you manage this and tracking the Privy Council at the same time?'

'We need time to set up covers and everything,

anyway,' Max replied. 'That will take a few weeks to do it properly. We can manage the surveillance while we're organising that.'

Leo grinned nefariously. 'This is good news, gentlemen. I will use Imperial assets to secure Brazil, while you go and get us the entire Asian Coalition.'

Chapter 20

R oyce watched Monaghan sparring from under the marquee. He was intrigued. Although the Australian was much larger, Monaghan was big enough to be powerful, but small enough to be fast. It was a rare and dangerous combination. It was the first warrior Royce had seen in a long time where he thought a fight between them might actually be a contest.

There was a ring of soldiers, in which stood the combatants. They all had head guards and gum protectors, with padded gloves. Monaghan had offered the local warriors five hundred pounds if anyone could knock him down. They were allowed to come in teams of four, but if he struck them, then they were out of the game. Five hundred pounds was a fortune in this part of the world. There was a long line of enthusiastic participants.

The Irishman was wearing his combat trousers

and boots, but no top. He was muscular, pale and lean, glistening with sweat and covered in dirt from the dustbowl arena. Royce had seen the way the local women looked at Monaghan. He was a handsome man and his physique was impressive. But he did not seem to notice at all. He was focused on the fight.

This was the third team to attack him. As soon as they had their equipment on, they ran in. Monaghan hit the first soldier in the chest with a spinning kick. The combined impact of the kick and the run caused the man to fly backwards, landing in the crowd several metres away. Number two waded in. She was fast.

Monaghan towered over the local soldiers, which was good for power, but also meant he could not duck anything. So, he needed to find more creative ways to evade them. He had to flip backwards to avoid her punch, bringing his foot out as he did so and catching her under the chin. It was a hard strike. She screamed and laid on the ground, squirming.

Numbers Three and Four co-ordinated their attack, something which, Royce had noted, none of the others had done, so far. Presumably because they wanted the whole prize for themselves. These two young men, however, seemed to have discussed their attack and formulated some kind of plan. They came from opposite sides, Three feigned an attack and then Four flew in with a high kick.

Monaghan was momentarily fooled by the fake attack, but Four moved too early. Monaghan had not committed to his defence, so was able to switch his feet and bring his arm up to block. At that point Three also attacked, this time trying to sweep Monaghan's leg.

Royce was reasonably impressed with them. They clearly both had some fight training, perhaps martial arts. Their attacks were quick and strong, with straight arms and legs. Monaghan only just managed to lift his leg to avoid the sweep.

Three was already spinning, this time in mid-air, aiming a kick at Monaghan's head. Royce thought it was an athletic and impressive move, but ostentatious and risky. It seemed to be more for the crowd than because it was the correct strategy.

Because it was so high, it gave the Irishman a good opportunity to duck. But Four was already coming in with a punch. If he did not move, the strike would land. Monaghan ducked down, but ran towards Three, catching him in mid-air from underneath and tossing him down to the ground. Three landed on his back with a loud 'oof' noise and then laid gasping for air, having had the wind totally knocked out of him.

Monaghan had distance now, and he could make his extra reach count. Four's punch missed, so Monaghan stepped to the side and used the Nepalese soldier's own momentum to end the battle. He grabbed the wrist and performed a throw. The soldier's heels went over his head, and he landed on his back, also. It was softer, though, so Monaghan followed it up with a firm chest punch to ensure victory was his.

The four combatants picked themselves up slowly and gave their equipment to the next four. Royce studied their new commanding officer keenly. He barely seemed out of breath at all. He had bested twelve soldiers, some of whom were, admittedly, of limited ability, but he was not even tired yet. Even the Australian was impressed. And he had not been impressed with anyone for a very long time.

He watched teams four and five fall easily. Team six gave Monaghan a scare and them number two from team seven finally got him with a kidney punch. The Irishman laughed and smiled, paying the woman in cash and then ending the game.

He walked over to the wash barrel and started to clean himself down when the gate opened. Two trucks drove in and the gates closed behind them. Monaghan smiled as he saw them, striding over towards them.

The passenger door of the first truck opened and a small blob of a man bounded out. Royce recognised him instantly. The Haggis was here.

David McNeary was only just legally allowed to join the British army. He was 150cm tall and inexplicably fat for a man who was a professional warrior. He had flame-red hair, which was combed over his bald dome, different-sized grey eyes, a bulbous, scarred, hairy nose and black, crooked teeth. He also only had one ear, having lost one to the grenade that also gave half of his face a large burn scar.

The Empire had strict new-born and teenage health screening programmes, designed to remove genetic weaknesses from the population, and Royce had often wondered how McNeary had escaped them. He guessed it would have been easy for his parents to hide him and avoid the authorities in the Scottish Highlands.

The local health service might have missed him, but it had transpired that it would benefit The Empire greatly. By the time they were aware of him, so Royce had heard, he was already fourteen, so past the legal age limit for detecting genetic abnormalities. McNeary was now allowed to carry on as normal. As a grown man, he was not legally disabled, but the rumour was that the British army had invested a lot of money in hormone treatment for him, once they discovered his talent.

McNeary had joined the Scottish Venture Scouts at fourteen. The story Royce had heard was that he had been such a natural, the Scout Master had alerted the local mountain rescue crew about him. They had, in turn, told the army, once they saw his talent up close. The army had recruited him at sixteen and he never looked back.

To say McNeary was an expert on mountain terrain seemed not to do his talents justice. The man could negotiate any terrain. Not only that, he could guide a team through it, with minimal training. He could sense danger, he knew which plants to eat and avoid, he knew where any animals were or might be. Put him in a desert and he would die in days. But, in any mountain range, he could get anyone though it and read it like it were a story he had been told a thousand times.

Royce knew that, if Monaghan wanted McNeary and his team here, then he planned to chase The Dayak wherever they might try to run. This was going to be a hunt. There would be no escaping The Scots.

Royce also knew that The Scots were not all Scottish. The moniker came from their training headquarters, up in the peaks somewhere near Ben Nevis. They were actually highly talented climbers from all over the world. He had only worked with them once, in the Idaho Rockies, but he recalled that they were not especially good, nor fierce, warriors. Their job was to get the dangerous soldiers to the hidden enemy.

He had to admit it was a smart move. He should, probably, have thought of it himself. That was why Nesbitt wanted a different commander, he supposed.

He sipped his water and noticed Monaghan and McNeary ambling in his direction.

The Haggis arrived next to him with a huge smile on his face, proffering his hand. 'Hey, Bob. It's been a long time.'

Royce shook it gently. It was less than a tenth the size of his hand. 'How are you, Dave?'

He took a cup and filled it with water. 'Can't complain, I guess. Hungry as fuck.' He laughed and wobbled his enormous stomach. 'When the general told me you were here, I was excited. I thought The Tracker retired a while ago?'

He forced a half-chuckle. 'He got me out of retirement for this. Just one job, though.'

The Haggis turned to Monaghan. 'Bob and I worked together in America one time. Have you ever seen him in action?'

The Irishman looked at Royce and shook his head, but smiled broadly. 'No, I haven't had the pleasure.'

'Wait until you do,' McNeary replied excitedly. 'It's a sight to behold.'

Monaghan continued to stare at the Australian. 'I'm very much looking forward to it.'

The Haggis downed his water and slapped Royce on the knee. 'Mate, I was looking at maps all the way here from Scotland. Since you're The Tracker, and nobody reads maps better than you do, I wanted to get your opinion on something. Is that cool?'

Royce nodded. 'Of course.'

McNeary pulled out a folded-up, paper map

from his pocket and started to unfold it. 'Awesome. Just give me a sec'.'

Monaghan stared at the map and laughed. 'What the fuck is that thing? It's not 1900, you know that, right?'

The Haggis shot him a deathly stare. 'This is my method. I grew up using these, because they're unregistered.'

Monaghan held his hands up in a gesture of surrender. 'No offence intended, Dave.'

He placed the map on the table and flattened it out as best he could, then indicated a circle he had drawn on it. 'Bob, you think they're probably in this area here, correct?'

He nodded. 'That's my best guess, although I never actually saw them.'

The Haggis waved the remark away. 'If you say there, that's good enough for me.' He pointed to a peak. 'If it were me, I would be up there somewhere. It's high enough to be able to see a long way, but low enough to be temperate. That means you don't need fires all the time and plenty will grow there. Also, there will be trees and bushes for materials and to help hide people.'

'Looks the same as all the other mountains to me,' Monaghan remarked.

He fired the Irishman an amused glance. 'There are quite a few in that area that are similar, but I'm pretty sure this will be the best one. Plus, it has several points of ingress and egress, but they're not big. If you saw someone coming, you could get out of there quickly, although you wouldn't be able to march an entire army through there in one go. If it were me, I would be here.' He looked up at Royce. 'What do you think?'

'I concur,' he grunted.

'Good!' he exclaimed happily. 'So, that's where we'll start.' He pointed to an area to the north of the peak. 'We can get to this area with a few people, but we'll never get an army through there.'

'I have an idea about that,' the Irishman suggested, suddenly adopting a serious expression. 'I think we flush them out of there and push them somewhere else where we can engage.'

The Haggis met him with a curious look. 'My team can't take on an army.'

'You won't need to.' He looked at Royce. 'Didn't you conclude that it's likely a very small army?'

The Australian nodded. 'To hide and cover tracks so well…yea, I think so.'

'So, we flush the prey out of their hiding hole,' Monaghan continued. 'They won't know how big the approaching force is, so they will assume it's the full force of The Empire. They always ran before, they're not going to change that strategy now. Don't you think?'

McNeary considered the idea for a few moments, rubbing his bald dome. 'They've never fought us? Ever?'

'Nope,' Monaghan replied confidently. 'Not even once. They run and hide, every time.'

He smiled. 'Then I agree, that would be a better plan. We can flush them out and kill them all.' He turned back to Royce. 'What say you, Bob?'

Royce looked at them each, in turn, with a quizzical glower. 'What about the kids? We will flush them, too.'

'What about them?' Monaghan shrugged.

'Fighting the soldiers is one thing, but the kids…?'

Monaghan sighed loudly. 'They're all part of The Dayak, Bob. Anyway, I have my orders. We're not to leave a bunch of people who can remember what happened and grow into enemies. That was very clear. Is that going to be a problem?'

'No.'

'Good.' Monaghan turned back to the map. 'So, I was looking at this area. Look at it, you have this valley that really thins here, looks kind of like snake, with the plain as the head then get thinner all the way to the tail. We wait at the tail.'

McNeary nodded. 'Well, also, it's not too far and it's the escape route I would use. I think that's the best place, too.' He looked at Royce. 'Bob?'

'Yea, looks good.'

Monaghan punched the air. 'Wonderful! We have a plan!' He looked at The Haggis. 'Get your team rested and settled.' He turned to Royce. 'Get the locals prepped and make sure we have all the equipment we need. I figure we can get really close to that tail by truck, maybe even all the way.'

'We will need to go a different way,' The Haggis confirmed. 'And we will need at least half a day to get up there, I guess. Maybe more. When do you want to leave?'

Monaghan smiled. 'You can go in the night and travel the road part by car, yea?'

'Of course. I don't need daylight until we start climbing.'

'Okay, then,' he replied. 'So, the rest of us will leave at first light tomorrow.'

THIRTY-FOUR MILES NORTH-EAST OF ANBU KHAIRENI, NEPAL

The monks sat in a circle on the plateau. The sunshine was warm in the afternoon at this altitude and the mountains seemed to shelter them from the wind. They sat around the map of the area that Duro had drawn in the dirt. He was very talented, Pearl mused.

'We have scouts here, here, here and here,' Krayak informed them, placing small rocks in various positions around the mountain. 'That covers north, south, east and west. They're static posts, switching every six hours. Nobody can sneak up on us.'

'How many soldiers have they seen going into Anbu base?' Deco asked eagerly.

'Not a lot, but enough,' Pearl answered. 'They're planning something and we think they're coming to look for us.'

'When did we last hear of extra troops moving into that base?' Lindo enquired quietly.

'Intake is every six months, like clockwork,' Pearl replied. 'That's still two months away. The locals in that area confirmed that they haven't seen any extra soldiers arrive there, outside of regular intake, ever since it was established about fifteen years ago.'

Krayak stood up. 'We are fully confident that The Empire is coming into our territory. The council has decided to stay and fight.'

'Is everyone aware of what this means?' The Canadian fired at the group and then proceeded to answer her own question. 'They will know where we are and they will come back in greater force. Does everyone understand the risks?'

Krayak picked up a stick and pointed towards the cave. 'We have spoken to the civilian contingent of The Dayak and they held a secret ballot. They have decided to stay and help us. They understand what might happen and they want to stay and help us protect, and fortify, our home. We all believe we can make this location a fortress.'

Pearl smiled. 'They can't get choppers in here and no laser-targeting system in the world can hit us in there. If we're ever going to stay in one place and build a home, this is the place.'

'It's important everyone understands the risks,' Krayak continued. 'There is a small village that will take in anyone who does not wish to stay. Nobody will be upset with you. But you must leave now.'

Deco spoke up next. 'This is what we have been training for. None of us will leave.'

Krayak was nodding. 'It is time to stand and fight. We were running for a long time, learning and practicing. We have been waiting for the right time to announce to The Empire that they are not welcome here. This is *our* home. This is *our* land. It is time for them to leave. If we ever want the support of the people, we need to act. We need to show them that they do not need to live under the heel of tyrants. They can be free. Once they see us fight, others will rise up. I'm sure of it. They're tired of having their children conscripted and homes taken. They are ready to revolt.'

Pearl stared at her friend. She had never seen him so impassioned. 'Once we win this battle, gentlemen, we need to send envoys out to all the local towns and villages to tell them of it and get more support. We can establish secret training schools in all of them, maybe even Pokhara, too. *This* is where The Dayak is truly born.'

They all cheered and Krayak continued. 'It will be unpleasant to fight. This time is different to the other battles we have fought. They were small and The Empire did not even notice them, but we were defending ourselves. But you must all remember that any one of them would kill us all, even all the families in the cave.'

'Without compunction,' Pearl added, vehemently. 'They would cut every throat in that cave and celebrate. To them, none of us are human. We are vermin, to be exterminated before we spread a disease. A disease called free will.'

They all cheered again. Lindo stood up. 'We are all agreed. Now is the time to fight. We will save ourselves and our people. Then we will find others to save. Eventually, maybe, we can save everyone.'

'That would be lovely,' Pearl replied, 'but one step at a time.'

Krayak took over, his voice the most authoritative it had ever been. 'Our plan is simple. Our people will hide in the cave and we will leave a small detachment to guard them, but we will conceal the entrance. It's unlikely anyone will see it, especially when we plan to intercept them so far away from here.'

'How far?' another monk, Jinto, fired.

'About five miles,' Krayak explained. 'We want to be far enough away so that they still don't know our exact location, but close enough to get back quickly. We have pinpointed a perfect location, with lots of places to hide and good vantage points.

We have an idea to stop them getting trucks any further, so they will need to come on foot. We plan to spread them out after they leave their trucks. We have spoken about it extensively and it's when they're going to be the most disorganised and vulnerable, but all still be together, not too spread out over a long distance. There is one place that we know will help us with that.'

'Where?' Jinto enquired zealously.

Krayak pointed to a valley on the map that looked a lot like a Cobra. 'The Valley of the Serpent.'

Chapter 21

Jude Astor studied herself in the mirror as she followed the guard towards the office. She looked more grey and wizened than a few weeks ago, but she held her shoulders straight to retain every inch of her six feet. She could not remember the last time she was this excited. Invitations to the private office of the King Regent were rare, even for the Imperial Chief Justice.

The door opened and the guard ushered her inside. The door closed behind her and she looked across to see Leo talking to his wife in the corner. He motioned for her to wait.

He finished his conversation and beckoned her over, as Tiffany strode out. Astor walked over quickly, her enthusiasm almost causing her to skip.

Leo shook her hand and welcomed her with a warm smile. 'Come in, Jude. Sit down. Sorry about that. Tiff is taking the twins to France for a couple of days and I'm in trouble for being too busy to go with them. Would you like a drink?'

Astor eyed the bottle of Remy on the side. 'Is that Louis XIII?'

He nodded. 'Would you like to try some?'

'I would love to,' she replied, eagerly.

The King Regent poured two glasses, handed one to Astor, then sat down. 'Chief Justice is an important role,' he said quietly.

'Thank you, sire.'

'It's crucial to The Empire to have the right person in that position and you're certainly the right person. However, despite that, if you ever utter a word of what I'm about to tell you, to anyone, then I will have you executed. Is that clear?'

She paused with the glass at her lips, looking over it at her host. 'Excuse me, Your Royal Highness? What did you just say?'

Leo grinned menacingly. 'I'm about to tell you something so secret that, if it ever gets out, I will know it was you. And I will have you executed. Do you understand?'

The judge's face turned white, and she slowly lowered the glass. 'I do, sire.'

'Good.' He gulped down his drink in one mouthful. 'The current population of Anglesey is just over one hundred and fifty thousand, is that correct?'

Astor's skin was ashen and clammy. She was

very seriously concerned that she might have a heart attack. 'I would need to check the number, but it sounds about right.'

'I need that up to a quarter million in four years. Can you do that?'

'W-w-w-why?'

'Don't ask why,' he scolded. 'Just tell me if it can be done.'

Astor's hands were shaking. She downed her drink, barely even tasting it. 'I don't see how it could be.'

'Raise the mandatory minimums, especially on any kind of violent crime.'

She paused to think about it. 'We could, but I can't just do it. There's a process.'

'I will give you a choice of Imperial Chief Constable and, together, you will introduce a zero-tolerance policy to all territories and increase the amount of violent offenders by at least sixty percent.'

'Everywhere?'

'The whole British Empire,' he reaffirmed with a nod. 'Violent crime is a blight and all our citizens should be free of it. Don't you agree?'

Astor nodded slowly. 'Forgive me, sire, but this seems like a law you could put through Parliament quite easily.'

'And yet I don't want to!' he replied in a menacingly low voice. 'Have I made myself clear, Jude?'

'I totally agree with the principle, sire, but your grandmother tried to keep people out of Anglesey because it's not conducive to rehabilitation.'

'Jude, I'm sorry if I haven't been clear enough. I'm not asking your opinion. I'm telling you what I want you to do, offering you a choice of cohort and commanding that you never, ever breathe a single word of this conversation to anyone. I can't emphasise that point strongly enough and the repercussions, should you fail to do that, will not be agreeable to yourself, I suspect. Or your family. You have two years to get it started and four years to get Anglesey up to a quarter of a million. Does that provide some clarity for you?'

'Yes, sire.'

'Wonderful!' he declared, a broad smile appearing. 'Now, let's have another drink and you can tell me all about Sophie and Jane's recital last night.'

LONDON, ENGLAND

MacLoughlin watched the young Englishman sleeping, drool running from the corner of his mouth, and yawned. He checked the clock on the dashboard. Over five hours since they got here.

He was concerned. That was a long time.

He saw a man enter the park and sit on the

correct bench, but it was not him. Then, forty-seven minutes later, a woman and child used the bench. Still no sign of him.

Bayston stirred, then woke and stretched as he yawned. He smacked his lips as he rubbed his bleary eyes. 'Still nothing?'

'I would have woken you if there was,' he snapped querulously.

'What did the message say again? Just wait?'

MacLoughlin met the young man with a blank stare. 'I can read, you know? I checked it five times. It says wait here. He will show.'

Bayston smiled awkwardly. 'Okay, okay, sorry. I was just checking. It just seems like a long time. Is that normal?'

'There's not really any such thing as normal in this line of work.'

He took the cold coffee from the holder in the centre console and took a sip, wincing as he swallowed. 'This coffee definitely isn't normal. Shall I go and get some more?'

The American handed him some cash. 'Put your hat and glasses on. Be quick.'

He nodded and put on his thin disguise, getting out of the car. He spent a few moments looking across at Finsbury Park. The trees were bare and the heavy cloud above made it seem dark, even though it was just past midday. The bench was just inside the heavy, black, metal gate and remained conspicuously empty.

He ran across the street, bought two white coffees, and ran back, noting that the bench still did not have anyone sitting on it as he returned. He got back to the car and found it unlocked and empty. He placed the coffees in the cupholders, stood up and looked around, panicked.

Where the hell had he gone?

He checked the bench. Still empty. Then he looked up and down the street several times. No sign of him.

'Jamie!' The call came from behind him.

He spun around and found him, standing next to a man, just inside the park. They were next to a large tree, concealed from view by a closed news stand.

Bayston walked towards the American and the stranger slowly.

'Sorry about that,' MacLoughlin explained, once Bayston was close enough. 'He wanted to speak to me alone first.'

Bayston eyed the stranger. He was small, old and had hexagonal glasses. He turned back to the American. 'Okay.'

The stranger held out his hand. 'I'm Peter Smythe.'

Bayston shook it. 'Hello.'

He continued. 'Do you know who I am?'

Bayston shook his head. 'No.'

MacLoughlin chuckled. 'Must be doing it well, then, Pete.'

'I'm the Director of MI6. Can I assume you know who they are?'

'Of course,' he replied, a little shocked.

'Is he not coming?' MacLoughlin asked, looking around.

'It's too risky,' the elder Englishman replied. 'Too much is going on. He's not ready to reveal himself yet.'

'Who are you talking about?' Bayston asked.

MacLoughlin ignored the question. 'Pete runs MI6, but is also involved in another organisation. They don't really have a name, some call them The Resistance, but really it's just a bunch of small organisations that are connected by the same objective.'

Bayston waited for the American to continue but, when he didn't, he asked the question in his head. 'Which is?'

'The independence of Imperially-controlled nations,' Smythe answered. 'It's very compartmentalised, with every small movement being totally self-contained. Most of them don't even know about the others. But there are a few threads that connect them and I am one of those. I have friends and contacts all over The Empire. Plenty of agents, too. Mostly I spend my time connecting pro-independence people, so they can help each other. It might not seem like a big deal, but they're all gathering momentum, especially in the past three months.'

'How many are there?' Bayston asked, suddenly intrigued.

'Mostly it's just people who share the same values getting together and talking, but that's how it all starts. There aren't many actual, cohesive organisations. Yet. Maybe five.'

'The Dayak is one of them and I'm getting something going in America. So, that's why we have been travelling around the country and why we needed to see Pete,' MacLoughlin explained. 'Ulinov had some names for me of some Americans with access to Russian money.' He looked at his friend. 'Did something happen to Tyler in Milton Keynes? I wasn't able to check.'

He shook his head. 'He got away because they came after you.'

'Good. He has three, maybe four, recruits ready to join me in America.'

Smythe smiled and turned to Bayston. 'I'm so sorry for keeping you waiting. I saw you, and Ed had not mentioned that he was travelling with someone, so I waited for you to leave before I made contact.'

Bayston looked at the American. 'I thought you were checking me out?'

He grinned. 'I did it the first night I met you.'

'Ed has briefly explained your situation to me,' Smythe continued. 'I can't tell you how sorry I am to hear about it. I can help with it, if that's still what you want.' He turned to the American. 'Sorry

273

about taking so long to get back to you. It's been manic the last, few weeks. I'm only checking our account once a week now. I don't trust that I'm not being watched.'

'You were careful about coming here today, though, right?'

He nodded. 'Of course. They don't suspect me of anything, I'm sure of that. But Leo has operatives working for him, so who knows what they're up to or what they might think?'

'Royal Guards or British ops?'

'Neither,' he replied, starting to walk slowly through the trees, indicating they should follow. 'I met these guys the other day and they're clearly pros, but I never heard of them and can't find anything about them.'

MacLoughlin stopped and stared at his friend, his face screwed up in concern. '*You* couldn't find anything about them?'

'Yes, that worries me, too. You ever heard of any ops called Maximilian or Gugano?'

He rubbed his chin. 'I have, actually. Those names came up in an investigation I ran maybe ten years ago, when I was still in the American SAS. They were in Colombia doing deals with drug cartels and executing some local politicians.'

Smythe was confused. 'I wonder why I can't find them. I have access to those files.'

MacLoughlin hacked into his hand. 'I will look up the op and send you the name. I can't remember it off-hand, but it will be in my notes somewhere.'

'Was it official?'

He nodded slowly. 'Orders came from someone. Nesbitt, I think.'

'That would be great,' Smythe replied, smiling. 'So, Jamie, do you still want help to get out?'

'Yes, please,' Bayston replied assuredly. 'I'm going wherever Ed goes, I guess.'

'Smart move,' Smythe replied. 'You can learn a lot from him. Except table manners.'

Bayston and Smythe laughed. MacLoughlin grunted. 'Nobody gives a fuck about using forks in the right order.'

'You should learn that at school,' Smythe replied. 'But I was more referring to that noise you make when you chew.'

'The grinding and slopping noise?' Bayston chortled.

Smythe chuckled. 'That's the one. I don't even know how it's possible. It's not a human noise.'

'It's the size of his nostrils,' he replied.

'Ah, yes!' the MI6 Director exclaimed excitedly. 'It is, you're right. That's been bothering me for years.'

MacLoughlin scowled. 'Don't we have bigger concerns, guys?'

'You're right, Ed, sorry,' Smythe conceded, stifling his laugh. He looked at his watch. 'We need to make our way across to the other side of the park, actually.'

'Why? What's up?'

'I have another meeting with another friend.'

MacLoughlin stopped and grabbed his arm. 'What you on about, Pete?'

Smythe looked at the hand on his arm disapprovingly. 'I was watching you for so long I'm running late. I have other friends doing other important things that The Empire wouldn't approve of, Ed. Did you think you were the only one?'

He released his grip, smiling apologetically. 'Of course.'

'This has got you on edge, I see.'

'Something is going on. They're more brazen than usual.'

'I agree,' Smythe replied. 'I see Leo upping the expansion ante and, I'm hoping, my friend has something with him to explain why. He seemed as spooked as you are.' He looked up and pointed towards another man by a tree. 'Ah, there he is now.'

Bayston looked over to see a lean-looking older man, with grey hair, a grey moustache and a PSG cap. They walked over and Smythe embraced him warmly. He gave MacLoughlin and Bayston the same curious look they were giving him.

Smythe grinned. 'This is Ed and Jamie. I'm sure you've heard of Ed.'

'I have,' he replied, offering his hand to both. They both shook it.

'Sorry to dovetail your meetings, but it's difficult for me to get away, so I had to squeeze both in here. Actually, it might work out because, from what I know, you might be able to help each other.'

'I know you,' Ed remarked. He turned to Bayston. 'Jamie, this is Trevor Layttle.'

Chapter 22

Bayston gave the American a blank look.

'You never heard of K6?' MacLoughlin asked him.

He shook his head. 'Should I have?'

Layttle was laughing. 'That's kind of how we like it.'

Smythe led them to a bench in the trees. 'I trust nobody was followed here today, but we'll soon know. I have some stuff I need to tell you both and, I guess, you both have stuff to tell me.'

Layttle, MacLoughlin and Bayston all sat down on the bench, while Smythe remained standing. Bayston watched them all curiously as each of them surveyed the area for any signs of danger before they proceeded. When they all seemed to relax a little, he guessed they were safe.

'I'll start,' Smythe remarked firmly. He turned to Layttle. 'I was just telling Ed that Leo has told us all his agenda. He wants to expand. He has operatives, called Maximilian and Gugano, who appear to be private contractors, helping him. I don't know what they're doing, exactly, but I couldn't find any record of them at all, although Ed might have something on them. He's going to check.' He paused to see if Layttle had anything to add about these men and, when he remained silent, continued a few moments later. 'He also invited two Asian generals, Nimko and Tarnat, to a Privy Council meeting.'

Bayston held up his hand and Smythe paused. 'The Privy Council?'

He nodded. 'You must have heard of that, surely?'

'I thought it was just a bunch of old men sitting around talking.'

'Far from it,' he scolded. 'It's the most powerful members of The Empire making huge decisions.'

Bayston shrugged his shoulders. 'Sorry, I didn't know.'

MacLoughlin laughed. 'This is what I mean when I say you don't know Britain anywhere near as well as you think you do. All sorts goes on in the shadows.'

'Anyway,' Smythe continued, a little irritated at being interrupted, 'Leo said this is meant to be part of ushering in a new era of British-Asian relations, but it all just felt wrong. Something's not right with it. I can't investigate too much without raising alarms, so I was hoping you would look into it, Ed?'

'Sure,' he said, with one, firm nod of the head. 'Is that it?'

'Not quite,' he replied. 'They're coming after your people sometime soon.'

'The Dayak?' MacLoughlin enquired, furrowing his brow.

Smythe nodded. 'But I didn't hear anything about it at all, and Nesbitt didn't update at the last meeting, so I don't know how seriously they're taking it or if they made any progress. Alfred backed Leo on it, but it seems like the new King Regent has other priorities. Either way, it's worth warning them.'

'I will,' he replied. 'I'll send an email now and tell them The Empire is searching for them.' He pulled his Device out.

'You're with The Dayak?' Layttle suddenly asked the American.

He was frantically typing his message, before he pressed send and looked up. 'As much as I can be.'

'I didn't even believe they were real,' the German replied, seemingly impressed.

MacLoughlin laughed. 'As real as you and I, buddy.'

'They must be good if the K6 hadn't even confirmed their existence,' Layttle said through a grin.

The American frowned. 'They're good, they're peaceful and they're small. I guess it all helps.' He turned to Smythe. 'Is that all you have?'

'Pretty much. Venezuela was us, but I'm sure that doesn't surprise either of you. Brazil will be next. The Empire is going to concentrate on expansion and Outpost, with Alfred working on the latter and Leo on the former. I'll keep you updated as and when I find out more, but I don't imagine there's much we can do to stop any of it.' He looked at Layttle. 'You had something you wanted to tell me?'

He smiled uncomfortably and looked sideways. 'Well, I did…I wasn't going to tell you with Ed and Jamie here, but they seem trustworthy. You vouch for them?'

'With my life.'

'Okay then,' Layttle continued, reaching into his jacket pocket and taking out a small USB drive. 'I managed to get hold of details of a large amount of The Empire's illicit financial accounts. There's a lot there, as you can imagine. On it is an account that traces back to Jacques Fontane.'

They all sat silent for a moment. Smythe spoke next. 'I only wish I was surprised.'

Layttle handed it to the MI6 Director. 'The evidence is on there. It's an account under the name Lillian Cheroux. Do you have any contacts that can make use of it and get the information out? Be warned, though, there's a tracker on it so they probably only have a minute to get the data and run. Got anyone who can do that?'

Smythe grinned and put it in his pocket. 'I have

just the person.'

'I thought you might,' the German replied, pleased. 'Also, as I was looking into this, I came across a new name of someone working for The Empire, but heavily involved in the EU. Anyone ever heard of The Chairman?'

'Chairman of what?' Smythe asked.

'I don't know,' he replied, looking at the ground. 'Could be anything, could be nothing. Could be just a name. Nobody heard that name, I guess?' They all shook their heads. 'I figured as much.'

Smythe turned to MacLoughlin. 'Okay, your turn now.'

He sighed. 'Pete knows this, but you guys don't. I have been investigating allegations that The Empire is using Groundbreakers to target poorer regions in their territories to recruit young people to their armies. They're cherry-picking gifted young students and trying to train them to be specialist operatives, too. I was hoping I could gain some support for American independence and maybe even some for The Dayak, at the same time. Anyway, as I was meeting some people Pete set me up with, and catching up with some old contacts, a professor called Ulinov was assassinated and this kid saw it all.' He nodded his head in Bayston's direction.

'Who's Ulinov?' Layttle asked.

Smythe answered. 'She ex-FSB and one of our

most useful Russian allies. I spent a long time getting her over her and in a secure placement. She wasn't active any more, though. She hadn't been for at least five years, so I don't really understand why anyone would target her now.'

'She was with us,' MacLoughlin replied.

'She was with The Dayak?' the MI6 Director snapped. 'Why didn't you tell me?'

'I thought you preferred not to know everything?'

Smythe growled. 'I could have protected her.'

'She wasn't doing much. A little recruitment, a little consulting if we had Russian entanglements. Nothing else. Nothing that should have brought her to The Empire's attention. Otherwise, I would have, I promise you.'

'Her name never came across my desk even once,' Smythe replied. 'If she was a person of interest, I would have known about it.'

'Exactly,' the American replied. 'It makes no sense to go for her now, unless there's more to it. Maybe she was into stuff I didn't know about.'

Layttle was looking at Bayston with sorrow in his eyes. 'You saw the whole thing?'

He shivered. 'Just the end product.'

MacLoughlin placed a firm hand on Bayston's shoulder, but spoke to the German. 'He managed to get away and even tried to fight. Fair play to the kid.' He turned to Smythe. 'It was Driscoll.'

Smythe paused and considered it for a few

moments. 'He was meant to be stationed in Rio. That's a hell of a coincidence considering that's Leo's next target, don't you think?'

'Not a coincidence at all, is it?' Bayston commented blandly.

MacLoughlin laughed and playfully slapped the young Englishman's back. 'He's a quick study, this one. With his brains and guts, I have high hopes for him.'

'I'll try to discreetly look into it,' Smythe continued. 'Technically, Driscoll works for Nesbitt, but he's pretty well known for his surveillance work, so it wouldn't be too weird for me to requisition him. I think I can figure something out.'

Layttle laughed. 'You're going to be busy, Peter.'

'You two are nothing but trouble. You always have been,' he laughed.

'We just need a new passport for the kid,' MacLoughlin stated. 'I need to get him over to Europe and then I can take him back to America with me and get him set up.'

Smythe looked to Layttle. 'That would take me a couple of weeks. Can you get one faster?'

He nodded. 'But my contact is in Paris. I would have to leave and come back again, but I can do it. To be honest, though, I wanted to get back on tracking Fontane and figuring out who The Chairman is.' He turned to the American. 'No offence.'

He waved it away. 'It's fine. I can hide him for a couple of weeks.'

Smythe looked at the young man apologetically. 'If I ask for expediated papers, they need a dual signature and get inspected. It's riskier, because I don't have control over the inspection process. Can you lay low for a little while? I'll make it as quick as I can.'

'Of course,' Bayston replied.

'Give him your details,' MacLoughlin instructed. Bayston took out a piece of folded paper and handed it to the MI6 Director.

He unfolded the paper and started to read it. 'Maybe I can get it in ten days, you nev-' His face dropped and he stared at the young man on the bench. 'Your name is Jamie Bayston, from Hull?'

Suddenly, Bayston's body filled with panic. 'Yes. Why?' He looked at MacLoughlin, who was also alarmed at the reaction of his friend.

Smythe's complexion was suddenly pallid. 'Please tell me you're not related to William Bayston.'

'He's my dad.'

He turned to MacLoughlin. 'He's one of my anti-Imperial activists. He's not an agent, but helps me put Republicans in touch with other Republicans.'

Bayston could barely muster words. 'My dad was MI6?'

'No,' Smythe returned firmly. 'He's a part of my work to help countries work towards independence, but he works with The Republicans. They're a bit like Ed and The Dayak. Except they're based in northern England. He uses his position as an MP to travel around and sometimes he makes introductions for me.'

'He's part of The Resistance?' Bayston gasped, his mouth gaping.

'Not exactly,' Smythe replied sharply. 'But he's definitely connected to it. And so was Ulinov, by an equally delicate thread.'

MacLoughlin stood up. 'And Jamie just happened to walk in on an assassination of another Resistance contact? That's sounds to me like...'

As the American trailed off, Smythe finished his sentence. 'It's definitely not a coincidence. The whole Bayston family is in serious danger.'

SIXTEEN MILES NORTH-EAST OF POKHARA, NEPAL

The sound of laughter and song filled the cave. The children were performing a recital as a farewell gift to the monks before they all left. There were soups, breads and even some momos and jeris smuggled in from the nearest village.

Letitia Pearl sat together with the monks and watched the children dancing by fire light, applauding and cheering. The families chatted and smiled. It was the most fun any of them had seen for a long time and, with what loomed over them, they were aware they might not have another evening like this to enjoy ever again.

The laptop sat in a tent, on a small bench, at the other end of the cave. It pinged.

But nobody was there to hear it.

Chapter 23

The convoy bounced down the mud track, if it even qualified as that. Royce sat in the passenger seat of the fifth truck and wondered how long they were going to persist with this. The vehicles were all 4x4, but the enhanced suspension was not built for this. He was no mechanic, but even he knew they could not take much more punishment.

The sun was high and warm. It was only mid-morning, but it seemed much warmer than usual. Or maybe it was just his perception amidst the heightened excitement and tension that emanated from those around him.

He rolled down the window and closed his eyes as the breeze stroked his face. Sucking in a deep breath through his nostrils, he caught the scent of the wildflowers and it made him smile. He opened his eyes and looked at the vivid kaleidoscope as they idled past.

They hit a large hole and it threw his head into the roof. He looked across at the driver, who smiled apologetically and shrugged his shoulders, as if to say it was Royce's fault for being so big.

He took out his Device and checked their location. They were getting close but, at the speed they were able to travel on this terrain, he mused, they were probably still an hour from parking up and progressing on foot.

He saw the blue, blinking dot on the far side of the mountain. The Scots were on cliff sides and still seemed to be moving faster than this convoy.

He looked at the vehicles in front and behind. They were all dark green and the panels had the British Army crest on each side. The only windows were in the cab at the front, the rear being made of a pair of fortified doors. Royce looked at the wheels. The tyres were huge, probably the size of an average-sized man. He would have preferred tracks, but knew it would have taken too long to get the equipment in from the East India Company's largest divisions.

There were thirty-one vehicles in total, each with around thirty soldiers in. Monaghan had divided them very specifically. There were members of his team, and his Beta team, in each truck, except Royce's. He commanded that one.

The leading truck was the only different one. It did not have a solid body, but was a curtain-sider.

Monaghan travelled in that one with just a few soldiers. Royce was not sure what was in there, but guessed some kind of heavier artillery. He also noticed that this vehicle had tracks, rather than wheels. It had arrived late last night and, he suspected, was one of the reasons Monaghan had wanted to wait.

He looked in the mirror at the soldiers sitting in the back of his truck. They were all Nepalese soldiers, most of whom would be there as a result of conscription. There were a few faces, though, that seemed a bit older, so perhaps they were criminals, on the run from the authorities. Nobody was going to look too hard for them here.

Anglesey was a long way from here and, if they were sent to The Island, they were unlikely to ever come back.

Some of them seemed to be nervous, primarily the younger troopers, but he also felt an energy exuded from others that felt something like excitement. He knew the British Butchers had been making a concentrated effort to bond with their Nepalese cohorts, telling them exciting tales of war and doing their best to dehumanise their opponents. It was a ploy The Empire often used and was especially effective with young, disaffected males. Knowing this, Imperial base commanders assigned women conscripts to support duties and men to fighting, more often than not.

Royce could not help but notice, though, that his truck had slightly more women than men, which he found curious. Sexism had been illegal in The Empire for over a century, but it was a scientific fact that the amount of testosterone in young, male bodies made them more aggressive and easier to manipulate. The enrolment officers, Groundbreakers and Missionaries did not even bother to hide that fact. They encouraged their local commanders to exploit it. The East India Company managed this part of the world for The Empire and their defence department was the Gurkha Command, led by Sir Rohit Bista. There were suggestions that they added testosterone to the meals, because they were keen to be fierce.

Royce had thought about this a great deal, as he witnessed the local troops fighting with each other so regularly. Bista was renowned for coveting a knighthood for his son and, since they could only be earned by feats achieved in combat, he had gone to extra lengths to discourage the Asian raiding parties on the borders of Nepal. It seemed feasible that he would order such a thing to create an eager army, rather than a well-trained done.

From what Royce had seen, these soldiers were highly motivated and aggressive, but lacked any tradecraft or genuine combat skills. He suspected Monaghan had noticed the same thing and was curious to see what plan the Irishman had to use this.

They hit a large bump and it threw him into the door. His shoulder cracked against it and he grunted in pain. He looked across at the driver, who was smirking. 'The next time you hit one of them, I will put your head through the fucking window.'

The driver's smile vanished and Royce turned to face the soldiers in the back, SA80s on their laps. He could see the fear in their eyes, the shaking hands, the bouncing knees. 'How many of you have seen active combat before?'

A couple of the slightly older soldiers raised their hands. 'We have, sir.'

'Where?' he fired.

'At Popti Pass,' the woman replied.

He noted the pair of V's on her arm. 'What happened there, Corporal?'

'A unit of the Chinese were raiding a few villages up there and we were sent to intervene,' the man replied. He had a single V on his arm.

'I asked your senior officer, Lance Corporal,' Royce admonished, turning back to the woman. 'You were sent from Anbu?'

'We were stationed at Darjeeling back then,' she replied. 'The EIC had not recruited us long before that, so we were new.'

'You're Gurkhas, right?'

She nodded. 'Yes, sir. Fully accredited.'

'How long did training take to complete?'

She paused to think about it. 'Six weeks, give or

take a little. Some people take longer, I think.'

'That's basic training. How long to get Gurkha-accredited?' he scowled. He had heard they were a higher level.

'You need it to complete basic training. Otherwise you have to start again or get reassigned.'

He snorted. 'So, the accreditation is basically completing the same basic training that every other branch of the British Army completes?'

She shrugged. 'I don't know what they have to complete, sir. I never went there for training.'

He chuckled. 'So much for that theory. At least some of you have some experience. Anybody else ever done any fighting?' They all looked at him blankly, so he expanded his question. 'I mean in the streets, in a bar, anything where you could have got hurt, basically.'

Almost every hand went up apprehensively. 'School,' said one woman. 'Club,' said another. 'Boxing training,' remarked a young man.

'You remember that burst of adrenaline that makes your hands shake and your vision blurry?' he fired back. Most of them nodded slowly. 'I have a trick for dealing with it. Close your eyes, take five deep breaths and then open your eyes.'

They looked at him and each other, uncertainly. The Corporal smiled. 'Thanks, sir. We'll remember that.'

'Is it true The Dayak are like ghosts?'

293

He turned to the young Private who had asked the question. 'How can they be ghosts? What are you talking about?'

'They say that they're the ghosts of The Empire's victims. That's why nobody has ever seen them.'

Royce was about to reply when another Private replied for him. 'No, that's not true. But I heard that they're not really monks. They're actually the last ninja clan on Earth.'

'Not ninjas,' another Private corrected. 'They're just the greatest warriors that ever existed.'

'I heard that some rich anti-Imperialists paid to get all the best fighters in the world together,' claimed another voice.

'Some people think it's Asian special forces trying to destabilise us.'

'I still think they're ghosts,' someone else said.

'Be quiet!' Royce snapped. 'They're just people. They bleed and die like everyone else. And they're not even military, so they will be weak, easy opponents.'

He watched them all fall silent, knowing he had not convinced any of them of anything, grunted and turned back to face the front, watching as the convoy started to come to a halt. He peered out of the windscreen. The second truck had stopped and its wheels were spinning furiously in some mud. Others were getting out and going to help, but he already knew that was as far as they were going.

'Come in, Captain Monaghan,' the radio suddenly crackled, It was The Haggis.

'Receiving,' it buzzed.

'We're almost in position. About a mile away. Are you ready?'

'Not quite, but soon. Have you found anything yet? Any resistance so far?'

There was a static-filled pause. 'One scout and one lookout, both disabled without trouble. We're definitely in the right place.'

'Great. We will be in position. You have permission to engage.'

'Roger that, Captain. Get yourselves ready. It will be soon.'

The radio went silent and Royce watched as Monaghan jumped out of his vehicle and walked over to inspect the truck causing the delay. He spoke to a few people and then moved the radio to his lips.

'All units, disembark. Only take what you can carry and plenty of ammo. We go on foot from here.'

ONE MILE NORTH-EAST

'Are you sure that mud pit will work?' Deco asked, concerned.

295

Lindo nodded. 'I don't think any vehicle will get past it. They will come by foot, but they will be spread out to get through there.'

He was pointing to the entrance to the valley, when it thinned down to a single track between the two mountains that stood guard over it. The gap was only wide enough to get a single truck through and even that would be a squeeze. Any forces would need to pass through two or three at a time.

Pearl studied the rock formations either side of The Gate, as the monks were calling it. They were craggy and steep, quickly growing into separate mountains on either side. They might be able to get a few soldiers over the cliffs, but it would be a dribble. That was not going to be a concern.

She had considerable doubts, but she had to admit that this topography was perfect for a stand. She looked across at the men around her, all taking position in the cliffs, trees and bushes of the valley tip, and beamed with pride. Battle was not their natural inclination. They wanted peace. It had taken years for them to accept that this was the only way. They needed to make a statement to The Empire and the whole world.

The Dayak were not going to gain any support or momentum by running and hiding every time. To affect The Empire in any meaningful way, they needed to grow. For that, they needed the world to know who they were and galvanise the anti-Imperial emotions already entrenched in every territory.

Her main concern, though, was the cave. The families. She wished they had ensured the civilian and support functions of The Dayak were far away, but they knew the risks and most had chosen to stay. Only a few people had gone to the village.

She watched Deco finding a position in the rocks opposite her. She remembered The Empire moving a stolen crate of Chinese-made QBZ-95s through Kathmandu, many years ago, and how they had stolen it with nothing more than knives and a single Smith & Wesson. The Imperial soldiers couldn't report it, as they had stolen the weapons from the Asian Coalition, presumably to sell on the black market. Nobody ever came looking for them. Now The Dayak had automatic weapons. To begin with, they had not been good at using them. With a little training and lots of practice, however, they were now very capable.

Lindo moved up next to her, high on the cliff, and placed a rucksack full of ammunition clips and grenades between them. She saw Krayak moving towards the rear of their troops, hiding in a copse of thick birch trees with the other elderly and senior monks. They all had QBZ-95s, but also some QBU-88 sniper rifles, stolen in the same shipment. They were very good with those, too.

She watched as the other, younger monks took their assigned positions. Most were high in the cliffs. The sun was behind them, which they knew would provide an advantage for the snipers, so she hoped The Empire would arrive soon. She looked at a few of The Dayak stationed on the ground, behind trees or in bushes, with large logs placed for them to use as cover. They were ready.

She sat in silence and listened. They had all agreed that Deco would judge when to make the first shot and the rest of them would follow. She could see him, laying on his front, weapon balanced on a rock, with his eyes closed. Everyone gaped at him nervously.

After about an hour, he raised his fist and they all suddenly turned towards The Gate, weapons primed. Pearl strained her ears and, after a couple of minutes, she could hear it. It wasn't what she hoped or expected to hear. It was the sound of an engine. But something else mechanical, too. It was a loud, repetitive clinking that she vaguely recognised, but could not place.

She looked across at Deco and could discern that he had similar questions. Had their truck trap not worked? She could only hear one engine and the noise did not sound like a truck. What was it?

She tried to crane her neck for a better view, but not so much that the Imperial forces could see her. She felt the panic starting to spread through them all.

Already there was something they had not thought of. Maybe this was a huge mistake, but it was too late to turn back now. They had to keep going. The fight was here. There was no more waiting.

The noise got louder, echoing off the cliff faces all around them. She watched The Gate intently. After another long, few minutes, she saw the front of it and she saw the tracks. Was it a tank? That was the sound, she now realised.

A few moments later, it came through The Gate. It was not a tank, she was relieved to see. But what was it? It had tank tracks, but was a curtain-sided truck. Whatever it was, it had been able to evade their trap. But it was just a single vehicle with no visible weapons. She turned her attention to the soldiers walking behind it. They were looking around, but did not seem to be especially cautious. They walked quickly and loudly, chatting to each other. They laughed and joked and smiled. She almost felt bad about what was going to happen, but reminded herself who they were and what they represented.

The monks all returned their gazes to Deco, who still had his fist in the air. He waited for them to get further through the gate. And further. And further. Pearl could feel the weight of the apostrophe of metal against her finger. It felt hot, too. Her fingers were sweating and she wiped her brow with her shirt sleeve.

Deco kept his fist in the air, his eyes trained on the soldiers pouring through The Gate. She knew he was trying to judge the right moment, when enough were through, so they did not have lots of reinforcements on the other side, but not so many that they could not defeat them quickly. She was glad it was his decision. They did not even know how many they were facing, so she had no idea how he would decide when to strike, but she trusted him.

The Dayak all watched that fist, their fingers hovering over their triggers. More Imperial soldiers came through The Gate. A dozen, two dozen, three dozen, now fifty, now maybe one hundred.

Pearl did not bother trying to count. She looked at their faces. They were mostly young locals, she quickly deduced. She noted a few non-Nepalese soldiers amongst them, presumably the commanders. They were looking around them with more attention than the local soldiers, she realised. They knew what they were looking for.

Suddenly, she was very aware that some of The Dayak were visible from their positions if the Imperial soldiers got further into the valley. They could not be seen from The Gate, but they could be from as little as fifty metres inside it. Their robes were good camouflage against the brown of the rock, but they could still be seen. Trained eyes would spot them and then their element of surprise would be lost. She knew that was the most crucial part of their attack. She doubted it could succeed without that.

She looked over at Deco, willing the fist to drop. The truck was maybe forty metres into the valley now, serpentine lines of soldiers following close behind. She knew the driver would soon be able to see some of The Dayak soldiers, hidden on the slopes and in the trees.

She was panicking. She could feel it. She thought about pressing the trigger, but did not. A single surprise gun was not going to do enough and every other Dayak warrior was watching the fist.

She looked down at the soldiers pouring through The Gate. There must have been one hundred and thirty by now, maybe a few more. The Dayak consisted of only just over one hundred warriors.

Time seemed to slow down. They seemed to be walking in slow motion. Pearl looked back at Deco, almost ready to scream at him.

Then the fist dropped.

There was a pause, just for a second, as they all turned back to their sights and took aim.

Then, in unison, The Dayak all squeezed their triggers.

Chapter 24

The gunfire made the birds flee the trees. The sound of it bounced around inside the valley, a deafening cacophony of death. Only a few moments later, the screams began.

There were all types of screams. Some were loud, some were dulled, some were high-pitched, some were guttural. They filled the air like the backing vocals to the most horrific song that any of them could ever imagine.

Men and women dropped. There was blood spurting up in the air, spilling out in every direction, covering the green valley floor in a dark crimson. The bullets flew in from everywhere. The Imperial soldiers had no chance. They could not even react, the attack just cut them down. Their camo shirts suddenly turned a deep shade of purple and they started falling to the ground.

It took a few moments for them to realise what was happening. They started to run, in any direction they could, but they were too exposed. If they found somewhere to hide, bullets followed them.

The truck stopped and the doors opened, but there was no cover nearby, so the doors closed again.

The Dayak were concentrating on The Gate and the front of the convoy. They wanted to trap everyone in the middle and maximise the efficiency of their ambush. Imperial soldiers on the other side of The Gate quickly realised what was happening and stopped pouring through it.

Royce could hear the fusillades and wails from the other side. He was still thirty or forty metres from the valley entrance when the panicked cries started over the radio.

'It's a trap!' Monaghan shouted. 'Everyone fall back!'

Royce could see the Imperial soldiers rushing back through, watching many of them fall as they ran. Many were diving over the rocks, desperate for any kind of protection they could find. He could hear the panicked commands over the radio before it went silent.

He could just discern the sound of the engine over the cracking of gunfire bursts in the valley. He ran towards the gap, but stopped behind a tree to assess the situation. He looked around him. They were all looking to him, even Monaghan's warriors. They needed a leader. He sighed. He was not that man. He was already thinking about how

303

to ensure his own survival.

He suspected the mission was lost already.

The radio was crackling, but he could not hear anything over the din of warfare. Was that a Scottish accent he heard?

It did not matter. The Dayak had planned this ambush. He thought back. Yes, there were signs. The mud pit. It had not rained in a few days and the drainage on this soil was exceptional. He should have seen it.

He heard the rumble of the truck as the engine screeched. It crashed near the gap, into one of the sides. The door opened and Monaghan fell out, three of his soldiers following him. The driver flopped out, a huge hole in the back of his head.

The Imperial soldiers were grouping up near the gap and hiding. None of the bullets were coming through it. They were safe this side. For now.

The truck had blocked the path even more, though. The soldiers trying to retreat suddenly found the space even more restricted. They could only get through a few at a time. They were falling as they tried. As the bodies filled the gap like some kind of macabre Polyfilla, soon none of them were getting back through it.

In the valley, one of the Monaghan Marauders had managed to organise a group of about twenty soldiers and found them cover in a small group of Utis trees. They were managing to target The Dayak and return fire. One monk fell from the cliffs, then another.

Pearl saw Jura fall from his position and stopped shooting at the few soldiers that were still trying to make it to The Gate. She noticed the small group that had found a way to fight back and tried to target them, but they were too well hidden from her position. She fired anyway, out of pure hope, but all that succeeded in achieving was to telegraph her position to the enemy. They began to target her and Lindo. They both ducked down and the fragments of rock showered down upon them.

Pearl gritted her teeth and stayed low. She knew these precious moments were causing a huge delay. The plan was to move up the cliff so they could fire over The Gate and beyond. But they could not do that with that small circle of enemies in that position. Those soldiers could pick off anyone trying to advance.

The sound of gunfire started to trail off, although the agonised screams did not. Then there was suddenly a loud crack. She knew it was not one of the assault rifles, but she knew the sound very well.

It was a sniper rifle.

The attack on her position had stopped, so she stole a look over the ridge, just as another loud crack filled the valley. She saw one the entrenched soldiers start to run as one of their heads became a gruesome cloud of blood and bone. The woman that ran was soon cut down by one of The Dayak high on the flanks.

The sniper fired again, splintering a branch above the Imperial heads, but it forced them down, so they could not return fire, nor target anyone else. Pearl looked around the valley entrance. There were no more targets. There were a few injured and screaming soldiers, but most of them were dead or quiet, resigned to their fate. She did not have time to count, but estimated at least a hundred Imperial warriors had fallen, perhaps more. Now they needed to press their advantage and finish the battle before the enemy could organise themselves. She looked at the rucksack next to her and picked up a grenade.

Royce walked over to Monaghan. 'They're coming soon. We need to retreat.'

He turned on the goliath angrily. 'We're not being beaten by a bunch of fucking farmers, Royce!'

'If they were just farmers, we wouldn't need to retreat,' he scowled. 'They've surprised us, divided us and have us flanked in territory that they know and we don't. We need to retreat, regroup and come up with a new plan.'

'No!' he shouted.

'Do you have a better idea?'

He snatched Royce's radio from his belt. 'McNeary?' he yelled into it. 'McNeary? McNeary, come in!'

Just as the answer came, there was a thunderous

crack from the other side of the gap. The two men looked at each other wide-eyed. 'They have snipers! We need to go now!' Royce roared.

'You want to run? A target of your size?'

'We can't just stay here in the open. It's suicide.'

The Irishman ignored him, opting to holler into the radio instead. 'McNeary, where the fuck are you? McNeary? McNeary?'

The radio crackled. There was a response, but it was drowned out by static. He walked away, locating a ridge that would be out of view of any sniper and scaled it quickly.

Royce watched him reach the top, bark into the radio and slide back down. He tossed the radio back at the Australian and he strode past. 'Get your fucking troops into position and get ready to advance.'

'What?' he asked incredulously.

'We have one last move to make and we're going to do it.'

'They'll all be slaughtered.'

He met Royce with a confident look; a nefarious, yet arrogant, glint in his eye. 'Just be ready when I give the signal.'

'What's the fucking signal?'

The corners of his mouth creased upwards. 'You'll know it when you hear it.'

There was a loud explosion on the other side of the gap. Royce looked at the pillar of smoke snaking away into the sky. They had a lot more munitions and training than anyone knew. 'That was a grenade, Captain. We don't have long.'

'We don't need long,' he scoffed. 'Just shut the fuck up, stop being a giant-sized pussy and get ready.'

He strode away and Royce watched him leave, then looked at the terrified troops around him. They had heard the order, but did not seem to believe it.

'Get ready to advance,' he ordered and watched one pair of trousers darken at the front. 'We go on his signal.'

Pearl tossed another one through the air, hiding behind the rock and waiting for the boom. She peered over. Close, but not there yet. Lindo smiled and took one. He launched it and it landed near the Utis trees, then rolled just inside.

The explosion made the ground shake and parts of tree flew out in every direction. The blast caught one Imperial soldier, who screamed in agony for a couple of seconds, then fell silent.

There were a few moments of stillness in the valley, filled with an air of disquiet, as both sides paused to consider their next move.

Lindo grabbed another grenade, ready to shatter the impasse. He then stopped before pulling out the pin. He screwed his face up in confusion and cast a worried glance at Pearl, before peering out from behind the rock, down into the valley.

She did not hear it at first, but the break in

hostilities soon made it audible. There were short bursts of gunfire and screams coming from deeper in the valley. From the direction of the cave.

The wails were loud and panicked. They were close. Then she saw it. Three figures came sprinting down the narrow pathway. One of them was larger than the others. Because those two were children.

She met Lindo with a horrified expression as more people arrived. 'What's going on? Why are they here?'

The answer came in the form of more fusillades from deep within the valley. Pearl sat up and saw that many monks were already abandoning their posts on the cliffs, rushing down to meet the civilians that were appearing in increasing numbers.

The Imperial soldiers entrenched in the trees noticed immediately. Suddenly they leapt up and started firing at anyone they could see.

The monks had not yet reached ground level. The Imperial bullets pierced the on-rushers.

Pearl watched a young woman fall. She was holding her son's hand and yanked him to the ground as she fell. The Imperial soldiers all opened fire.

The swarm of bullets cut through everything. The trees, bushes and flowers spat out shards of flora, but they did not offer any protection. They began to tear through the people.

The cries filled the air.

Pearl started to fire upon the group of Imperial soldiers in the trees. They were starting to target the monks that were running to help the defenceless civilians. Very few of The Dayak were stopping to return fire. Volleys poured out from behind the Utis, but almost nothing went back.

Maybe she could scare them back into hiding. She managed to hit one soldier, but could not pierce the trees. She tried to target anyone she could, as Lindo joined his fellow monks and dashed to the aid of anyone he could get to.

Royce heard Monaghan issue the order, turning to dash away. The Irishman dove through the gap and landed near the truck. Nobody fired at him.

Royce thought he heard more screams, but gunfire took over. He saw Monaghan vanish into the truck and looked around. Everyone was waiting for Monaghan's signal, but nobody knew what it was. They all exchanged confused glances and the Marauders shouted at them to be ready. Royce's unit looked at him for guidance, but he just frowned and shrugged his shoulders.

The he heard the distinct loud, deep, echoing bang. Then there was another, then another.

Only one thing made a noise like that. A .50 cal.

That was the signal, it seemed. Monaghan's Marauders poured through the gap and his unit followed them eagerly. Royce could see the Imperial soldiers firing almost as soon as they were through the gap.

He idled towards the truck, the loud rings of the .50 Cal now cracking through the sky and disappearing into the valley. The curtain on the truck was open and he could see the Irishman standing astride the flatbed base, both hands on the handles, thumbs on the trigger buttons.

It was mounted on the truck and fed from both sides, allowing for it to load more quickly. Each time it spat out a bullet about fifteen centimetres long from either side. Monaghan aimed and fired, aimed and fired, his teeth gritted, his arms locked, with every sinew strained. He was roaring.

Royce looked around him again. There were only about three other Imperial soldiers still this side of the gap, all of whom were sitting and crying, totally consumed by fear. Every other trooper had flowed through. He strode through the gap and surveyed the scene. He only managed to look at it for a few moments before he vomited all over the ground next to him.

Royce had seen plenty of horror in his time, but even he was unprepared for the macabre scene that filled his eyes. There were body parts all over the floor. People laid screaming, or wandering somnambulistically around, with limbs missing. The .50 Cal thundered and he watched it cut a young boy in half, in an explosion of blood and bone.

Children were sitting on the ground and crying

next to their dead parents. The monks were scurrying around, trying to return fire, but they were so outnumbered that their efforts were futile. He watched the battlefield for a few seconds in dismay. The glee with which the Imperial soldiers attacked infuriated him. They were enjoying it.

He saw one of his unit trap a young mother and her baby next to a tree. He pulled the baby from her grasp and pushed her to the ground. He dropped his trousers and was about to rape her when another woman emerged from the cliff and shot a round through his eye.

The mother dashed to her baby, which had miraculously landed in some long grass, scooped it up and ran to hide. Royce looked at the woman with the gun. She looked around, found another target and killed it. Then she noticed him. There was a note of recognition in her eyes. She knew him.

He watched her closely. She did not look local, unlike everyone else he had seen from the Dayak. She soon looked away, aimed and fired. Then she was gone.

He continued to descry the horrors before him, the bile rising in his throat. This time he managed to calm his stomach before his mouth ejected it. It was barbaric. He could see a few Dayak warriors, but most of their enemies appeared to be civilians. There was an inhuman amount of damage being done to children and their mothers.

His head was spinning. He could not remember ever having such a fog in his brain. His devotion to duty had been a huge part of his life. It was at the very core of his being, the crucial fabric out of which he was made. But he had never seen anything so repugnant in all his years of unwavering service.

He closed his eyes and counted to five, but could not seem to open them again. He remembered being here just a few days before and could not comprehend the difference. The were no insects buzzing. There was no birdsong. It had been replaced by gunfire, explosions and agonised wails. The scent of wildflowers was masked by the metallic tang of blood and death.

He forced his eyes open.

He had made a decision. The mists cleared from his mind and he felt a clarity and assurance he could not ever remember feeling before.

Royce strode away towards the truck, knowing exactly what he needed to do.

Chapter 25

Monaghan stood atop the truck. Aim, fire, aim, fire. The weapon was powerful and difficult to control. He focused on a target. A small monk crouched and fired at the Imperial soldiers. Monaghan aimed and pressed the button.

The rifle boomed and Monaghan flexed every muscle to stop it spinning away. He watched the bullet take the target's head off. A smile creased his lips. That might have been his best shot yet.

He felt the truck tip slightly and looked around. Royce was here to join him, maybe to take over and give him a break. He grinned and was about to greet his colleague. But then he saw the look in Royce's eyes. They were filled with pain and anger. They were filled with malice and intent.

Monaghan drew his Glock from the holster on his hip, but it was too late. Royce was upon him in two, quick steps, smacking it from his hand and into the long grass. With his other hand, Royce grabbed the Irishman's neck and picked him up into the air.

Monaghan's eyes widened as he felt the iron grip on his throat. The hand closed with a power he had never felt before. He grabbed Royce's wrist with both hands and tried to pull himself free.

The two men stared into each other's eyes, Royce's full of fire, Monaghan's starting to fade. The Irishman wriggled and pulled himself downwards with all his strength, but Royce barely flickered. He was a strong man, but he knew he could not buckle the Australian with that. He was completely outmatched.

He punched Royce in the face several times. Without having his feet on the ground to employ his weight in the attack, it barely seemed to register. Royce just glowered at him, teeth-gritted, and dug his fingers deeper into Monaghan's flesh.

The Irishman could not breathe and he could feel the lack of oxygen making him weaker with every passing second. He needed to think of something quickly. He suddenly had an idea. He wrapped his legs around Royce's tree-trunk arm in a scissor hold, crossing his feet up near the shoulder. He put both hands on Royce's wrist and twisted his hips. With every ounce of power he had left, he pulled his head downwards. He pushed all his weight in that direction, as he pulled with both his arms and legs.

Even Royce could not hold on. Monaghan broke the grip and sent them both tumbling off the side of the truck and into the long grass underneath.

Royce landed with a loud thud and a grunt. Monaghan hit the ground and rolled away as quickly as he could, getting to his knees and gasping for air.

He looked over towards the giant, who was already getting to his feet, albeit slowly. He heaved the air into his lungs, clearing his mind and finding his focus. He got up and briefly considered running, but knew a .50 Cal bullet would soon be following him if he tried to escape. That was what Royce wanted. The weapon. He did not know why, but he knew he could not allow it. Yet he did not know how to stop a goliath. Monaghan drew the bayonet from the sheath on his thigh and took as many deep breaths as he could. His vision was back, his strength returning. All he needed was one, good strike against an enemy he already knew was powerful, but cumbersome. He might not have been strong enough to damage the Australian, but the blade could cut through anyone's flesh.

Royce studied the Irishman carefully. He had lost the element of surprise and was still a bit shocked that Monaghan had managed to escape his grip. Now he needed to end it. Not just Monaghan, but the battle. The suffering. He had to stop them. They would slaughter everyone. They would skin all the innocent children. They were the British Butchers and he knew that his mission, now, was to stop them.

He waded in with a fake jab and then a real uppercut. Monaghan was too quick, though. He saw it coming and returned with a slash of his dagger. The blade sliced through Royce's forearm. A line of crimson suddenly appeared through the fresh cut in his sleeve.

Monaghan danced away and grinned. Then he came in with a stab. It was quick.

Royce saw it late, such was the Irishman's speed. He twisted his torso and tried to arc his body, but he was too big. The tip of the dagger entered the side of his hip and cut a small chunk out of him. Monaghan did not stop to enjoy his success. He followed up by spinning around and jumping, crashing an elbow into the back of Royce's head.

The colossus staggered forwards, slightly dazed. He saw the glimmer of the blade in the sunshine, flashing towards him. This time he dove forwards into a roll, away from the slice and giving himself a little space. As he came to a halt on his knees, he saw a branch from a nearby tree on the floor, presumably blown off by either gunfire or one of the explosions.

Monaghan was slightly surprised by the agility of his foe, but was determined to use his advantage. Royce was leaking blood all over himself and still seemed to be slightly discombobulated from the ferocious blow that had landed only moments before. He knew this was his best chance. The giant was still on his knees, his back to the Irishman. Monaghan ran at him and swiped his weapon downwards.

Royce turned just in time, holding the branch firmly in both hands across his face. The bayonet cracked through the wood, stopping centimetres from his eye. Monaghan needed a moment to process what had happened and tried to yank the dagger back out, but it was stuck. Royce twisted the branch, tearing it from Monaghan's grip, and tossed it through the air. The weapon and the branch landed thirty metres away.

The Irishman was undeterred by this. He danced in towards Royce, thrusting two punches at the injury on the hip and then two more in the kidney. Royce felt them and grunted but, by the time he moved to block, Monaghan was already targeting his face. The knuckles burst his nose open and crunched against his jaw, chipping three of his teeth.

Royce attempted a grab, but the Irishman was gone. He came back with a spinning kick to Royce's chest that forced the giant to take a step back and knocked the wind out of him. Monaghan continued his onslaught with another kick, this time jumping and spinning. The boot cracked against Royce's jaw, snapping his head around painfully.

He tried to sweep Royce's leg next, but found it was like kicking a cement post. Springing up, he aimed four fast, powerful punches at Royce's kidneys and then uppercut his jaw, jumping up as he did so to get as much power into it as possible. The Australian's head snapped back and he roared in pain.

Monaghan paused for a moment to analyse his opponent. He had hit Royce with four blows that would have felled any other enemy. Two of them would have killed an average man. But he was winning. Royce was bleeding profusely and could not take much more. He might have been a man mountain, but he was just a man. He knew Royce's reputation, so he knew to be careful, but the man in front of him was a bloody, confused, lumbering mess. It was now just a matter of how long it would take.

The Irishman sped in with several more kicks and punches, but they bounced off arms and a chest. Then Royce managed to get a punch out from behind his guard. Monaghan saw it at the very last moment, only just getting both arms around to block it. It was faster than he would have expected, but every bit as powerful as he feared it would be. Even with both arms shielding his face, it knocked him from his feet.

Royce followed up with a stomp, trying to crush his adversary with his boot. Monaghan rolled away, flipping to his feet and returning with a kick. Royce blocked it and almost caught it, but the Irishman managed to flip backwards and then somersault away, putting several metres between them.

Monaghan could see that the giant was far from beaten. Even with the damage he had already done, it was going to take a long time using his fists and feet. He needed a weapon. He eyed the area where the dagger had landed, but dismissed it. It wasn't much use to him attached to a branch and the wood was too thin to hurt this gargantuan. He looked at the dead soldiers nearby. They all had weapons. That might be his best bet.

Royce ran towards him and Monaghan was almost caught out. Focus, he told himself. He ducked under the punch, pivoting up and elbowing Royce in the face. He spun around again, aiming a kick at the Australian's hip. But Royce managed to counter with a backhand swipe as he stumbled backwards.

The blow only glanced Monaghan, but it was still enough to knock him from his feet. He landed on his back in the long grass and felt it.

The pistol Royce had knocked from him on the truck.

The Australian had stumbled back, but was now on the offensive. Monaghan knew he could get away. He was fast enough. Or he could get the gun. There was not time for both. Royce was only a few metres away and was charging. He chose to end this duel.

He reached under his back and took the Glock,

pulling it out and aiming it. Royce was on him already, there was less than a metre between them. The hulk was reaching down to grab him.

Royce saw the flash of the gun early. The bright metal twinkled in the sunshine like a jewel. He knew he could not stop the shot, but he could try to limit the damage. He leapt and twisted in mid-air.

Monaghan aimed quickly and pressed the trigger. But the giant was twisting as he dove and, he knew, the bullet would miss. He also knew he would not get a second shot.

Royce landed on his side, on top of the Irishman. Monaghan could not escape, not with that weight on him. There was a flurry of punches and kicks, but Royce grabbed the wrist with the gun with both hands. And snapped it.

Monaghan screamed like a banshee. The punches and kicks stopped. Royce got up, keeping a grip on the limp wrist, grabbing the Irishman with his free hand and pulling him up by his neck. He picked him up, with Monaghan's feet scrambling against the truck.

They looked at each other for a moment. Monaghan's face was contorted in agony, the gun dangling harmlessly from his limp arm. Royce growled in his face and then let go of the wrist. The gun fell to the floor and Monaghan watched it with the hope draining from his eyes. He looked up at his enemy and knew it was over.

Royce took the back of Monaghan's head and

smashed it on the iron corner of the flat bed. It almost went through the skull, but stopped at having crushed it. The Australian let go, leaving the lifeless body to flop to the ground next to his feet. He did not even look down.

He wiped the blood from his nose with his shirt and checked his wounds. He had lost a good amount of blood, but he did not feel faint yet. He could still do what he had set out to do.

Climbing up on to the truck, Royce took a firm hold of the .50 Cal. He looked across the battlefield. There were still unarmed civilians running in every direction, but they seemed to be congregated around a thick group of birch trees, where he guessed The Dayak were mounting their defence. He saw dead monks all over the ground and then he saw her again. The woman. She had taken up position on the side of the valley, behind a rocky outcrop, with a few other monks. They were successfully defending their position, but he saw they were trapped.

The Scots had taken position further up the valley and were attacking from the safety of an elevated position and a few boulders that had fallen from above. The small Imperial force in the group of Utis had grown and the other soldiers were advancing carefully upon both Dayak positions, using any cover they could find for protection.

He watched it all for a few moments. There were no monks exposed any longer, but they were trying to guide their civilian cohorts to safety. It seemed all the monks that were not behind cover were dead, aside a few screaming injured strewn about the ground.

There were not many exposed Imperial troopers, either. Those that had rushed through the gap were either dead or had found their units, directed by the remainder of the British Butchers. None of them seemed to have noticed that he was now at the .50 Cal. Their Captain's corpse was well-hidden by the truck and the long grass around it, so they would not realise that he had chosen a new objective until it happened.

Royce knew he needed to get it right. He was exposed up there and The Dayak might not realise he was now an ally and might take their chance to shoot at him in the confusion he was about to cause. He needed to pick the right target. It needed to let them know the .50 Cal was now an ally at the same time as inflicting enough damage on the Imperial forces to change the course of the battle.

He looked at the Utis force, mostly well hidden. He knew the .50 Cal bullets would cut the copse to shreds. He eyed the various units grouped together around the battlefield, trying to gain ground and inflict any damage they could to their enemy. They were too dispersed. Then he looked at The Scots. All grouped together and blocking the escape route, but hidden behind boulders. Even the .50 Cal would take a long time to break down their defences. Yet they were the only Imperial forces on the other side of the battlefield. He looked at their position and then realised the boulders had to have come from somewhere.

He looked up and smiled to himself. He had found his target.

Chapter 26

He moved the huge weapon and studied the trajectory. He closed one eye and checked it again. Then he triple-checked and then once more, just to be sure.

He was aiming for an unstable-looking outcrop of rocks around one hundred and fifty metres up the cliff face. He did not know how loose it was. It might not have been unstable at all. He might be about to waste The Dayak's, and his own, best chance at survival.

But it was their only chance. He knew it, deep down somewhere in his gut.

If he targeted the Utis, he would not do enough damage before they started to return fire. If he went for any of the units dotted around the valley, it would be the same. He could not get to The Scots, for they were too well protected in their defilade position.

Yet they were the most strategically sound target. It gave the children a way to escape and removed an elite fighting force from the battle. He knew it was the only, real choice.

His enormous thumbs pressed both buttons and he held his breath. The rifle boomed several times. He saw both Imperial and Dayak faces turn towards him, the former full of excitement, the latter draped in fear.

The enormous rounds zoomed through the air, hitting the rocks in a flurry of sparks. The cliff spat out large chunks of rock and the shower of stone chips splattered the ground beneath.

Royce watched keenly, almost forgetting to breathe.

He saw most of the faces turn away from him, looking to see what he had hit. None of them seemed to realise why. Not straight away.

Not until the rumbling began.

It was almost indiscernible at first, low and muffled. Then it got louder and the splintering began, emanating a loud cracking sound. None of The Scots moved, though. They seemed to be uncertain what the noise was, even though the boulders above them were visibly starting to peel away from the side of the mountain.

They began to fall away slowly but each inch they parted from the cliff face increased the unattached weight and that, in turn, sped up the process. It was as if it were in slow motion to begin with and then someone had used a remote control to speed it up.

The first boulder fell, crashing down the side of the mountain. It bounced three times and then settled into a roll, picking up speed despite the uneven surface it travelled down. It reached the bottom within a few seconds and rolled past the hidden Imperial commandos, crunching into some trees on the opposite side of the valley.

Other large chunks of rock and boulders soon followed. The first seemed to be a keystone for a large part of this area of the mountain. Within moments, rock fell like rain. There were tiny shards, pebbles, stones and giant chunks all rolling down the cliff or plummeting to the ground. There were crashes and cracks, smashes and crunches.

The Scots finally seemed to realise what was happening. They darted out from their hiding place, rushing into the valley, but they were too late. Royce saw The Haggis panicking, running towards one of the Imperial units hidden in valley. Then a huge boulder landed and the blob was gone, leaving a spray of red on the ground, like someone had taken a hammer to a ketchup sachet.

The Dayak saw their opportunity and suddenly opened fire on The Scots. They started to drop and the Imperial troops around the valley began attempting to protect them. Royce heaved the .50 Cal to a new position and pressed the buttons again. The booming echoed all around him, cutting through the trees and those hiding behind them.

He targeted the Utis force. The trees

disintegrated under the fusillade, the air soon filled with a cloud of brown and silver wood blended with the green leaves. The bullets were hitting some of the troopers hidden there, but not as many as he hoped. The foliage there was dense and even the .50 Cal could not penetrate it immediately. It was chipping away, though, and doing considerable damage.

The trees soon splintered so much that they started to collapse, scattering the soldiers hiding in there. The Dayak had finished with The Scots and turned their attention to the Imperial soldiers evading the trees that threatened to crush them.

Royce turned towards a unit near Utis and pressed the button again. They seemed to be the closest and he noticed that they were now realising what was happening. They trained their weapons on him, but they were too slow. He pressed the button and cut them all down within seconds. The bullets cut through the bones and sprayed blood in every direction. One direct hit could cut even an armoured torso clear in half.

He had to duck as a different unit, on the opposite side of the valley, opened fire on him. There was a shield on the .50 Cal, but he was too tall for it to protect him. He aimed in the general direction of where the gunfire was coming from and he pressed the buttons again. The attack did not stop, however, so he repositioned the turrets and tried again. This time he was closer. They had to stop shooting to try and find cover.

He peeked back over the shield and saw that The Dayak were moving swiftly. They were guiding the civilians out of the valley first. Once they were safely on their way out of the battlefield, the monks started targeting the Imperial units and creating an enfilade to give him time to stand up and aim. He used it.

He stood up sharply, wiping the sweat and blood from his face with his sleeve, making sure his vision was as good as it could be. He found one. Boom. Another one. Boom. And another. Boom.

A bullet whizzed past his head and he found the source. Boom. Another flurry of bullets was too close, so he ducked again and waited for a pause. The moment it came, he popped up, took aim and fired. Aim, fire, aim, fire. The enormous bullets split soldiers in half. The Dayak encircled their enemies, splitting into three separate splinter groups. The Imperial forces now had predators on all four sides. There was no escape for them.

They fought back bravely. They found any cover they could, but it did not last. Soon, a .50 Cal round or a Dayak grenade demolished it. The monks were moving in and the Imperial soldiers were completely surrounded. Royce continued to fire at anything he could see in a green uniform.

A few moments later, he saw the woman again. She appeared to be directing the monks to cease fire and they obeyed. Royce stopped, too. He could not hear what she called to the Imperial survivors, but they subsequently dropped their weapons and slowly came out of their hiding places. They paced carefully, their hands behind their heads, towards the woman.

The Dayak moved in towards all the Imperial positions swiftly, quickly determining that the threat was over. They swept from location to location, then starting to inspect any location that was, conceivably, large enough to hide a person.

Royce let go of the handles and sat down on the edge of the flatbed truck, watching the scene keenly. The monks were methodical, checking every inch of the valley, sweeping left and right. A group of elderly-looking men emerged from a hiding place further down the valley with sniper rifles, placing them on the ground and shuffling over to talk to the Imperial soldiers. He inspected the small group of around thirty men and women. None of them seemed to be Monaghan's Marauders. He could not see any of The Scots, either. They had been two of The Empire's most elite units.

The Dayak had made an enormous statement here today.

Royce knew the repercussions were going to be swift and brutal. The Empire could not allow this and, more importantly, they could not allow news of it to travel. He briefly considered Nesbitt, his old friend and commander. When the reports went back to The Empire about the dead soldiers, a man of his dimensions would be conspicuous by his absence.

He would be a hunted man for the rest of his days.

He could take the .50 Cal and execute everyone if he really wanted to. They were all closely grouped now. He could probably kill all Imperial and Dayak troops in less than two minutes. Then he could run back to Nesbitt and tell a bunch of lies, with nobody alive to tell anyone otherwise. The only remaining Imperial troops still had not come through the gap. They had no idea what had happened and he would make them corroborate his version of events.

But he did not want to.

He was finished with The Empire. He had now seen what they really were.

Child-killers.

He saw some Dayak rushing back into the valley from their hiding places on the other side of the boulder pile. They seemed to be mostly women, but there were a few men. They rushed to fallen Imperial soldiers, monks and civilians, dispensing whatever first aid they could manage. He saw one woman screaming and rocking, her dead child in her arms. He sighed. If only he had acted sooner.

He slid off the truck and limped to the cab, opening the door and locating a first aid kit. He was still bleeding heavily and found some bandages to stymie the flow. He knew there were antibiotics back in his truck, but he would rest a little before making that journey.

That was assuming The Dayak let him leave.

He might have saved them, but he was part of the initial assault and he was the reason The Empire knew where to go. He did not know how forgiving The Dayak would be.

He hoped they were more altruistic than he would be in the same situation.

Royce cleaned his wounds out with a bottle of water he found in the driver's door then started to rip open the field medical packs with his teeth. He held it on his hip and found the tape, trying to hold it and tear it simultaneously. It was slippery with so much blood. He dropped it a few times and was about to give up when a voice suddenly appeared in front of him.

'Need some help?'

He looked up, a little startled. Nobody had been able to sneak up on him in a long time. It was the woman from the battle. He smiled weakly. 'If you don't mind. I'm struggling here.'

She motioned for him to lift his shirt and lean back on the truck. He obeyed and she adeptly covered the wound in a few moments. 'I'm Letitia.'

He watched her work. She was a skilled medic. 'I'm Bob.'

She continued to apply tape to keep the dressing

in place, not looking up. 'You really saved our asses there, Bob. Thank you. But what made you do it?'

'I didn't know they would go after the kids,' he grunted.

She finished with the wound and stood up, looking him squarely in the eyes. 'That *was* you I saw in the valley before, right?'

He nodded ashamedly, looking away. 'I didn't know. I just had to find you.'

She grabbed his wrist and started to clean the deep slice on his forearm. 'I thought it was you.'

'I-I-If I had known what they would do, I would never have-'

Pearl held her hand up to silence him and waited for him to look back at her. 'You didn't. We let you see us, Bob.'

He felt the guilt wash away and looked down at the woman. She was beautiful and her accent was North American. He could see she had indigenous ancestry, but had no idea where from. He saw that she had dirt smudges in every smear of sweat on her face and a few scratches on her forehead. 'You let me do what?'

'We let you see us so we could ambush the forces here. Sorry, did you think we were just accidentally walking to those positions on the cliff?'

He shrugged his shoulders. 'I was pretty far back in the column. I didn't see anything at the start.'

She looked around at some of her dead friends. 'We're as much to blame for this as you are. We should have known they would flank us. The only difference is that you did something to save us. None of us could have done that.'

Royce was almost crying. 'I'm sorry for bringing them here.'

She looked down at the body and where Monaghan's face used to be. 'Was he the commander?'

He nodded. 'Captain Monaghan?'

She raised her eyebrows. 'The British Butchers, huh? Good job you intervened, Bob.' She finished dressing his forearm and started to inspect the corpse at their feet. She soon found his Device and then located his wallet. She found the chip and opened the Device.

'Maybe we could sort that stuff out later?' he suggested.

Pearl shook her head. 'They will soon know what happened here, Bob. They will disable this in no time. There isn't a later, there's only now. That's life in The Dayak.'

'Oh, sorry. I don't really know how it works to be in that situation.'

She looked up at him and smiled sweetly. 'Well, you'll pick it up quickly, I don't doubt.'

'Excuse me?' he asked, confused.

'You're one of us now, Bob. The elder monks

asked me to come and speak to you about joining us. I'm going to assume you're not dumb enough to refuse.'

He shrugged his shoulders. 'I'm pretty dumb sometimes. What happens if I refuse?'

Her smile was kind. 'Then we'll patch you up and wish you well.'

'You'll let me go?' he asked doubtfully.

'Anyone who doesn't want to join us is free to go. We don't take POWs. But I think you saw enough today to show you that you can make a difference with us. So, what do you say? Want to make a difference?'

Royce smiled, flashing his chipped, blood-stained teeth. 'I would like that.'

He held out her hand and he shook it. 'Well, then, Bob. Welcome to The Dayak.'

Chapter 27

The Ford engine screamed as MacLoughlin swerved inside a truck and undertook it. He pulled back out just in time to miss a broken-down car in the hard shoulder and then weaved through the next four vehicles.

Layttle gripped the dashboard. 'Ed, slow down a bit, you're going to kill us.'

MacLoughlin grunted. 'Not far now.'

Hull was a four-hour drive from London. They had been on the road for less than two hours and were not far away, maybe thirty miles. Layttle eyed the digital speedometer. They had only just joined the motorway, having taken a shortcut that MacLoughlin knew, which he drove like a rally course, and now they were up to ninety-five miles per hour.

'You need to slow down a bit. There weren't any police on those smaller roads, but there will be here,' he insisted.

'Tough shit,' the American growled. 'We can't afford to lose even one minute.'

'If we're spotted and captured, then it will cost us even more time.'

MacLoughlin cast him a stern, sideways glance. 'Let me worry about driving. You check on the kid.'

The German knew when an argument was a waste of his time and closed his eyes as they raced between two cars. He peeked through one of them, realised they were still alive and took a deep breath, before turning to face the back.

Bayston could do little but stare out of the window. He was catatonic with fear. Smythe's words bounced around his mind, replaying like they were a scratched record. His family was in danger. Serious danger.

Layttle watched him for a few moments, before employing his professionally-crafted sympathy smile. 'How you doing, Jamie?' After about ten seconds without response, he tried again. 'Jamie?'

The Englishman looked at him, fear etched across his face. 'How long now?'

'Maybe twenty minutes,' MacLoughlin called over the wails of the engine, as he dropped a gear, whilst still at seventy-eight, to overtake a van in half a second less than he would have done otherwise. 'Depends on the bridge.'

Bayston looked at Layttle. 'What happens if

they're okay?'

'We hide them and get you all out together.'

'And if they're not okay?' he gulped.

Layttle frowned. 'Let's just get there and see them.'

'I can't believe my dad is in this Resistance.'

'From what Peter said, he's been active for a long time,' the German replied softly. 'He's been doing important work. You should be proud of him.'

Bayston met him with an icy glare. 'If he gets them all arrested, then what good is that to anyone?'

'He probably had a contingency,' MacLoughlin shouted, yanking the steering wheel to avoid crashing into the rear of a Mini. 'Pete always tells everyone to have contingencies.'

Bayston shrugged his shoulders. 'What does that mean?'

'It means don't worry if they're not there,' the American answered.

He sat up quickly. 'You think we're too late?'

'He didn't say that,' the German replied. 'What Ed means to say is that if they're not at home when we get there, don't panic. It doesn't mean they were arrested. Your father probably had a contingency plan in case anything happened and is in hiding. He will contact Peter in due course and then we will go and get them all.'

'Okay,' Bayston said, unconvinced.

338

'Try calling them again,' Layttle suggested.

Bayston pulled out his Device, opened it and tried again. His father, his mother, Tony, Deb, Claire and Matt. A few minutes later, the tally was up to eleven missed calls. 'No, nothing.'

'Is that normal?' MacLoughlin asked.

'Is what normal?'

'That you can't get hold of any of them in the middle of the day?'

Bayston looked at his Device and then peered back out of the window, the worry starting to make his chest tighten. 'No, it definitely isn't normal.'

Layttle watched him for a few more moments, with sorrow in his eyes. He turned back around to the front and looked across at MacLoughlin.

The American checked Bayston in his mirror and looked at the German in the passenger seat. 'Speed up?'

'Yes, please,' he replied.

They zoomed on for just a couple more miles when Layttle noticed a noise above them. He peered upwards out of the window to descry a helicopter. He watched it for a few minutes before deciding it was following them.

'We have company,' he informed MacLoughlin, pointing to the sky.

'Fuck,' he growled.

'They found us quickly.'

'Not really,' the American replied gruffly. 'Jamie turned on his Device a couple of hours ago.

That's not fast for The Empire, especially on home turf.'

Layttle checked on Bayston, but he continued to gawp out of the window, oblivious to the fresh danger. He turned back to the American. 'You know any more shortcuts or anywhere to hide?'

He scoffed. 'I drove around here maybe three times, Trev.'

Layttle pulled out his Device. 'I'll look for somewhere under cover.'

MacLoughlin nodded towards the mirror. 'That won't help. Look.'

He looked back to see three large, silver SUVs racing up towards them. He looked at their speedometer. Ninety-three. 'Will this thing go any faster?'

MacLoughlin rammed the pedal to the floor. It went up to ninety-four then, a couple of seconds later, to ninety-five. 'A bit. Not much, though.'

Layttle took the Sig Sauer out from the holster under his jacket. 'I guess they're going to catch up pretty soon, then.'

The American eyed the weapon. 'Are you as good with one of those as I've heard?'

He shrugged his shoulders. 'I'm a bit rusty, but I used to be.'

'Let's hope you haven't lost too many steps, then, Trev.'

MacLoughlin steered the Ford around a BMW and swerved in too close, forcing the driver to slam on his brakes. He did this another three times and watched as the traffic behind them started to congest and block the way for the SUVs. To his dismay, all three of them simply moved to the hard shoulder.

He saw that they were coming up to a row of lorries on the inside lane, so accelerated past them all and, once reaching the lead vehicle, he slowed down and waited for a couple of cars to get behind him. Then he swerved in even more closely. So closely that the driver would not be able to avoid the Ford just by hitting the air brakes. He had to steer in towards the hard shoulder because of the other cars driving in the outside lane.

MacLoughlin dropped a gear and zoomed away as soon as the huge lorry got within a few inches of the Ford's rear bumper. He checked the mirror and smiled.

'Nice move,' Layttle congratulated, see the trio of SUVs skidding to a halt.

'Our turn is here,' the American replied. 'I'm hoping they don't see us take it.'

He sped up the slip road and did not stop at the roundabout, screeching around it and forcing the other panicked drivers to stop as he sped through past the queue and away down the first exit.

MacLoughlin overtook a row of cars and then slotted into the middle and waited. 'Is it still up there?'

Layttle looked up and nodded. 'It looks like it.'

'And the others?'

The German looked out the back, noting that Bayston seemed ignorant of the danger they were in, and smiled. 'Nothing.' Then his smile vanished. 'Oh wait.' The SUVs appeared at the back of the row of traffic. 'They're back there.'

'We'll never lose them with that chopper up there.'

'Agreed. Let's get to Hull and find cover there.'

'The bridge is only just up ahead, maybe a mile, or so,' MacLoughlin replied. He pulled out and sped up, forcing an overtaking Audi to make an emergency stop and slow both lanes for a few moments.

The Ford reached ninety quite quickly but then stopped getting faster as they began to go slightly uphill. The American flashed his lights and honked his horn to get people out of his way, but a quick glance in the mirror showed the SUVs gaining ground.

Layttle looked ahead and could see the grey concrete towers, almost orange in the sunset and fading light. They almost seemed to touch the clouds. There were two enormous cables either side, which came up sharply from the approach, to the top of the nearest tower, swept down almost to the road, then back up again to the top of the far tower. The hanging cables rooted the main cables to the concrete base either side of the road. When MacLoughlin had referenced 'the bridge' several times, he had not been expecting such an enormous structure.

They sped up the approach, the SUVs getting closer with every passing metre. The German watched them in the mirror and then looked ahead as they came on to the bridge. 'How long is this bridge?'

'A bit under a mile and a half,' MacLoughlin replied.

'What's that? Over two kilometres, right?'

He nodded. 'Yes. Why?'

'They're going to catch us before then.'

The American nodded his head towards the Sig Sauer. 'Then stop them, why don't you?'

Layttle checked the mirror again. They were only, perhaps, a hundred metres behind them now and closing the gap swiftly. 'I'll try.'

'Try hard,' MacLoughlin scowled.

The German pressed the button to lower the window and cast a quick look back at Bayston. He remained motionless, staring at the sky like a zombie. He looked in the mirror again and they were within range.

Leaning out of the window, he needed to steady himself. The wind on the bridge was strong and they were travelling at ninety-four miles per hour. It took all his strength not to drop his weapon. He aimed and fired. The bullet flew off into the sky, nowhere near his target.

He took a deep breath. He was nervous, more

than he had been in many years. He knew that his own life, and the lives of so many others, depended on them completing their journey. He had been responsible for people's lives for years, but they were at a distance, most of the time. Those that were closer to him knew the risks and accepted the dangers.

This was different.

This felt much more personal.

He steadied his hand and squeezed the trigger again, but it was just as MacLoughlin swerved to undertake a Jaguar, so he missed by even further. Once the Ford was realigned with the SUVs, he tried again, trusting his instincts and the muscle memory gained by so many years of training and active service.

The bullet cracked the windscreen, red covering the inside like a paint bomb had just gone off inside. He had hit the driver.

He saw the passenger try to grab the steering wheel, but the vehicle was already out of control, careering into the central reservation and flipping over in a screech of twisted metal and smashed glass.

'Nice fucking shot!' MacLoughlin cheered. 'Some more of that, please, Mr Rusty!'

Layttle smiled, but had to stop and duck back in as the gunfire started to ping off the metal work in a spray of sparks. 'Get down!' he commanded and Bayston did so, but only after the rear window shattered. The German looked at him from between the seats. He continued to stare out of the window, but from a new position.

The German looked at MacLoughlin. 'Can he use a weapon?'

He shook his head. 'Not yet. It's on my to-do list, buddy. Right below not getting killed on this bridge.'

Layttle nodded his understanding and took a deep breath. 'Okay.'

He peered out from behind the head rest, noting that the gunfire had stopped. MacLoughlin had managed to position the Ford the other side of a truck. The respite gave Layttle time to get back out of the window and prepare his next shot. As soon as one of the vehicles appeared on his side, he released a volley of bullets. None of them hit the windscreen this time, but several of them pierced the engine block.

Thick plumes of black smoke suddenly started to pour out of the front. Flames were not far behind. It skidded to a halt and all four doors opened. The driver and three passengers dove out and ran, thrown from their feet by the explosion a few seconds later.

Layttle watched them all get back up and scurry to safety as the final SUV smashed through the burning wreckage and chased after the Ford. The bullets pinged off the Ford and he took cover inside as MacLoughlin swerved inside a Toyota to get them out of the line of fire.

It was only a brief pause. The soldiers shot at the Toyota and the panicked driver screeched to a standstill. They were past it in moments, now only a few metres behind the Ford. They were too close for him to shoot from the window, so he got back inside the car.

'Stay down!' he commanded to Bayston, who was still paralysed by dread.

Layttle put in a new clip and then aimed through the back window. He fired four times and the SUV pulled into the other lane. There were no more cars ahead of them. Everyone had stopped, presumably because of the gunfight and exploding vehicles, so there was clear road ahead.

The SUV pulled up level with them effortlessly and then swerved in. The metal crunched and squealed.

MacLoughlin struggled to control the Ford but managed to keep it on the road. He pulled his weapon from his lap and lowered the window. He flicked his eyes sideways to aim, but he caught something in his peripheral vision. The windows of the SUV were coming down and there were muzzles clearly visible. They would beat him to it. He slammed his foot on the brake.

The Ford's tyres howled and smoke came from the wheels, but the fusillade cracked into the concrete of the central reservation and the SUV sped on alone. MacLoughlin had to drop his

Beretta to grab the steering wheel with both hands, but he managed to keep them from crashing. He saw the red lights at the back of the Imperial vehicle and then switched pedal, almost pushing the accelerator through the bottom of the car.

As the SUV slowed, the Ford flew past and away. The SUV soon started to accelerate again. It was a brief reprieve, but it got them a few metres closer to Hull and cover.

As the Imperial vehicle caught up again, Layttle saw the end of the bridge. They were close now. He could see Hull in the distance.

He took aim again and fired through the window as the SUV raced up behind them. It smashed into the back of the Ford as his bullets flew into it. There was a loud bang. One of the rear tyres burst.

MacLoughlin tried to wrestle with the steering wheel, but even he did not have enough strength to keep it straight. The Ford went into a spin.

Layttle ducked down and held on as they spun to a screeching stop. As soon as they did, he popped the door open and leapt out, ready to fire. He emptied his clip into the SUV, as it slowed down and stopped thirty metres away.

He went to replace his clip and realised it was still in the car. He walked back and found the seat empty. His eyes met MacLoughlin's. 'Ammo?'

'Flew out of the car when we were spinning.'

Layttle's eyes scoured the road behind them and saw the four Imperial soldiers from the exploding car were running up the road. He saw the clip. It was easily fifteen metres away.

He looked back at the Imperial vehicle in front of them and they were already approaching. All four of them shot at the engine and soon the Ford was smoking from the radiator. Precise shots, he thought, designed to incapacitate them.

He looked back in the car. 'You have a gun?'

MacLoughlin smiled. 'Back there a few hundred metres.'

'Alive! Take them alive!' someone roared from somewhere over near the SUV.

The Imperial soldiers put their weapons away and strode towards the Ford.

MacLoughlin looked at Bayston, still laying on the back seat and staring out of the window. He peered back at the German and opened his car door, getting out and cricking his neck. 'Are you a rusty fighter, too?'

He nodded sombrely. 'Office work does that.'

The American was cracking his knuckles and looking around. 'There's eight of them, buddy. Let's hope it comes back as quickly as the shooting.'

Layttle shrugged his shoulders. 'That could just have been luck.'

The eight Imperial soldiers were forming a circle around them. MacLoughlin scanned them and grinned at the German. 'Let's fucking hope you're not that lucky, Trev.'

Chapter 28

The soldiers stood for a few moments, analysing their foes. Layttle thought, perhaps, they were assessing them, but then he realised they were awaiting an order.

'Alive!' commanded a broad, angry-looking woman in front of him, apparently concerned that her subordinates had not heard her before. They all began to remove telescopic rods from a small hook on their belts.

Layttle inspected their uniforms. They were standard Imperial issue, not special forces of any kind. They had green camo trousers with knee pads and olive-coloured shirts. On the left-side shirt pocket was a small Union Jack and on the right-side was the British Army crest. They had black leather belts with a few small pouches, a pistol holster and a knife sheath, which doubled as the hook for their rods.

He looked in their eyes and could see their uncertainty. They waited for the order to attack and there did not seem to be much enthusiasm to do so.

He looked at their commander. She was also British Army, but she had the three-V badge on her arm to indicate that she was a Sergeant. He also spotted the Ranger eagle on her shirt. He knew the British Rangers were formidable warriors.

The Sergeant suddenly barked the order to attack and they began to close the circle, but they were nervous and hesitant. Layttle and MacLoughlin exchanged a knowing look. There was only one way to defend against adversaries who lacked confidence.

Attack.

Layttle skipped forwards throwing a punch at the nearest soldier. The girl did not react in time, turning away as his punch cracked against her jaw. She fell to the ground and he followed up with a kick to her temple. She did not get back up.

MacLoughlin was much quicker than his size should have allowed. He covered the ground in a lightning-fast sprint, pirouetting at the end to land a spinning kick in a young man's chest. He wailed and fell backwards, cracking his head on the ground and screaming.

Layttle had already moved on to the second enemy and none of the Imperial soldiers had even moved yet. He grabbed the nearest rod and shoved it into the face of the man holding it. It cut open his forehead and he wailed, as blood spilled into his eyes.

MacLoughlin had to block an attack from a tall, young woman, countering with a chest punch that knocked her over. He ducked a swipe and grabbed the large man attempting it, pulling him into a headbutt. The next attack landed as one young man swept in with his rod aimed at MacLoughlin's knee. It connected and the American roared in pain.

Layttle had two soldiers attacking from either side. He caught the rod and managed to get a kick in the opposite direction to stall the attack coming from that direction. He noted they were both quite physically powerful men as he shoved the first attacker away and saw them both coming back at him almost immediately.

MacLoughlin limped backwards as three attackers came at the same time. The large man with the broken nose stepped in with a lazy punch, which MacLoughlin caught. Twisting, the American hooked the arm and used a hip throw to get the man on the ground. He kept hold of the arm and stomped on the Imperial soldier's face. His eyes rolled into the back of his head and closed.

The other two came wading in, moving quickly around to take advantage of MacLoughlin's injury. The first swung with the rod at the American's face. MacLoughlin ducked and stepped towards the blow, coming up as the rod missed him. He grabbed the wrist and, with his forearm of his free arm held vertically, he crashed it into the back of the Imperial elbow. The joint buckled and gave way with a loud crack, bending the arm in the wrong direction. The woman yelled in pain and he pushed her to the ground.

The third attack came in and was another swing aimed for his head. He ducked under it and stamped on the side of the knee. The young man's leg buckled and he collapsed, crying.

Layttle evaded the attacks. He blocked, jumped and spun away, trying to give himself some space to move. He caught a glimpse of the other two soldiers moving towards MacLoughlin, including the Ranger, but he could do nothing to help. A jab caught him in the chin and he had to deflect another away.

He saw that MacLoughlin had managed to incapacitate three foes and he had managed one, but they were still four against two. Layttle caught an arm, belonging to the man with a gash across his forehead, but a rod cracked across his back and he had to let go. He ducked another attack and skipped sideways to avoid another, trying to get some distance to mount any kind of effective counter-attack. But they were young, fast and fit, so they kept up with him.

MacLoughlin faced up with the young man who had cracked his head on the ground. The Imperial soldier was swinging haphazardly, teeth-gritted and shouting. The American was ducking and blocking with relative ease, but he was hopping around and trying to balance on one leg, so could not muster a counter. After six manic swings, he managed to turn sideways to avoid number seven. As the solider missed, MacLoughlin was able to punch him in the stomach. When he doubled over, the American crashed his elbow into the back of his head.

Before he could turn around, though, the Ranger swept his good leg out from underneath him. MacLoughlin fell sideways and a rod cracked across his skull. It dazed him and he stumbled as he tried to get up, then fell back down again.

Layttle was waiting for his opportunity, but he was beginning to tire. He had been dodging or blocking them for almost a minute and they were emboldened by the fact he was unable to escape. He knew he needed to wait for his chance. These young men were trained. They were fast and strong. Any misstep would be the end of the battle for him.

He caught a wrist and used the rod in it to block another attack, then twisted his body and sprang away. They came again. This time he managed to duck under and sprint between them, to get behind them. He thought it might be his opportunity, but they turned too quickly and launched yet another offensive.

This time, though, they did not attack in unison. One of them was too slow. It gave Layttle the opportunity he needed. The attack was a mid-height swing and he leapt into it, catching the arm and trapping it next to his hip. The soldier was only inches away and Layttle could see that he knew his mistake as the German rammed his knee into their groin. By the time the next soldier came in, Layttle ducked away and the fresh rod attack cracked the other soldier across the head before he could grab his pained testicles.

Layttle was already moving to the rear of the late attacker. He grabbed the back of his head by the hair and rammed it down into the head of the man who was already collapsing in agony. They both flopped to the ground.

The German heaved air into his lungs and turned to see how his cohort was faring, but was met with the sight of the Ranger. She held a small, black box in her hand. It was a taser.

Layttle noted that none of the other troopers had one of these on their belts. He saw MacLoughlin was struggling to get to his feet and was about to dive away when a loud crack filled the bridge.

A gunshot.

For a few moments, everything seemed still. It was like someone had used the pause button on them all. Layttle was frozen, staring at the Ranger. The Ranger was frozen, about to press the button on her weapon. And MacLoughlin was frozen, sitting on the ground, confused.

Blood starting to seep from the Ranger's mouth,

then she collapsed and fell to the ground.

Layttle and MacLoughlin both looked over to the source of the noise to see Bayston standing near the Ford, astride one of the unconscious Imperial soldiers, whose holster was empty, holding a Sig Sauer at the end of extended arms. A wisp of smoke snaked away from the barrel.

The American slowly managed to find his feet and staggered towards his young friend, who continued to stand there, a look of tortured anger twisting his face.

'Jamie?' MacLoughlin said softly. 'Lower it, Jamie. It's okay.'

Bayston's eyes poured his hate into the fallen Ranger. He continued to glower at her as the American tentatively approached him.

Layttle looked around them at the fallen soldiers, who were either unconscious or writhing in agony. Two of them were starting to wake up, but their eyes had no fight left in them. He looked at the dead Ranger and his eyes moved to the young man still brandishing the gun. It was a good shot. Straight through her neck at a range of twelve, maybe thirteen, metres. Bayston had either had training, or he was a natural. And he seemed completely unphased by the fact he had just taken a human life.

In his experience, fear and adrenaline often focused the mind and brought out talents people did not even know they had.

MacLoughlin continued to gingerly approach the wide-eyed Englishman. He was not sure if Bayston was paralysed by the realisation of what had just happened or by fear for his family. He came level with the weapon and, very gently, placed his hand on top and pushed it down to face the ground. 'Kid, can you hear me?'

Bayston nodded very slightly, finally breaking his gaze from the Ranger. He looked up at the American and cleared his throat. 'Can we go now?' His voice was not shaky or croaking. It was firm, filled with resolve and purpose.

The American and German exchanged an anxious look. Bayston had just taken a human life and his face did not betray any kind of contrition. MacLoughlin seemed to look to Layttle for approval and he gave it. He knew the adrenalin created the apathy. He also knew the comedown would be considerable and they would need to watch him closely. But it did bode well for the future that the young man was able to maintain such intent focus on their objective through such an emotional experience. Perhaps the American was right about him.

Bayston released the pistol and MacLoughlin snatched it gratefully. 'Of course.' He looked over at the dilapidated Ford and shook his head. His eyes moved to the SUV. 'I guess one of them has the keys. Anyone see who was driving?'

Layttle marched over and peered inside.

'They're still in it.'

Bayston strode to the back and MacLoughlin leapt into the driver's seat. Layttle cast a last look at the bridge as he got into the passenger side. The sun had set now and the bright halogen lights made everything seem orange.

He could see the smashed SUV in the distance, upside down in the road. The second SUV remained ablaze, towers of black smoke billowing into the sky. All the traffic had stopped on this side of the bridge, behind where the fire burned. The Ford was covered in bullet holes and had a buckled rear wheel. There were prone forms on the road, although some were now starting to crawl and stagger away from them. He caught the sight of some lights in the distance.

He got in the car. 'Imperial police are coming.'

MacLoughlin started the car and revved the engine. 'Then that's our cue to leave, I think.'

He screeched away and sped across the remainder of the bridge. They were entering Hull only a few minutes later. Bayston, now free from his catatonic state, barked directions.

Layttle carefully watched the skies and the roads. The helicopter had gone and he could not see any lights that might be drones, so they seemed to be in the clear for a little while. He only hoped that was long enough to reach their destination.

'Next left!' Bayston commanded.

MacLoughlin obeyed, speeding up and bullying

his way through the traffic by honking the horn and flashing the lights non-stop.

'They might be waiting for us,' Layttle remarked. 'It could be a trap by now.'

Bayston turned on him. 'So what? Are you saying we don't go?'

'No,' he returned vehemently. 'I'm saying you two get out a couple of blocks away and I will drive in and distract anyone who might be waiting for you.'

'Okay, sounds good,' replied the Englishman.

'Is there a back way in?' MacLoughlin asked.

Bayston considered it. 'We can get through the garden behind us and over the fence. Next right.'

MacLoughlin skidded around the corner. 'That should work. How far away are we?'

'Next turn,' Bayston replied. 'Drive past my street and down the next one and we can get out there. Right again here.' He pointed to a road next to a chip shop.

'Got it.' MacLoughlin slowed down and made the turn at a normal speed.

'My road is the third on the left but just-'

They all saw it at the same time. There were Imperial police cordons blocking off the third road on the left and two police cars next to them with blue flashing lights.

'Uh oh,' MacLoughlin grunted.

'Just drive past normally,' Layttle instructed. 'They might not know what car we're in and the bullet holes are on the other side, so they won't see them.'

They cruised past the blockade and peered down the street. There were blue flashing lights all over the area. There were police, fire engines and ambulances everywhere. One of the houses had flames pouring out of it.

The fire engines obscured their view, but they all exchanged a look of dread.

They all knew immediately which house was on fire.

Chapter 29

Bayston began to scramble for the door. 'Stop the car!'

MacLoughlin did so, but the Englishman was already diving out of the vehicle. He could not wait for it to stop. He hit the ground in a roll, cutting his arms and legs, but sprung up immediately and started sprinting towards the blockade.

'Shit!' the American growled. He looked at the German. 'Go and get him. I'll ditch the car.'

Layttle nodded and jumped out in a run, already only a few metres behind the Englishman. He could see two police officers already starting to pay attention to the panicked Bayston as he sprinted towards the waist-high, yellow barricades.

Bayston darted for the gap and they converged to catch him. He was kicking and shouting. 'I need to get through!'

'Nobody gets through, mate.'

'That's my house.'

There was no way to see it from this angle, and

with the fire engines blocking the view, but they both looked around, anyway. Then they looked back at him.

Layttle approached carefully, and was still several metres away, when he noticed the glint of recognition in the eyes of one of the police officers. They were both men, one much older than the other, and it was the elder of the duo that started reaching for the radio on his jacket.

The German knew what was happening straight away. They would have been told to report anyone wanting to get into the street, but it seemed to be more than that. Bayston's image had probably been circulated in the area. It had not been on the television or any socials, but The Empire would notify law enforcement and emergency services, as they were the most likely to come across him.

Layttle flew into action instinctively. The police officers were about to put Bayston on the bonnet of the nearest car when the German came flying over it. He kneed the elder officer in the chest, sending him flying backwards into the other car. He slammed into the door and slid down to the ground.

The younger officer was holding Bayston and released him as Layttle appeared, but was not fast enough. Layttle jabbed him on the nose and his eyes filled with tears. He could not even attempt to fight the blur before him, so was defenceless as Layttle grabbed his head and crashed it into the bonnet with such force that the dent was several inches deep.

Layttle snatched the radio from the officer's chest as he fell to the ground, spinning and hurling it at the elder officer. The man had his radio to his lips, but the projectile cracked against the front of his skull, which smashed his head back into metal door.

The German watched a moment, as the officer hunched and then slid to rest in a prostrate position. Satisfied they were safe for the moment, he looked up to give Bayston permission to proceed, but the Englishman had already gone.

He turned to search for Bayston and found he was already sprinting down the street towards the sirens, shouts and flashing lights.

Other police were starting to notice him and Layttle knew that, if the barrier police had seen Bayston's image, the others would have, too. The German ran after him, turning around a couple of news trucks and seeing the house.

There were only a few small fires remaining, but the house was completely charred. The glass from the windows was all gone and the roof had started collapsing. He could see a few small patches of red brick beneath the black soot covering the walls, but the plastic on the uPVC doors and window frames had bubbled and melted. Even the guttering was dripping down to the ground.

Several fire crews poured water on the

remaining flames, but Layttle found his eyes drawn to the helicopter on the front lawn. The blades were still spinning, and he had not seen or heard it come in, so he presumed it was preparing to leave. Next to it stood a tall, slim frame, hidden by shadow, except for two pink skulls on their body armour and on the top of a face mask.

This person seemed to be issuing orders. Layttle saw that there were Imperial soldiers around the house, too. Pink Skull seemed to be organising them. There were not many, maybe six, so he guessed they had been in the helicopter.

The helicopter that had been following them.

That meant they knew Bayston was coming and were preparing for his arrival. He was running straight into a trap.

Layttle could not catch the Englishman. He was too young and fast. But maybe he could help him.

Bayston was approaching the inner cordon, which circled the burning house and a few either side of it. A pair of police officers, standing next to a fire engine were moving towards the Englishman. He had not noticed them and Layttle knew he was too far behind to help.

As they were about to move towards the panicked young man running at them, MacLoughlin appeared from the side, smashing their heads together. They both collapsed and Bayston ran straight past, now almost at his house.

Layttle kept sprinting, but could feel the burning

in his legs. He was starting to fade and Bayston was getting further ahead. He could see that other police were starting to pay attention and, soon, he suspected, Pink Skull would notice, too. Suddenly, he turned and raced off in different direction.

MacLoughlin chased after Bayston, ahead of Layttle, but slower. Within a few moments, they were running together. They sped past the cordons and around an ambulance. They could see what Bayston had also seen and had turned towards.

On a gurney, in the road, laid a large black bag.

A body bag.

There were others, too. Layttle scanned the area, counting three, but two of them were already in the back of ambulances, so there could have been more in the back of other vehicles. It seemed like Bayston had not seen the others. He had zeroed in on the gurney and was sprinting for it.

There were paramedics and police near it. They saw him coming and saw the desperate and fearful look on his face. The police moved to stop him, the paramedics just stood and watched.

MacLoughlin and Layttle were not far away, but could not get there in time. The police grabbed Bayston and held him back, only a metre from the bag. The paramedics started to move it towards the nearby ambulance, but he started screaming.

His frantic wails told them this was not some curious passer-by and they stopped, but the police were trying to wrestle him to the ground. Bayston sobbed and yelled as they forced him to his knees.

The screaming had not yet drawn much attention, such was the noise of the hoses, sirens and helicopter blades that were still chopping the air. But they knew this would not last long. Bayston was squirming and shouting too loudly.

MacLoughlin and Layttle arrived at the scene simultaneously. They took a police officer each, incapacitating them quickly and brutally, one with a punch, the other with a punch and a knee. The paramedics gasped and abandoned the gurney, escaping towards the crowds of fire officers still battling the blaze near the house.

They watched them leave, knowing they had limited time.

Bayston did not stop to thank them. He rushed to the bag and yanked the zip down furiously.

The body was so burnt it was impossible to see who it had once been, but then he saw the necklace. It was badly torched, but the initials engraved in it were easy to make out.

JAD.

Jamie. Anthony. Deborah.

Bayston collapsed, falling to his knees and screaming loudly. He had no strength left. A chasm opened in his soul and he slipped straight into it.

Layttle looked at MacLoughlin. 'Who is it?'

He shrugged his shoulders, eyeing the Englishman worriedly. 'No idea, but it doesn't look good.'

Bayston buried his head in his hands and curled up in a ball, his cries muffled as he rocked back and forth. He was shaking and cold. He felt the darkness overtaking him.

'How far away is the car?' Layttle asked the American.

'We should get a different one, anyway. They know that one. I saw one not far from here.'

The German looked around and saw that they were starting to attract attention. 'We need to go.'

MacLoughlin scanned the house and the area around it, nodding in the direction of Pink Skull. 'Who's that?'

He leaned down and took the Walther from the holster of the unconscious police officer at his feet. 'I don't know and I suggest we don't wait to find out.'

The American look down at Bayston, despondent. 'We can't leave him.'

'Can you carry him?' Layttle asked, now starting to worry as more people looked over.

MacLoughlin indicated the bags in the back of the other ambulances. 'Should we check them?'

He shook his head. 'I don't think we have time.' He pointed to Bayston. 'Anyway, I think he's seen more than enough.'

'Good point.' He reached down and scooped Bayston up. He went limp and rested over MacLoughlin's shoulder. 'Let's get the fuck out of here.'

Layttle heard some calls from behind him. He looked around to see there were police and Imperial soldiers heading their way. Pink Skull looked directly at him. 'Too late.' He turned to the American. 'Where was the car?'

'Two streets over from where I dropped you, on the left-hand side.'

'Go!' he insisted. 'I'll meet you there.'

MacLoughlin did not need telling twice. He started to run away, as quickly as he could with Bayston over his shoulder. 'Hurry up.'

Layttle nodded and turned back towards the men and women coming towards him. They were now running, too. He raised the gun and fired a few shots, hitting one in the chest. Everyone else, including Pink Skull, ducked and dove for cover wherever they could find it.

He crouched behind the bonnet of the ambulance and squeezed the trigger a few more times as silhouettes moved against the backdrop of fire. The fire crews dropped their hoses, which were still spraying water, and dashed to hide behind their engines. The paramedics, reporters and other civilians all ran, as did the small crowd behind the cordon.

Layttle needed to hide as a volley of bullets came back at him. He used the opportunity to look for MacLoughlin. The American was making good ground, approaching the outer barrier where the two police officers were still laying unconscious.

He would only need a few more seconds.

The German waited for a brief respite, when he guessed they would be approaching, and popped his head up, firing several times as soon as he viewed anything moving. He could see the streams of water firing up in the air and along the ground, making the front lawn of the house muddy and slippery. The flames were already starting to grow again, but it gave him a better view of the shadows and made aiming easier. He clipped another one and they all hid again until one of them managed to get a few rounds out in his direction. He ducked down again, noting that MacLoughlin was now gone from view.

He studied the angles of his position, those of his enemies and all the vehicles in the area, quickly choosing his escape path. It was between a fire engine and police truck. They would need to flank him to get a good line of sight and he could cover that ground quickly. All he needed was a few seconds head start and he would be able to get away. He just hoped MacLoughlin was ready for him.

The next lull came and he jumped up, ready to fire at anything in view, but there was a soldier directly in front of him. Layttle had no idea how she had managed to get so close, but he knew he had to deal with her before he could make his escape. She was aiming her weapon, but he knocked it up and the bullet vanished into the night sky.

He moved his Walther around to fire, but she kicked at it. The pistol flew out of his hand and under a police car. She was trying to get her weapon down to shoot at him, but he kept his grip on her wrist, pointing the gun into the sky. She pulled the trigger several times wastefully and he twisted her arm, snatching the gun from her as he pulled it around behind her back.

Using her as a shield, he surveyed the area in front of him. All the shadows were closer, but Pink Skull had remained near the back, cowering behind the bonnet of the car ambulance of a first responder. Layttle fired several shots at every silhouette he could see, in front of the growing flames, then he shoved the soldier forwards so hard she tumbled and fell. Then he turned and ran for the gap.

He reached it quickly, darting through as the shots began behind him. The bullets pinged past and cracked into the metal of the vehicles as he ran through. He had a slight lead. He did not want to waste it.

Layttle could hear them coming after him and rounded the fire truck near the barricade just as the bullets started to zing in his direction. Before they could reach the fire truck and gain line of sight, he was already through and around the corner.

He powered down the street and reached the second one, turning left. There were no more bullets missing him by inches, but he could hear the voices and footfalls behind him. He did not have much time.

He saw the car with the passenger door open and heard the engine roar to life. It was a big engine, he thought. That was a good thing. Something told him that they would need it.

He reached the car to find that it was a police car. Peering inside, MacLoughlin smiled. 'Get in.'

Layttle leapt inside and closed the door. 'They can definitely track this, you know that, right?'

He pulled out and sped away as bullets started to spark off the cars parked around them. They were around the corner in a few seconds and away. 'We'll switch it for another on the other side of the city and leave this with the keys on for some kids to joy ride in. Should buy us a couple of hours to make some distance.'

The German smiled. 'I like it.' He looked around at Bayston, who was laying on the back seat whimpering. 'Did he say anything?'

MacLoughlin checked the mirror and there was nothing behind them, but he did not slow down. 'Nope.'

He turned back to the front and winced as they narrowly avoided a young man crossing the road. 'Any idea who was in that bag?'

'Nope.'

'How many in his family?'

'Five, including him, I think. He also mentioned

a girl and a friend he thought they might target.'

'I only counted three bags. What about you?'

MacLoughlin grunted as he raced through a red light. 'Same.'

Layttle looked back at the sobbing mess on the back seat. 'So, maybe that's three that they didn't get.'

'He obviously knew who was in the bag, but there's no telling who were in the other two. Could be anyone.'

Layttle offered Bayston a gentle, sympathetic smile. 'Good point. He definitely has something to keep going for. There's still hope.'

'If not hope, there's revenge.'

The German looked across at the American and nodded fervently. 'Hope and vengeance? They're both powerful motivators, in my experience.'

MacLoughlin smiled wryly. 'And exactly the kind of thing that topples empires.'

Chapter 30

The sunrise looked spectacular from the fifty-eighth floor. Every time they met here, he insisted on a breakfast meeting on the balcony of his penthouse city apartment, even though it rarely got above freezing this time of year. Spring was coming, but was probably another month away.

Nimko sat twiddling his moustache, sipping his coffee and watching the apartment towers coming to life. The mountains in the background were still covered with snow, but managed to offset the ugly architecture that dominated the city scape from this angle. He ignored the huts on the outskirts of the city. To him, those people did not even exist until they joined the army.

Tarnat was eating. He often ate a lot at these meetings, since there were always freshly-baked pastries and bread, along with imported jams. He could afford to buy such things himself, and he travelled frequently enough to eat them regularly, but his mother had told him never to say no to a free meal and those words had served him well over the years.

They were discussing the problem this city had with pollution and how much they disliked coming here. If not for these meetings, they would never come. They both stopped and turned around when the balcony door opened.

Genghis strode out of his apartment in a grey three-piece suit, bought on Savile Row. He had a navy-blue tie, in a Windsor knot, gold cufflinks and Armani leather shoes. He was tall, broad and handsome, with a perfectly symmetrical, chiselled face and not a single flaw anywhere on his skin. He had a thin, but pristine, black moustache above his lip and a blade-shaped, thick wisp of black hair hanging from his chin.

He stood in the doorway for a moment and slipped on his thin, square Cartier sunglasses, adjusted his Bremont watch and then took his white stick out, before gliding to his seat. He always sat in the seat facing the sun.

He sat down and felt for the coffee that his butler left in the same spot every day, pouring it into the juxtaposed cup and blowing the steam away before he took a sip and placed it back down again.

He took a deep breath and smiled. 'The pollution isn't too bad up here.'

Nimko and Tarnat exchanged a knowing look and the latter replied. 'It's not that we don't like your city, sir.'

He held up his hand, moving his face in the direction of the speaker. He liked to do that when it was a friendly conversation, as he found it made people feel more comfortable. 'It's fine. I can smell it from up here. How does it look? Is there a cloud at ground level?'

'Not yet,' Nimko replied. 'Give it a couple of months and there will be, though.'

'What colour is it?'

'Normally depends on where the sun is,' he replied, still fiddling with his facial hair. 'But it gets really dark grey and smoggy.'

'I don't know what that looks like,' he laughed. 'Is it like a cloud?'

'Sort of.'

'I will look it up later on my braille Device,' he commented, sipping his coffee again.

Tarnat took another mouthful of bread. 'You know what a cloud looks like?'

'I remember them,' he replied, stroking his beard. 'So, gentlemen, to business. How was London? Am I correct in my assumption that Beijing are still happy for me to run this?'

They looked at each other, smiling. They knew that Beijing had not been given a choice. Nimko coughed into his hand. 'Nobody has informed us differently, sir. London was very useful. We met the Privy Council and can now identify all the members. Did you read our report?'

He nodded. 'I did, but you know what I'm really asking. Did you find someone?'

Tarnat was still chewing, so Nimko continued. 'Well, yes, we left it out of the official report, as you asked, sir.'

'I appreciate that, General. But update me now, would you, please?'

'Of course, sir. We believe we found the opportunity we were looking for.'

'You found someone you think you can turn?'

He nodded, even though the gesture was pointless to his current audience. 'Yes, sir. As luck would have it, one of our operatives had some information about these people already. We didn't know they were on the Privy Council so, once we put all the information together, we were able to verify it within three weeks. One member has a child with a genetic defect they have concealed from the system.'

'What is it?' Genghis fired.

'Turner's Syndrome, they call it. It only affects women and this girl is still young. They must have somehow avoided or cheated the post-natal tests, but the adolescent ones are not far away.'

'You believe they will be amenable to helping us?'

'Perhaps. They have committed treason, so the signs are good.'

Genghis sighed loudly and grinned. He enjoyed the irony that it was a genetic abnormality that was going to present him with the opportunity he had been waiting for. The British did not tolerate disability or defects unless sustained in service to The Empire. He would have been slaughtered as a child and that thought always haunted him. Now their policy would be the start of their downfall, or so he hoped. 'That's excellent news. Are you confident enough to make contact?'

'Not yet, sir,' Nimko replied assuredly. 'I have one of my best assets gathering more information and will present it to you, hopefully, at the Coalition Summit in Pohang next month.'

Genghis frowned and finished his coffee in one gulp. He felt for the cafetiere and poured himself another. 'That should work. I will be staying there for a while, so let's not rush this, gentlemen. We need to get it right. What do your instincts tell you, General?'

Nimko heaved a deep breath into his lungs. 'I honestly don't know, sir. These people are devoted to The Empire.'

He chuckled. 'Perhaps, but they're already a traitor, no?'

'It could be an oversight, or maybe it wasn't present in the birth screening. We don't know for sure. We need to get the evidence and then confront them with it to see how they react.'

Genghis was laughing. 'And they need to choose between their child or their empire. What a horrible decision to make.'

'It could be that they have already made their choice, sir.'

'When will we confront them?'

Nimko contemplated his answer carefully. 'I need to get the data first, sir. Do I assume I have your permission to proceed as soon as I feel I have it?'

'Yes, yes, of course,' he chuckled, waving the doubt away as if it could be dispelled by his hand. 'Don't waste precious time coming to me. I trust your judgement.'

Tarnat finally had an empty mouth. 'I think they'll join us.'

'I hope you're right,' Genghis replied, turning towards the voice. 'I feel a bit bad for them, but it's necessary. Gentlemen, that is fine work. I think you might just have finally discovered a chink in the British armour.'

LONDON, ENGLAND

Smythe walked down the street with a spring in his step. It was a pleasant, warm evening. The trees were green and the flowers in bloom. It was the first time this year he had removed his jacket on the walk home, draping it over his arm as he strode the half-mile from his office to his city flat.

His flat was in an old, white building in Pimlico,

on the top floor. The building had a reception because it was owned by MI6 and they used it for various guests. Sometimes it was a safehouse, other times just secure accommodation for especially contentious diplomats. He was the only person who lived there, using it as his city home in the week. Sometimes his wife joined him there, but she preferred to be in their country house now their daughter had left the city and moved to India to take over the PR department of the East India Company there.

Smythe thought about that as he greeted the guard/receptionist and scanned his Device for the elevator. He was pleased Tracey had moved over there. He had worried, for a long time, that she would want to join the SIS. She certainly had the capability and he knew the schools and universities were full of Imperial Groundbreakers trying to recruit the best and brightest.

He had also been concerned that Janice would get lonely up in Toot Hill, but she had joined a host of village social clubs and was a governor of their very successful secondary school. She also now had a six handicap at golf. He was stuck at fourteen and had been for years.

He considered retirement as the elevator took him to the fifth, and top, floor. It was not that the idea did not appeal to him, but he felt like he was not yet ready. He did not yet have a replacement to groom that he felt would continue in the right way.

He certainly could not help The Resistance from a small village in Essex, even if he could work on that golf handicap and his bowling.

The elevator pinged open and he walked to the only door on the floor, scanning his Device on the panel and waiting for the bleep before pushing it open. The light poured into the room and he plonked his Device on the table just inside the entrance.

The flat was open plan. The entrance was into the living room, the far side of which became the kitchen and dining area. There was a small corridor to the left, which lead to the bathroom and both bedrooms, although he used the smaller one as an office. This part of the flat comprised of a large corner sofa pushed up against the kitchen counter, which distinguished where the living area ended and the dining area began.

Beside the entrance was a small console table and, in the far corner, was a large, thick recliner and a lamp. The door closed behind him and shut the light out with it, but he was already next to the light switch and was about to press it when the lamp came on in the living room. Maximilian sat in the recliner.

Startled, Smythe reached for the drawer in the console table.

'It's gone,' Max gloated, a nefarious glint in his eyes, holding up a Walther P99. 'So are the ones in the fridge, bathroom and bedroom. You have a lot of guns at home, Peter.'

Smythe took a deep breath and tossed his jacket on to the sofa. He cast a quick look around the flat. It was dark and he noted his blinds were closed. He had not left them that way. 'I keep them in case of uninvited visitors.'

'Very wise. Your security isn't very good.'

'I shall be reviewing it,' he replied acerbically. 'What do you want?'

'You started asking about me, Peter.'

Smythe took a small step towards the recliner. He could see the weapon did not have the clip in it and he was certain the intruder would have removed the bullet from the chamber. He just needed to get close enough to strike. 'Are you surprised?'

He shook his head. 'I would expect nothing less.'

Smythe scoured the flat again. It was too dark to see anything, but he had not heard anyone else. It seemed that Maximilian was alone. It was a curious move, perhaps a sign of arrogance. The MI6 Director was old, but he could still kill a person with his bare hands. He had not forgotten how. 'So, what are you here for? To register an official complaint?'

'Not exactly. After you started making enquiries, we started watching you.'

Suddenly he felt a chill wash over him, but he hid it. 'I could have saved you the trouble. I play bridge on Wednesdays, golf on Monday mornings and have brunch at The Imperial Hotel every Friday.'

'Yes, we know your social schedule. We also know your work schedule. We followed you to every meeting and even had people in some of them. No, that's not why I'm here. It's the other meetings I wanted to talk to you about.'

He scoffed. 'What other meetings?'

Max allowed himself a menacing smile. 'You know which ones. Leo didn't believe me, at first. But we got the evidence eventually. You shouldn't have given the USB to the journalist. She came straight to us.'

'I have no idea what you're on about,' he lied, trying to hide his anger.

'She gave you up for a promotion and a move to Beijing. She's going to uncover the Chinese Dawn for us. Can't trust anyone these days, eh?'

Smythe shrugged his shoulders but was internally cursing himself. 'I still don't know who you're talking about. I never heard of the Chinese Dawn.'

'Not yet, anyway,' Max chuckled. 'I have to give you credit. You're exceptionally convincing. If I hadn't seen it with my own eyes, I would believe you.'

The thought of Layttle's flash drive passed through his head. What a waste. 'I don't know what you're talking about, but I'll be speaking to the King Regent about this very shortly.'

His grin widened. 'I doubt that very much.'

'What are you hoping to get from this?' Smythe asked, trying to stall, inching towards his target.

'I was hoping you would admit it,' he replied in a perfunctory tone. 'I already know torture would be a waste of time. You had too much training for that to work. Nothing coerced out of you would be of any value. We suspect you got it from Layttle, as he found something similar, according to our sources in K6. I doubt we could learn anything more than that.'

He sneaked another small step in as he spoke. 'I literally have no clue what you're talking about.'

'I didn't think you *would* admit it. But I was hopeful you might.'

Smythe shuffled another couple of inches closer. 'Then, if I might ask, what's the point of you being here?'

Max grinned but stayed silent.

Smythe was close enough to strike and was about to launch himself forwards when an arm emerged from the darkness. It was so fast he barely even saw it.

The enormous hand grabbed him from behind, covering most of his face, but pressing on his mouth.

He tried to scream, but no sound escaped the iron grip of the hand.

Gugano stepped forwards, into the light, and

moved his lips to Smythe's ear. 'The point of us being here is to keep a promise, Peter.'

He tightened the grip, digging his nails into Smythe's cheek. He pierced the flesh and the MI6 Director screamed in pain. Gugano moved his fingers under the jawbone and dug them in, getting a hold. Then he placed his other hand on the top of Smythe's head and held it firmly.

When he yanked the jaw, the bone came out and tore half of Smythe's face off with it. The muffled screams stopped instantly.

Gugano let the body drop to the floor and looked down. Smythe was still alive, but his tongue had come out with his jaw and he was choking on all the blood that filling his throat. He gargled for a few seconds, holding his face and kicking his legs, before the life drained from his eyes.

Max stood up and walked over to the giant, careful not to tread in any blood, leaning in and giving him a kiss. 'I didn't think you would find it so easy.'

Gugano smiled lovingly. 'Nor did I. You think he was only working with Layttle?'

'I don't know, darling. That's for Nesbitt to sort out. We did our part and have bigger fish to fry.'

Max gently took the jaw out of his lover's hand. Gugano growled. 'You still don't trust me?'

He laughed and bent down, carefully placing the jaw in position on the dead face. 'You're not always as good at precision, my love.' He took a box of matches from his pocket and shook them playfully. 'How are we wiping this one? Fire?'

He nodded. 'It's a classic. Hasn't failed us yet, has it?'

'No, it hasn't, honey.' He lit a match and tossed it on to the highly inflammable sofa.

They took each other's hands and walked out of the door, staring into each other's eyes lovingly as they strode happily down the corridor.

THE END